Horns of the Devil

A Jeff Trask Legal Thriller

MARC RAINER

ISBN: 1480030236
ISBN 13: 9781480030237

Library of Congress Control Number: 2012918557
CreateSpace Independent Publishing Platform, North Charleston, SC

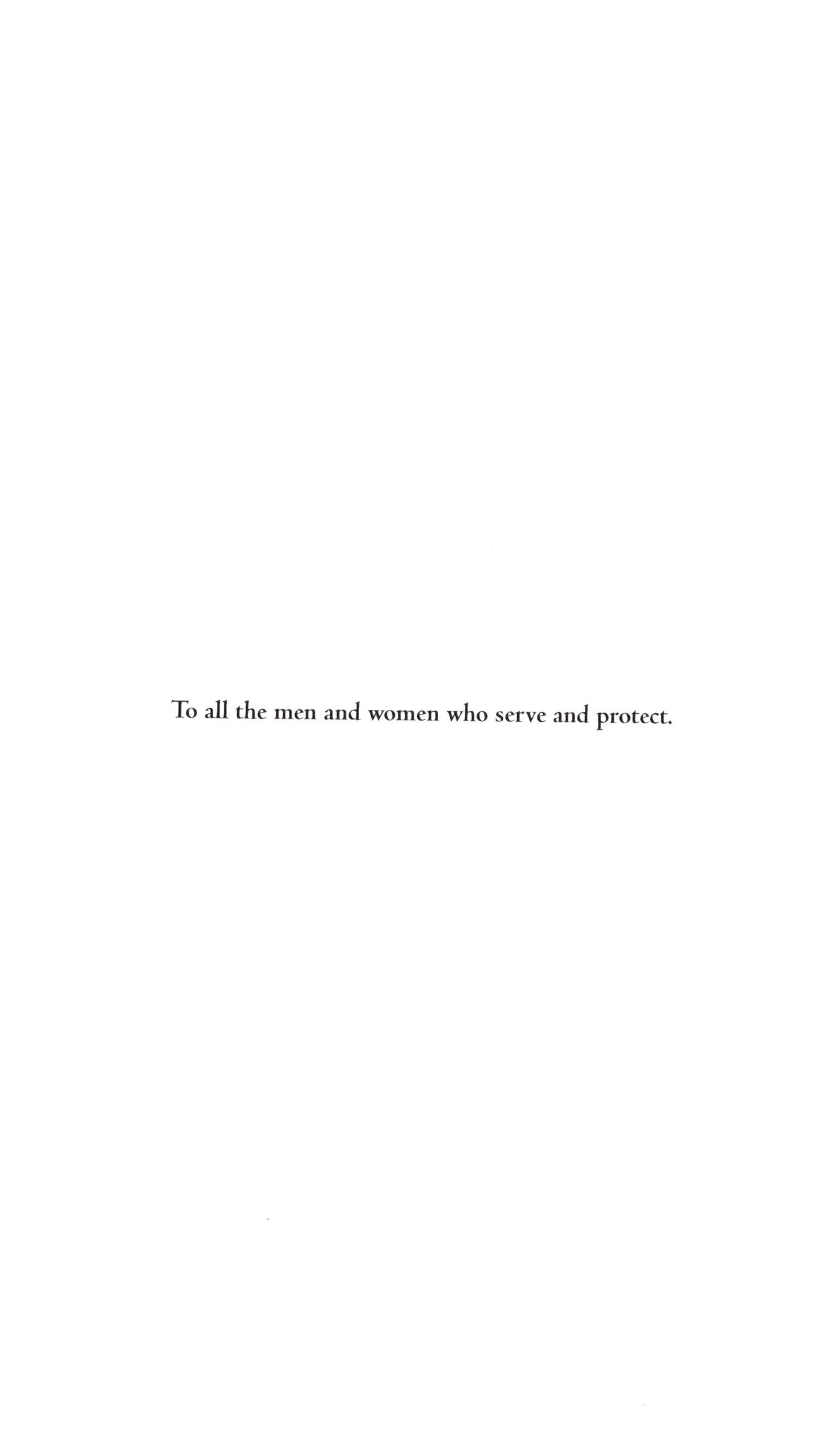

To all the men and women who serve and protect.

Chapter One

Washington, DC, August 8, 7:32 a.m.

"Unit Twenty-Four."

"This is Twenty-Four, dispatch."

"Unit Twenty-Four, see to report of an injured party at 1400 16th Street, Northwest. EMTs are en route."

"Twenty-Four, roger."

Officer Timothy Wisniewski of the Washington, DC, Metropolitan Police Department turned the marked unit southward onto 16th Street and activated his lights and siren. He glanced at his watch, noting the time he'd have to enter on the report when he wrote up the call.

Zero-seven, three-two hours. Seven thirty-two a.m.

He pulled to the curb in front of the building. A crowd had gathered around a figure lying on the sidewalk just inside the green barrier fence that ran along the curb.

They're sure not getting too close to the guy, he thought.

The spectators had established an invisible barrier of about fifteen feet between themselves and the man on the ground. Some shook their heads, some covered their mouths with their hands. Some turned and ran away. One mother ushered her child away from the scene, glancing back over her shoulder in horror.

Nobody wants to help. Nobody wants to get involved.

Wisniewski jumped out and jogged around the front of the cruiser. A male, dressed in jeans, tennis shoes, and a Philadelphia 76ers jersey was lying on his back, feet pointed north. His shoulders were facing south, toward Lafayette Park and the White House. A narrow rivulet of blood had left a dark-brown stain flowing down the sidewalk. Wisniewski leaned over the railing and looked at the figure, then reached for the microphone on the shoulder of his uniform.

"Dispatch, Unit Twenty-Four."

"Twenty-Four."

"Cancel the medics on that call for 1400 16th Northwest. Start homicide and alert the medical examiner."

"Medics are en route Twenty-Four. Are you sure—?"

"Yes, I'm sure. Turn 'em around. This body has no head on it."

He returned to the cruiser for a roll of crime scene tape and traffic cones, and was cordoning off the area when a green Buick pulled in behind his cruiser. A large figure in a navy-blue suit emerged, his shaved black head shining in the sun.

"Hello, Dix. I heard you'd gone back to Homicide."

"Tim." Detective Dixon Carter barely acknowledged the patrolman; he was already looking over the scene.

"Anybody here see anything?" Carter asked, still looking at the body.

"Haven't really had time to do anything but roll out the tape. You got here pretty quick. From what I've overheard in the crowd, he was lying here when folks started showing up for work this morning."

The bystanders closest to them overheard the exchange. Wisniewski saw them start to pull away, hoping to avoid the questions that were sure to delay them. They had things to do. Coffee to drink, newspapers to read. It was only another murder, after all. The District had hundreds every year.

"Just stay put for a minute, folks."

Carter's deep baritone froze them. He pulled out a small notepad and pen and started working the crowd.

"Anyone here see how this body got here? Anyone see any vehicles pulling away from this area?"

A chorus of no's answered him.

"Anyone have any idea who this might be?" Carter shouted.

A tall, distinguished-looking man pushed his way to the front of the crowd, flanked by four younger men in business suits. He looked down at the body, his shoulders slumping.

"It is my son."

Carter was by the man's side instantly. Wisniewski pushed the crowd back, assisted by four other uniformed officers who had just pulled up to help control the scene.

"How do you recognize him, sir?" Carter asked, his eyes sweeping the entourage that had followed the gentleman. Two of the four men kept reaching inside their coats. The older man saw the concern on Carter's face. He turned and spoke to his escort in Spanish, and they seemed to relax.

"Please forgive me, officer," the older man said. He was tall and slim with streaks of gray lining the temples in his otherwise coal-black hair. "I am Juan Carlos Lopez-Portillo, the ambassador to your country from El Salvador."

"Mr. Ambassador," Carter nodded, accepting the claim for the moment. "Can you tell me how you were able to make it here so fast, assuming this is your son, as you say?"

"My embassy is inside this building. Suite one-hundred." The man's voice was hollow and breaking, his gaze still fixed on the body on the sidewalk. "I am sure it is my son, Armando." He pointed toward the body. "The birthmark on the left arm. There is a high-school class ring on his left hand. You will find his name engraved on the inside."

A medical examiner's van arrived, backing in at the front of Wisniewski's cruiser. A second van had also pulled in behind his car. Wisniewski recognized it as one of the District's crime scene vehicles.

"Where will you be taking him?" Lopez-Portillo asked Carter.

"He'll be going to the morgue for an autopsy, Mr. Ambassador," Carter said. "We'll need to take a statement from you. If the ring confirms what you've said, we'll certainly let you know, and the body will be released to you. The medical examiner will want to get some DNA samples from you, too. We have to preserve any evidence at this point. When was the last time you saw your son, sir?"

"Three days ago. He didn't come home from school."

"Did you call the police or file a report of any kind?"

"I'm afraid not. It is not the first time."

"Do you have any idea who might have done this, sir?"

"No."

The ambassador motioned to his escort and turned to leave. He handed Carter a card.

"You can reach me at this number. Please call me when we can take him home. If you'll excuse me, I have to call his mother."

"Of course."

The ambassador walked back toward the building, his escorts separating the crowd for him.

The crime scene technicians were finishing with their photographs. There wasn't much else for them to do on this one. No shell casings. No footprints. No personal effects dropped by the victim. No neighborhood to canvass for witnesses. This was a business district, and the bystanders who had seen nothing were already trying to get away from the scene. Just a headless corpse dumped on a sidewalk. They'd comb the immediate area anyway, in case the head had been tossed into a trash can or bloodstains could be located nearby, but they'd probably find nothing. Carter nodded to the medical examiner's crew, who began to load the body onto a gurney.

"An ambassador's kid?" Wisniewski asked.

"That's the way it looks for now," Carter nodded. "An ambassador who knows more than he wanted to tell me."

"What makes you say that?"

"He acted like he'd seen this coming," Carter said. "His reaction was more like a father getting the news that his kid didn't make it through a risky heart surgery. No shock, just grief. I asked him if he knew who could have done it, and he paused just a second before saying no, meaning he has *some* idea, but didn't want to say anything. His kid's headless body is lying on the sidewalk, and he doesn't sob, doesn't even cry out in anger." Carter shook his head. "This one's going to be weird."

Inside the embassy, the ambassador returned the telephone to its cradle. His wife now knew. He dispatched an aide to be with her, telling the subordinate he would be on his way home shortly. He felt numb, sick, impotent. He picked up the phone again and dialed the international call from memory. When the voice answered, he did not say hello.

"You were right, old friend. I should have listened to your advice earlier. They have murdered my son. I want you here as soon as possible."

The man in San Salvador hung up. He adjusted the black patch over his left eye before picking up the cell phone again and selecting the third number in its memory. When the ringtone stopped, he spoke in Spanish: "I need six. Get them immediately. We'll be leaving this afternoon. Put them in a suitcase with a lock on it and meet me at the airport."

San Salvador, El Salvador
August 8, 3:05 p.m.

As the blue sedan pulled into the passenger-unloading zone in front of the Comalapa International Airport in San Salvador, Special Agent Jason Mays of the Drug Enforcement Administration pulled the digital camera up to his eyes with his right hand and held a radio to his left ear with the other.

"You in position?"

"Yep. We'll make the grab soon as he's inside."

"Stay out of sight for now. I'll let you know as soon as he heads that way."

"Roger."

Mays swatted a fly away from his face and leaned against the tree. He adjusted the zoom and watched through the camera's viewfinder as the driver of the sedan pulled a stainless-steel suitcase from the trunk of the car. Instead of heading into the terminal, however, the driver stood with the suitcase on the sidewalk, obviously waiting for someone.

"We may have a change in the ops plan—" Mays began.

He was about to direct the team outside, to the front of the terminal, when he saw a well-dressed man wearing an eye patch take the suitcase from the driver. The case was then transferred immediately to a team of six bodyguards who were following the man with the patch. One of them slapped some large, bright stickers on the outside of the case and tossed it on the top of a luggage rack already loaded with several other cases that all bore the same set of stickers.

Mays hit the auto-shutter button and clicked off as many shots of the group as he could before lowering the camera in disgust.

"Dammit." He raised the radio to his ear. "Abort."

"What? Why, Jay?"

"Just abort the damned operation. See if you can tail the guy who made the drop. I'll tell you why back at the office."

At 4:45 p.m., the man with the eye patch and the others left El Salvador on *Transportes Aéreos del Continente Americano* Flight 580, bound for JFK.

Washington, DC,
August 8, 10:17 p.m.

Diego Morales smiled nervously at the gathering of twenty-five tattooed men who had surrounded him in the backyard of the house in the 3100 block of Georgia Avenue, NW. He had looked forward to this moment for months, but had also dreaded it.

"You did well, Diego. Very well."

The leader of the group—a solidly built Hispanic male with a shaved head—nodded approvingly, and tapped the numbers inked into his left shoulder.

"Now it is *your* time."

"*Sí,* Esteban."

The leader nodded again and held up a stopwatch as six of the gang members stepped forward, circling the boy.

"Begin."

Diego covered his head as well as he could while the blows rained down on him. He felt the impact of a leather glove as it slammed into his forehead, opening a cut that started blood flowing into his left eye. He dropped to a knee and tried to bring his arms over the top of his head, but he was losing the battle now, his arms drooping from the pain of the punches and kicks. He felt himself sagging to the ground just before he lost consciousness. The beating continued.

"Not too hard. We don't want to kill him," Esteban cautioned.

He watched as the second hand approached the mark on the dial, signaling the end of the thirteenth second.

"*Halto.*"

He motioned again, and the six men who had beaten Diego picked the boy up and carried him gently toward the house.

Chapter Two

Washington, DC,August 9, 11:18 p.m.

Dixon Carter watched as Assistant Medical Examiner Kathy Davis cut the jersey from the upper half of the headless body. It was a procedure he had watched hundreds of times before. The corpse lay under the sterile white lights, stretched out on the stainless-steel autopsy table. Drainage holes waited to dispose of the fluids which, hours before, had sustained a life.

Kathy was short, only about five-four, and she was standing on a step stool as usual, working on the top of the body. She completed the cut with the scissors and pulled the jersey open, revealing the torso.

"My God." Carter couldn't help himself.

The kid had been through hell; his chest had been used as a carving board. The letters "MS" and every possible variation of the number thirteen—Arabic, Roman numerals—had been sliced into his flesh.

She pointed to the body's wrists. "Ligature marks on the wrists and bruises on each forearm. Straight lines. Looks like they had him tied to a chair with his arms behind him. They sure did a number on him, and all this happened *before* they cut his head off. See, the bleeding from all these cuts indicates that they're *ante mortem*."

"No cuts in the jersey, though," Carter observed. "Other than yours."

"Right, Dix. Just bloodstains. They put the jersey on him after all the slicing and dicing, and probably after the decapitation."

She held the shirt up with gloved hands.

"See? No cuts in the fabric. You were right about this being a body dump, too. Lividity shows he'd been laying face down somewhere after he was killed.

The blood—whatever didn't spurt out after the decapitation—had pooled on the front side. You said he was lying on his back in front of the embassy?"

Carter nodded. "Any tats or old scars?"

"Just one tattoo," she said. "Or what's left of it. You'll have to come over to this side."

Carter walked around the table. Kathy's gloved hand pointed to the two numerals that had been inked into the right shoulder. Several cuts had been made into the shoulder through the tattoo.

"Looks like someone wasn't happy about it," she said. "It's as if they tried to remove it."

It was the only conclusion Kathy offered that Carter disagreed with. If someone had really wanted to remove the tat, it wouldn't have been difficult, especially after the decapitation. Instead, the cuts through the symbol seemed to be more of a sign of contempt that the killer—or killers—had for the number eighteen.

The door to the autopsy room opened, and a tall, thin figure with silver hair and bright blue eyes entered. He walked up behind the assistant ME and kissed her on the cheek.

"Hi, babe." He nodded toward Carter. "What do we have, Dix?"

"Cap."

Carter still used the older, familiar title for Commander Willie Sivella, the chief of Homicide and his boss. It was his third stint under Cap'n Willie. The first had been as a patrolman, the second a long tour in the District of Columbia's Seventh District as a detective. When Sivella had been promoted out of 7D to take over Homicide, he'd persuaded Carter to come with him.

Carter hadn't been surprised to see his boss at the morgue. It was a gruesome case, with plenty of shocked citizens on the street gawking at a headless corpse, an ambassador's son as the victim, and certain press interest to follow. Sivella would have questions to answer, which is why he'd asked Kathy Davis, his live-in girlfriend of seven years plus, to do the body exam ASAP.

Carter pointed to the jersey.

"Seven plus six equals thirteen, Cap. And there's an '18' tattoo on the kid's shoulder." Carter paused for a moment. "Didn't Barry Doroz just move over to the gang task force at FBI?"

"Yeah. I'll give him a call. He'll let us work the case with him if they want to pick it up, and he can deflect some of the shit storm in the press. Did we confirm this was the ambassador's kid?"

Kathy picked up a ring from a metal tray on the side of the examining table.

"The inscription was pretty clear once I rinsed off the blood."

"Armando Lopez-Mendez." Sivella returned the ring to the tray. "Hispanic surname. First one's the dad, last one's the mom. You'll need to get DNA from the parents for confirmation, Dix."

"I already told the ambassador. He'll be expecting it. Do we have a prosecutor assigned yet?"

"Yeah," Sivella winked. "I called Bill Patrick at the US Attorney's office right after you radioed from the scene. Told him we needed his best on this one. It's Jeff Trask. Any objections?"

Carter shook his head. Trask was the best he'd seen in the US Attorney's office, with the possible exception of Bob Lassiter, and Lassiter was dead now. Trask was the best choice Patrick could have made. Aggressive, no-nonsense, and smart as hell.

"No, and I don't think Agent Doroz will have any, either."

"Good. Let me know when you hook up."

August 9, 6:20 p.m.

From a chair in the back of his favorite restaurant in Georgetown, Jeffrey Ethan Trask, Assistant United States Attorney for the District of Columbia, looked around the room. His back was to a wall, as usual. *No Jack McCall sneaking up from behind. I won't make the Hickock mistake. Wild Bill violated his rule only once, and it killed him.* He opened the filing cabinets in his mind and allowed the images and data to flow freely, waiting to settle on one in order to control the cacophony of his thoughts. The music being piped in was cycling through some late fifties hit parade and early sixties soft rock.

That music will do for now.

He had always found the songs to be a soothing way to focus when his mind wasn't concentrating on a task at hand. He closed his eyes and challenged himself to name the next song in as few notes as possible. It took him just two. *"It's All in the Game." Tommy Edwards' biggest hit. Number one on the charts for six weeks in 1958. Lyrics by Carl Sigman, music by Charles G. Dawes, who happened to be vice-president under Silent Cal Coolidge. The only hit ever to be co-written by a vice president of the United States.*

Trask smiled. His command of trivia had earned him many a t-shirt or free drink in bars scattered across the South while he was an Air Force JAG traveling prosecutor.

He was waiting for the next song to begin when he saw her enter from the street. He felt himself smiling. *No trouble focusing now.* She was still the most perfect thing in his life, the anchor in all the madness. Five-five and a nicely proportioned one-hundred-and-twenty pounds, dressed in black slacks and a teal blouse that perfectly set off her deep brown eyes. All the file cabinets in his head remained closed when she was with him. Lynn kissed him as he held her chair while she sat down.

She saw his fingers drumming on the table.

"What song is running through that fevered brain of yours?"

"*My Girl.* Temps." He smiled.

"Yeah, I'll bet." She rolled her eyes.

"Whenever I see you," he said. "How's the new job?"

"Not bad, I guess. I'm going to have to get used to the support role and not being an active street agent."

Trask smiled again and shook his head.

"What's the big joke?" she asked.

"*I'm* going to have to get used to the idea that I'm married to an old retired woman."

Lynn Preston had been a Special Agent with the Air Force's Office of Special Investigations. She had worked several long-term undercover operations, invariably resulting in perfect conviction rates and sending many military drug-dealers to spend hot summers and bitter winters at Fort Leavenworth, Kansas. Trask had met her at a base in Florida where she had done one of these undercover stints. That operation had generated dozens of courts-martial and a very strong mutual attraction. Trask had left the air force after fourteen years of active duty to become a federal prosecutor. Lynn had been reassigned to Andrews AFB, Maryland, and a chance meeting there on one of Trask's monthly days as a JAG reservist had led to their marriage a few months later. She had stayed on active duty for the retirement, but left the moment her twenty years were up. She'd just landed a job with the FBI as an analyst.

"You forget that I enlisted when I was six," she quipped.

"You look like that might be true."

"Thanks, but I suspect you have a very biased opinion."

"I admit the bias, but the opinion's still accurate. Where'd they put you?"

"Your friend Bear has me working for him in the gang squad."

"Good. He can keep all the young bucks in the Bureau from hitting on you."

"Fat chance," she said. She nodded to her left. "I think you're the one who needs watching."

Trask turned to see a little girl in a booster seat grinning at him from the adjacent table. She was only about sixteen months old, but she was smiling widely, showing off the few teeth she had managed to sprout. "What is it with you and babies?" Lynn asked. "You're a baby *magnet.* Mostly little girls. They're always smiling at you like that. I think they see some kind of halo around you and know that you're here to protect them."

Trask smiled back at the infant, who was beaming at him again.

"How old do they have to be before that stops?" Lynn asked.

"I've noticed that it drops off considerably after they hit twenty-five."

"You'd be wearing this salad if we weren't in public."

Trask laughed. "After dinner, we can go home and I'll show you how attractive I think *you* still are."

She smiled again, but it faded quickly.

"I might have to leave Barry's squad already."

"Why is that? I thought he'd be a great boss to work for."

"That's not the problem." She stabbed the fork into her salad before looking up again. "*You* are."

"What?"

"Barry got a call from *your* boss just before I left work to meet you."

"And what did smilin' Bill Patrick say to stir this up?"

"Tim Wisniewski took a call yesterday and Dixon Carter picked it up at Homicide. The vic was an ambassador's kid. Decapitated. Somebody threw his body out in front of his father's embassy."

"Which embassy?"

"El Salvador. Willie Sivella called Barry. Willie said he'd already talked to Patrick and that the case was going to be assigned to you."

El Salvador, Trask mused. *Decapitation. The signature of a political retaliation by the MS-13. I'd read that they were moving into the area. Doesn't make a lot of sense, though. The new government was supposed to be more favorable to the gangs. . .*

He looked back up at Lynn.

Focus, dummy. Don't ever tune HER out.

"Great," he said. "The case of the headless diplomatic dependent. What does that have to do with your squad assignment?"

"The murder's probably gang-related; at least that's the initial theory."

Trask nodded as if the information were new to him.

"Barry had wanted me to work on gang intelligence stuff," she continued. "He was worried that with you taking the case, it might conflict me out of the squad."

"There's no conflict of interest as long as you're not a potential witness. I'd have to call the witnesses who wrote whatever you're reading, not you. As long as you're an analyst and not a witness to an event, no conflict."

"You're sure?"

"Yep. Just make sure there's a second set of eyes on everything you do. As long as I don't have to call you to the stand, I don't have to kick you off Bear's squad."

"Great!" She dug into her salad. "We can work together again, I can stay on the desk, and I don't even have to talk to dumb-ass lawyers in court!"

"Thanks, I guess."

"I didn't mean *you*. Besides, I never thought of you as a lawyer."

"Thanks again."

"You know what I mean. You're as much of a cop as I am. All the guys who've done cases with you say that. Plus, you're a hell of a prosecutor, and you're not bad at some other things."

"Like what?" He prodded, arching his left eyebrow.

"Like showing me how attractive you think I still am. I plan to take you up on that offer when we get home."

"I think this salad will be enough, then, don't you?"

"Not so fast, Romeo," she laughed. "You promised me a dinner, not an appetizer."

"All right. Just chew fast."

They were home in Waldorf, Maryland, two hours later. When Trask unlocked the front door to the split foyer, he could see the light on the answering machine blinking from the table at the bottom of the stairs. He pushed the message button, and after listening to the recording, complied with the instruction to call Ross Eastman.

"Thanks for getting back to me, Jeff," the United States Attorney for the District of Columbia said. "Sorry to disturb you at home."

"Not a problem."

"You've heard about the murder of the ambassador's kid, I assume?"

"Yes."

"Commander Sivella called about it this morning, and Bill Patrick and I agreed the case should go to you, at least for now."

"For now?"

"*For now.* The conclusion at the autopsy was that the killing was probably the result of a feud between Salvadoran street gangs. 'Eighteen' versus 'thirteen,' Sivella told me. Barrio 18 against MS-13. That being the case, it's probably a drug-related murder, just with a lot of special interest from Main Justice. If it turns into something else, like a politically motivated hit on the ambassador's family, you can expect the Office of International Affairs to take the case, or at least assign somebody to it. I spoke to them today, and they're OK with us keeping it, *for now.*"

Wonderful, Trask thought. *I bust my hump and some departmental weenie with no idea of how to walk into a real trial steps in at the last minute for some high-quality TV face time.*

"I understand."

"Just keep me informed so I can keep the Department informed," Eastman said.

"Will do."

"Good night, Jeff."

"That sounded heavy." Lynn came down the stairs, a glass of Diet Coke in her hand. She handed it to him.

"Yep. I'm afraid things are going to get goofy for a while. Thanks for the drink."

"Let them get goofy tomorrow," she said. "You're going to concentrate on me tonight."

He downed the glass in three large gulps.

August 9, 11:32 p.m.

The man with the eye patch looked up and nodded as two cases, each still bearing the bright stickers that identified them as diplomatic pouches, were brought into his room at the embassy compound.

"*Gracias,* Hugo."

He handed Hugo a scrap of paper bearing a telephone number and pointed to one of the cases.

"Tell Marcos to take this one and make contact at this number. Keep one, sell five. Twenty-one thousand dollars each, not subject to negotiation. Bring the cash back to me in the same case."

"Sí, Señor."

After Hugo left, the man with the eye patch walked to the mirror above the sink in the bathroom and removed the patch, staring angrily with his good eye at the sunken socket and the scar stretching across it.

I have one eye left. It is all I need for shooting.

He replaced the patch and returned to the bedroom and the other case, a long, narrow one. A key from his pocket opened the lock. He began disassembling and oiling the weapon, a Knight's Armament Company XM110 sniper rifle. When the weapon was properly reassembled, he mounted the laser scope, loaded the rifle, and returned it to its case.

At least we can thank the Americanos for providing this tool to help deal with the problems they have created for us. I think I'll go hunting tonight.

He picked up the phone and pressed the intercom.

"Hugo, get the car ready. We leave after midnight."

Chapter Three

August 10, 1:18 a.m.

The man with the eye patch watched the sidewalks carefully as the sedan with diplomatic plates rolled by the streetlights in Langley Park, Maryland. He was alert for the usual telltale signs: the flash of a sky-blue jacket, the sound of a familiar accent, the sight of a number or the letters he hated.

"There. Slow down, Hugo."

From the backseat he pointed to a group of three young men standing in a parking lot beside an all-night convenience store. One was wearing a jacket bearing the logo and colors of the North Carolina Tarheels. It was three in the morning. No one else was on the street.

The driver stopped the car parallel to the targets, and the rear window rolled down. The man with the eye patch could hear them talking and recognized the speech patterns. He heard one of them mention *soyapango,* one of the neighborhoods in San Salvador that had produced the leftist guerrillas he had fought for so long.

"Get ready, Hugo."

He leaned the flash suppressor of the rifle against the bottom of the rear window and fired. The wearer of the Carolina jacket was the first to fall, followed by the one who had mentioned *soyapango.* He was unable to get the next shot off before the third man ran to cover around the corner of the building. The sedan turned the corner and sped away. The man with the eye patch returned the rifle to its place in the concealed drawer under the rear seat. Once a few blocks had disappeared in the rearview mirror, the sedan slowed again, appearing to be nothing more than a chauffeur taking his VIP back to the embassy following a party.

August 10, 10:30 a.m.

The status hearing was a nuisance, but part of the job. A crack dealer had been arrested plying his wares in Anacostia, and due process had to duly proceed. The initial appearance was a hearing in which nothing ever happened, but Trask was required to attend. The complaint would be read, the not-guilty plea would be entered for the defendant because he had no attorney appointed yet, bond would be set because this guy was neither violent nor a flight risk. The only purpose of the whole drill was to start the clock for an indictment. Trask would have thirty days to get the case in front of the grand jury, or the complaint would be dismissed.

He was irritated a bit more than usual because the magistrate presiding over the hearing was even later than usual. The Honorable United States Magistrate Judge Kathryn Hightower was known for keeping attorneys waiting thirty minutes or more past the scheduled start of a hearing, but God save the unfortunate lawyer who counted on the usual judicial tardiness and was late himself. There were cameras in the courtroom that fed the images back into the judges' chambers. An empty counsel chair at the appointed time was an invitation to a contempt hearing, and so Trask waited. While he waited, his mind began to work, as it always did when he was unoccupied. To the others in the courtroom—the court reporter, security officers, the defendant at the table—he appeared to be asleep.

The pictures floated through his head.

I'm outside the principal's office. Third grade. Teacher doesn't like me very much. Mom's inside talking. I can hear them if I block out the other sounds. Talking about "attention deficits." Saying maybe I should be on some kind of meds. Mom's mad, says that if they knew how to really educate me, they wouldn't have any trouble. I haven't been any trouble. My homework's always done. I do it in class, always finish before school is over. I can't help it if I daydream after that. I hear what the teacher's saying, I just look at other stuff, read other books while she's talking. "Give my son one of your stupid zombie pills without my permission and I'll sue you sideways."

His eyes flickered open for a moment. Courtroom still quiet. No judge yet. He closed his eyes again.

Back at home now. "I know you're being good, Jeff. Your grades are good, you do the work; they just don't understand you like I do. You're already a grade ahead of the others your age. We don't want to move you ahead any faster right now. We just need to make a game of it, OK? Can you look at the teacher while she's talking? Pretend to pay attention to her? If she thinks you're listening to her..." I AM, Mom, but— "Yes, I know, but she *doesn't. You have to make it a game so she thinks you're focusing on her, even if your mind is somewhere else at the time. It's just a matter of appearances." She kisses me on the head. "No pills for you. I promise."*

"All rise."

Trask appeared to wake from his nap and stood respectfully as the magistrate entered the courtroom. He glanced down at his watch. *She's thirty-five minutes late today. Ten minutes late even according to MST, Magistrate Standard Time.*

Trask left the federal courthouse following the hearing and decided to cut through Judiciary Square before heading back to the "Triple-nickle," as most of the prosecutors referred to 555 4th Street, NW , the home of the United States Attorney for the District of Columbia and his more than five hundred assistants. He stopped in front of the National Law Enforcement Officers Memorial and quietly stared at two names etched into the marble. Images of both came flooding back into his mind. Robert Lassiter, his mentor and sponsor in the United States Attorney's office. Detective Juan Ramirez, Dixon Carter's partner.

"They were good men, Jeff."

Trask turned to see Barry Doroz standing behind him. He acknowledged Doroz with a nod and turned back toward the Memorial.

"Yes, they were, Bear. I can't help but think that my name might be on that wall instead of Bob Lassiter's if he hadn't signed the indictment on the Reid thing. It was really my case."

"Yeah, and *my* name would be there if you hadn't bean-balled that punk who was about to back-shoot me."

Trask shrugged. The film running through his head changed for a moment to an afternoon over a year ago, a surveillance van screeching to a halt in front of the alleyway where the two armed rapists were dragging their screaming victim. He was with the others, bailing out of the van on the run, Dixon Carter taking a bullet in the thigh and Juan Ramirez kneeling over him, Doroz taking down one of the gunmen with a shoulder shot, but not seeing the other circling behind him. Trask's lucky throw with a rock had made the shooter pull his shot. Doroz' return fire had not missed.

"We all do our jobs, Jeff. Some of us get lucky and dodge the bullets; others don't."

Trask nodded, stopping the movie and returning it to its place in his mental archive. "Juan would have probably preferred a bullet, given the choice." Trask looked at the name of Juan Ramirez etched into the wall of the Memorial. Demetrius Reid had ambushed Juan, knocked him unconscious and then killed him. They'd tracked Reid down and charged him with the murder. Reid had charged Trask during the trial and died in a struggle in the courtroom.

"You took care of Reid." Doroz patted the younger man on the shoulder. "You read your e-mail today?"

"Not yet," Trask replied. "I had a hearing first thing this morning. Never turned my PC on."

"If you had, you'd have seen an e-mail from me informing you about a meeting on your new case."

"OK. When and where?"

"My shop in fifteen. Shall we go?"

The Washington field office of the Federal Bureau of Investigation was located at 601 4th Street NW, just across the street from the Triple-nickel. Doroz led the way into the gang squad. Eight low-walled cubicles—carpet over gray metal and each with a computer station—occupied the center of the bullpen. They passed the cubicles and entered the squad conference room, bright and well illuminated by several rows of energy-saving fluorescents. Trask made a mental note to alert Hollywood that their portrayals of the Bureau in the *X-Files, Fringe,* and other shows were a bit off. The FBI had lightbulbs, and actually used them.

Trask and Doroz shook hands with Willie Sivella and Dixon Carter. Trask held out his hand to Lynn, who pushed the hand away and kissed him full on the mouth, prompting cleared throats from six other FBI special agents standing around the conference table.

"I knew this would never work," Doroz quipped.

"It'll work just fine," Lynn replied. "We have the best cops, the best agents, and now the best prosecutor working the case."

"And as soon as she gets up to speed, the best investigative analyst?" Doroz asked.

"Of course," she said.

"Good."

Doroz looked toward the door as a very young-looking man in a light-gray suit entered the room.

"Everyone here remember Puddin'?" Doroz asked, using the squad moniker for Special Agent Michael Crawford. An aging secretary had seen the new agent as he arrived for his first day of work and had loudly proclaimed that he looked like a fresh bowl of the dessert. The nickname had stuck.

"I never forget a face," Sivella said. "Especially one that looks twelve."

"Thanks, Cap," Crawford said. "You can help me buy some beer after I give this spiel. I'd just get carded again. It's such a hassle."

"Just look at it this way, Mike," Lynn offered, "when you're forty, you can still date cheerleaders."

"Thanks, but they're pretty high-maintenance," Crawford said, blushing.

"As if you knew," Doroz laughed. "Get on it with it, Puddin'."

Crawford walked to the front of the conference table as the rest of the group took their seats. A button-push on a remote caused the lights to dim and a screen to drop from the ceiling. A projector in the rear switched on, displaying the silhouette of a small country.

"The Republic of El Salvador," Crawford began. "A small nation on the Pacific side of Central America, about the size of Massachusetts. The capital is the city of San Salvador, one-point-six million people, about one-fourth the population of the entire country. Until recently, the government was controlled by the *Alianza Republicana Nacionalista,* the National Republican Alliance, or ARENA party. Hard-line conservatives and very friendly to the US. The last national election, however, was won by the *Farabundo Marti para la Liberacion Nacional,* the Farabundo Marti National Liberation Front, or FMLN."

"Liberation front?" asked Trask. "That doesn't sound too friendly." *You've done your research, Puddin.' Don't leave out the politics. It could matter here.*

"Probably not," Crawford said, "unless you're Castro or Hugo Chavez. It's a fairly new administration, and we have to see how far to the left the country will swing. Anyway, that's how this all started. In the eighties, there was a helluva civil war going on down there—left versus right—and about one hundred thousand people died, mostly in the rural areas. The country's agricultural industries got caught in the middle, and with nothing to sell or eat, about two million Salvadorans decided to come to the US. Thousands of them settled in California, and as their kids became teenagers, they faced the same problems any other teenagers face in LA and Oakland."

"Gangs?" Carter asked.

"Precisely. The black and Mexican street gangs were already established, and originally the Salvadorans banded together in self-defense. They created *Mara Salvatrucha 13. Mara* is short for *marabunta,* a word for gang or for army ants; *salvatrucha* can be translated as 'shrewd.' The thirteen comes from the 13th Street area in LA, where a lot of the original members lived. In fact, their chief rival gang is usually just called the 18th Street Gang, Barrio 18, or M-18, another Salvadoran crew originally from LA. The *Maras* originally only admitted Salvadorans, but later they were taking in anyone from Central America. Of course, in the proud history of LA street gangs, self-defense soon took a backseat to every kind of criminal enterprise you can think of."

"What kind of colors and tats are we looking for?" asked Carter.

"For MS-13, colors are light blue and white. Tattoos include 'MS,' '*Salvatrucha,*' the number thirteen or any numbers adding up to thirteen—"

"Like a Philly 76ers jersey," Sivella noted.

"Yes. And also tattoos of their signature hand sign." Crawford held his left hand up in a sideways rendition of what any Texan would have recognized as a tribute to the University in Austin. "Think hook 'em horns, but held down or sideways. They call this the Horns of the Devil. The 18ers use similar numerical tats and tags: 666, XVIII, or just eighteen. They wear black mostly, sometimes black and blue."

"We need to start concentrating on potential charges," Trask said. "Tell everyone what the gangs are into."

"Drugs, prostitution, extortion, and most of all, violence." Crawford hit the button on the remote. "Some examples."

The screen changed to a photograph of the bodies of two young men and two young women who had been shot in the head, execution style. The women had also been slashed in the face with a machete.

"Newark, New Jersey, 2007. One of the girls actually survived. There's a MySpace entry we took off the web from a sixteen-year-old MS-13 gangbanger bragging about his role in this.

"They've got absolutely no respect for authority," Crawford continued. "In 1997, the son of Ricardo Maduro was kidnapped and beheaded after the government of Honduras started a crackdown on the gang. Ricardo Maduro is a former president of Honduras."

"Sound familiar?" Doroz looked at Carter, who nodded. It was evident now why the Bureau had the case. Assassinations, even if drug-related, were federal business, not local.

The screen changed again, revealing an incredible scene of carnage. A mass of bodies, including several women and small children, lay strewn about a shattered bus.

"Honduras again, 2002. Some MS-13 members stopped this bus on the outskirts of Tegucigalpa and sprayed it with AK-47s. Killed twenty-eight, including seven little kids, then left graffiti tags on the hood of the bus bragging about it."

"Assholes." Lynn Trask had no tolerance for those who abused the helpless.

"That they are," Sivella agreed. "How many of these assholes are we dealing with?"

"Not that they faithfully return their census forms, but we estimate at least twenty thousand nationally, with as many as ten thousand in the metro DC area."

"Shit!" exclaimed Sivella. "Have you guys had any luck penetrating this bunch, Bear?"

"Only occasionally," Doroz said. "They have the same code as the mafia. *MS por vida.* Once you're in, you're in for life. The *Mara* kills cooperators, so they're hard to recruit. We had a seventeen-year-old female give us some info back in 2003. Four of her high-school classmates stabbed her to death and left her body on the banks of the Shenandoah River. They even whack their own just for trying to leave the gang."

On cue, Crawford clicked the remote again. A photograph of a single blood-soaked corpse filled the screen.

"This is the body of Ernesto Miranda. They called him Smoky. He was actually one of the *Mara* founders. They murdered him at his home in El Salvador after he refused to attend a gang party. He'd decided to go straight, was attending law school, and was trying to keep kids from joining the gang."

"Thanks, Puddin'." Doroz stood and switched the lights back on. "I just wanted everyone to go into this with their eyes wide open. This is not going to be a normal investigation. We aren't going to find every street dealer tied to this organization wanting to sing to us in order to avoid a five-spot at Lorton or in some federal pen. They'll probably want to go down swinging."

"That being the case," Trask said, "let's look for the hangouts, businesses, wherever they do their dirty work. Without informants, we've got to think T3's." Title III was the short name given to that section of the federal code covering electronic surveillance: wiretaps and hidden microphones.

"I agree," Doroz said. "Willie, I'd like to deputize any of your people working with us on this, so we can cross state lines without having to make a phone call every five minutes. They'll be our TFOs." Doroz used the common acronym for federal task force officers. "Any problem with that?"

"Nope," Sivella answered. "I'll assign Dix here and get him a new partner."

"What?!" Carter objected. "Dammit, Cap, we've talked about this, and—"

"And I've changed my mind, Dixon. I don't want anybody—even you—riding alone on this thing. Too risky. Discussion closed."

Carter shook his head and stormed out of the room. Most of the others headed back to their desks.

"Dix still has Juan Ramirez hanging over his head, doesn't he?" Doroz asked.

"Yeah, but it wasn't his fault, and he's going to have to get over it," Sivella said. "I shouldn't have let him fly solo this long."

"Who've you got in mind?" Trask asked. "Anyone we know?"

"You'll recognize him. Lots of experience, and a good young cop. Just passed the detective's exam."

Chapter Four

August 11, 2:37 a.m.

Esteban Ortega pulled his car up to the back door of the deli and pulled the gasoline can out of the trunk. The convenience store where his soldiers had been killed the night before was not that far away, and the shootings had him worried. Not afraid, just worried. If the cowards from the 18th Street *Mara* were trying to move into his territory, the deli was not the kind of place from which one could properly manage a war. It was too close to the street and virtually indefensible against drive-by assaults like the one that had killed his troops. There was also too much glass in the front. Glass exposed those inside to the view from the street, and ordinary plate glass didn't stop bullets.

The deli had served its purpose—to provide a legitimate cover for the laundering of the funds generated by the sales of cocaine—but his people needed a new home. He had found one with concrete walls, a spacious attic, and set well back from the street. He just needed to get the final drop of financial funds out of the deli in order to crank up the new business. He unlocked the padlock on the back door and poured the gasoline around the base of the walls in the storage room, then dropped the container where he was sure the investigators would find it. Returning to the car trunk, he pulled a tire iron out. After relocking the padlock, he smashed the frame around the lock and ripped the hasp out of the door, leaving it dangling. He struck a match and threw it into the pool of gasoline.

At 3:12 a.m., the man with the eye patch low-crawled along the wall of the vacant house. When he reached the rusted air-conditioning unit on the concrete platform at the side, he balanced the rifle barrel on top of the unit.

He was close enough to the backyard of the house in the 3100 block of Georgia Avenue NW that he didn't really need the scope, but he preferred to use it anyway. It lessened the slim odds of a miss, but more than that, it allowed him to see the faces of his targets.

There were three of them sitting around a patio table on the elevated deck in the back of the house. There was a lantern in the center of the table, providing enough illumination for the man with the eye patch to read the *Cerveza Caguama* labels on the beer bottles. The one in the middle seemed to be very proud of the tattoo across the top of his back, since he kept pulling his shirt up to display it to the others.

The man with the eye patch focused the scope on the face of the center target. Looking through the scope gave him a small sense of contentment. The view was the same as before his loss; his left eye was closed, not needed, as it had always been while he shot. The difference would come when he took his right eye off the scope. His left eye was no longer there for him to open. They had taken it from him, along with so much more.

He took in every detail of his target's face. The round shape, the flat nose, a bruise here or there, the bloodshot eyes and drunken smile. His first shot arrived at the center of the forehead. The dead man tumbled backward. The two other targets stood reflexively, first looking down at their friend, and then whirling back toward the rear of the yard, toward him. His second shot hit the man on the right, the bullet striking the center of his chest. That target had been closest to the door of the house, and he fell, blocking it and slowing down target number three as he tried to pull the door open. The third round struck this target in the back, squarely between the shoulder blades.

The man with the eye patch paused to pick up the brass casings on the ground before turning toward the car waiting for him on the curb.

"Home, Hugo." He pulled the drawer open beneath the seat and dropped the rifle into it.

Trask got out of the Jeep and started walking up the hill past the perfectly lined rows of white grave markers. It was half-past ten in the morning, and Lynn had said that Dixon Carter hadn't checked in yet.

Arlington was an awe-inspiring place. Trask stopped and looked out at the silent ranks, wondering how many were buried there, what their stories were. One of his three academic majors had been history, after all. He knew that some lying here really had been heroes, while others had just been unfortunate. He had been to military bases named after those whose only accomplishment had been to get themselves killed on their first mission. Other bases had been named after combat or service legends. All had assumed the risk by putting on the uniform. Many here had paid the ultimate price for their service. All rested quietly now.

Not all the heroes chose to come here. Major Richard Bong, our Ace of Aces. Forty kills in the Pacific during World War II. Crashed and died on a test flight in San Francisco. The Japs couldn't kill him; forgetting to switch on a fuel tank in a new plane did. They took him home to Wisconsin for burial.

Trask couldn't help but feel a little inadequate among these honored dead. He'd never seen combat. His knees had been almost destroyed by the time he'd graduated from the Air Force Academy. Too many innings playing catcher in baseball, too many football games. It would have been a waste of the taxpayers' money for him to try to make it through pilot training. The flight surgeon who did his graduation physical told him that once he started pulling a few g's in a fighter trainer, they'd have to pull his kneecaps. There just wasn't enough cartilage to hold them in place anymore. So he'd stayed on the ground, gone to law school. His only fighting had been in the courtroom. He was still fighting those battles while his pilot classmates were all retired or flying desks of their own.

He remembered the burial site from the ceremony. The route through the headstones and trees was still vivid in his mind.

The grave's just beyond the crest of the little ridge, toward the right.

As he reached the top of the hill, Trask saw him sitting on the grass in front of the grave. Carter turned as he approached.

"Hi, Jeff."

"Dix."

Trask looked past him to the marker bearing the name of Sgt. Juan Ramirez, United States Army. For a moment, the images returned. The pallbearers in their dress uniforms, the mournful notes of the bugle, the rifle shots fired in salute. The folded flag presented to Juan's partner who was sitting here now, still blaming himself.

"Are you here to give me the lecture?"

"No. In fact, I was at the LEO Memorial today and got one myself."

"You? Why?"

"I've always thought that Bob Lassiter took a bullet that was meant for me. Barry Doroz agreed that it probably was, but said there was nothing I could do about it now but move on."

"Sometimes that's easier said than done."

"I know."

Trask waited for several long minutes for the big man to say something. He didn't. Trask turned to leave.

"Thanks for coming out," Carter said.

Trask turned back.

"Nobody else thinks it was your fault, Dix."

"What anybody else thinks doesn't matter."

Trask walked back over and sat down. Not too close. He looked at the gravestone, not at Carter.

"Saint Thomas Aquinas wrote that the greatest sin of all wasn't even written in the Ten Commandments. He said that you had to be a man to accept responsibility for your actions, but that you had to be a bigger man to forgive yourself when you didn't measure up. Otherwise, you were committing heresy by throwing the Maker's forgiveness back in his face and substituting your own judgment for his."

"I didn't know you were Catholic."

"I'm not. They just made me read a lot in school."

Carter nodded. "Saint Thomas sounds like a good man who never got his partner killed."

"Even if that happened, and I don't believe it did, there's another partner waiting for you who's willing to bet that you'd never let it happen again."

Carter scowled at him. "Who is it?'

Trask stood up and started back over the rise. "You'll have to see for yourself when you're ready. I thought it was a good pick."

He walked back toward the Jeep.

Hell if I know who Willie picked to survive your self-loathing, to try to measure up to Juan, but you're a detective, for Christ's sake. You've got a curiosity chip in your head that's just as big as mine, and I'm betting that right now you're really pissed that Sivella told anybody before he told you. You're also trying to figure out who he picked and who I thought was a good choice. I'll bet you're in the Cap's office in an hour.

He opened the door to the Jeep.

I hope it really is a good pick...

Trask crossed the Potomac on the Arlington Memorial Bridge, circled around the Lincoln Memorial, and headed east on Independence Avenue, driving along the south side of the Capitol Mall. He saw the usual crowds of tourists on the sidewalks on either side of the Mall, gawking at the huge granite buildings, heading for the Monument or the Smithsonian.

Stay on the Mall, children, he thought. *Six blocks the wrong way and you might end up as a statistic. We had hundreds of murders here last year, more if you count the 'burbs.*

He turned southeast where Independence turned into Pennsylvania Avenue and crossed over the Anacostia on the Sousa Bridge. Just past Branch Avenue, he pulled into the parking lot of the Penn Branch Shopping Center. From the street the place looked like a 1960s-vintage shopping mall. There was a tax preparation office, a sandwich shop, and some other storefronts along the façade. Once inside, he found the room number for the Violent Crimes Unit of the District of Columbia's Metropolitan Police Department.

Trask walked past the detectives' cubicles in the main room before he found the office of Commander William Sivella. The door was open, and he saw that Barry Doroz was already inside, sitting in one of the worn leather armchairs in front of the desk. Sivella looked up from behind the desk and waved him on in.

"Hello, Jeff. Any trouble finding the place?"

"Not at all. This one's a lot easier to get to than your old command at 7D."

The police precincts in the District of Columbia were called districts. Sivella had recently commanded the Seventh District, or 7D, including the southeast area of the city next to the Anacostia River.

"That it is. We're on a main drag here. The city owns about half the building now. Just a few shops and other offices left. Otherwise, it's kind of City Hall East."

"I would have thought that Homicide would be in the headquarters building."

"It was at one time. Then they split it up and splintered the detectives out to each one of the districts, the theory being that the guys could concentrate on certain neighborhoods and know them better. That system didn't work. It ignored the mobility that individual killers and gangs enjoy these days. You have one victim in 7D one day, another in 4D the next... same shooter.

"They reunited the unit and stuck us out here. Good thing. Murders grab attention, and high-profile cases mean high-level interest. If I was still in the Daly Building, the chief would be either walking down the hall every five minutes or summoning me to her office every time she got a phone call. I'd never get a damn thing done."

He looked at his watch and frowned.

"You didn't see Dix outside, did you?"

"Yeah. Way outside. I just came from Arlington. He was camped out on Juan's grave."

"Dammit." Sivella walked out from behind the desk and sat on the front of it, shoving a stack of case files aside to make room. "I never should have let him partner with Ramirez that long. Over ten years. It's just hard to break up guys who work that well together. They were the best I had. Cracked every big case I ever gave 'em. Still, if I'd split 'em up, Dix might not be where he is right now. I can't pull his head out of this. He blames himself for Juan's murder."

"How long has he been solo?" Doroz asked.

"Ever since Juan died. I tried assigning another experienced guy to ride with him, but that lasted all of two days. His new partner came in and threw his badge on my desk. Said I could either reassign him or he'd quit. Dix was giving him hell the whole time. I just let Dixon ride alone after that. He's still a helluva good detective, even working alone. His casework hasn't suffered, but the rest of his life has. His wife left him last week."

"Melody's gone?" Doroz asked. "Christ, they've been married over twenty years, haven't they?"

"Yep. High-school sweethearts. She called me after she moved out, said she'd tried to make a difference after Juan died, but Dix wouldn't let her. She said he still wakes up with nightmares, just sits in the den and cries at times. If I'd noticed anything on the job other than Dix just being a cranky asshole—I've got lots of those—I'd have given him an order to see the department shrink."

"You can't let him ride alone on this case, Cap," Doroz said. "The MS-13 crew's too dangerous and won't be reluctant at all to take out a cop working alone."

"I know that. I hope I picked the right guy for the job. If not..."

Trask looked up after hearing the knock on the frame of the open door. He stood and held out his hand. "Good to see you again, Tim."

"You too, Jeff."

Wisniewski was wearing his tailored patrol uniform. About thirty-five, he still had the look of a California beach lifeguard: blond, blue-eyed, and buff. The uniform looked like someone had painted it on him.

"Come in, Tim." Sivella offered his hand. "You remember Barry Doroz, right?"

"Of course. Bear, how are you?"

"Better than you're going to be, if my hunch is right." Doroz glanced at Sivella, looking for confirmation. Sivella nodded.

"What's going on?" Wisniewski asked.

"I've got some good news and, of course, some bad news," Sivella began. "The good news is that you've passed the detective's exam."

Sivella tossed a new wallet to Wisniewski, who caught it and opened it to examine the gold shield inside. He smiled and looked up.

"OK. Thanks. What's the bad news?"

"Because you're from New Mexico and had the foresight to become fluent in Spanish, the Latino Liaison Division had their sights on you when your name came out on the list. You know, showing the city flag on Cinco de Mayo, translating on high-school career day in certain neighborhoods, being the junior guy with the language skill on somebody else's cases—"

"That's OK. I know I have to start somewhere," Wisniewski said.

"Oh, you won't be getting off that easy, young man." Sivella laughed. "I pulled rank and got your ass assigned here. You'll be working for me in Violent Crimes. Homicide cases. I'm assigning you to the Bureau, Tim. You'll be a TFO on Barry's squad working an investigation into at least one murder—probably committed by members of the MS-13. You know the case."

"The ambassador's kid?"

"Yeah, the one you called in. Here's the *really* tough part. I'm assigning you as Dixon Carter's partner."

"Wow." Wisniewski sank into one of the chairs, even though the others in the office remained on their feet. "I don't know that I can fill Juan's shoes. . .not in Dix's eyes."

"Don't even try to." Sivella sat down on the front of the desk again. "Just do your job and give him time. You'll need a thick hide. Think you're up to it?"

"I guess we'll see. If not, I'll be translating and playing the community-relations game in the liaison unit, huh?"

"That's about the size of it. What do you know about MS-13?"

"A good bit, actually. We used to run into them fairly often in Santa Fe. They spread west from LA and started taking over any turf they moved into. At first they were fighting everybody else: the others gangs, locals. Just before I left New Mexico, they'd started a truce with the Mexican Mafia and were helping to bring dope across from Juarez through El Paso. The guys down in Las Cruces had fits with them. Tough bunch."

"They're here now in force," Doroz added. He patted Wisniewski on the shoulder. "I think the commander here has the right man for this assignment. You'll need some more civvies. Nothing flashy. Mine is not a formal squad. We'll see you in the morning across the street from the Triple-nickel. Prepare to be federally deputized."

"And to meet your new partner," Sivella said. "I haven't told him yet."

"I think I have some body armor in the car," Wisniewski said.

"Good," Sivella laughed. "Keep the sense of humor. You'll need it. Take the rest of the day off. I'll tell Dix, and you may not want to be here for that."

Chapter Five

August 12, 8:15 a.m.

It was one of the most surreal days Trask could ever remember.

He got to the gang squad early. His original excuse to himself was that he wanted a copy of Crawford's PowerPoint so he could show Bill Patrick, his immediate supervisor, exactly what he was going to be dealing with. The truth was that he wanted to see how Dixon Carter was going to react to the designation of Tim Wisniewski as his new partner.

As he entered the squad room, Lynn saw him and smiled. He walked to her desk.

"What's up?" she asked.

"I came here to find out. You guys are supposed to tell me."

Trask saw that Wisniewski was pulling some personal stuff out of boxes and setting up his cubicle. He nodded toward Trask. Trask heard the exit bell from the elevator. Carter emerged, walked briskly into the squad room, and tossed a file into the chair in front of his desk.

"Tim?"

"Yeah, Dix?"

"Let's go."

"Where to?" Wisniewski asked.

"Baltimore. Some MS-13 bangers got whacked in Langley Park a couple of nights ago. They're doing the autopsy today in the chief medical examiner's office. I want to see what they have."

"Mind if I ride along?" Trask immediately regretted asking the question. He was intruding on the new partners' first job together. The withering look he got from Lynn made him regret his gaffe even more, but he couldn't un-ring the bell.

"Sure. Come on," Carter said flatly.

They took the elevator down to the garage and piled into Carter's green Buick. Trask remembered it as the supposed undercover vehicle that Carter had shared with Juan Ramirez. Everyone in Anacostia had known it was a police car, and they had known the cops in it. "The Twins," the rest of the force had called them. The very large black guy and the small, wiry Hispanic. Jawing at each other constantly, keeping everyone around them in stitches with their comedy road show, and all the while never missing a thing. Solving cases. Working twenty-hour days. Loving their work.

Poor Dix. Can't even bring himself to get new wheels. Probably still feels Juan in the other seat.

Carter drove, with Wisniewski riding shotgun. Trask sat behind Tim. The drive up Interstate 95 from DC to Baltimore took the usual hour, an hour in which not a single word was spoken.

Trask's mind began to drift again. He closed his eyes and released the latches on all the files. Not all of them floated out at once. He'd learned to control them. He was back with his mother, with a doctor of her own choosing, not one of those the school wanted him to see, the ones with the pills. This one was different. He didn't have to strain to hear voices behind closed doors. This doctor talked directly to him.

There'd been some tests. A deck of cards, more than a hundred shown to him, kept in order. The second time through he'd been able to recall the order perfectly, predicting the next card in the deck time after time. The doctor nodded. "*An incredible eidetic memory, photographic recall,*" he'd said. "*Most lose this ability by your age. Do you have a lot of things that seem to float through your mind all at once?*" *Yes, sir.* "*The key to living with your ability is learning to focus on one thing at a time. We'll work on that. Do you like any games, sports?*" "*He loves them,*" *his mother had said, surprised.* "*I'd always thought that was kind of...*" "*Inconsistent? Not really. Athletic drama. No predetermined outcome. No plot he's already read a hundred times. What kind of sports interest you, Jeff?*" *Football, baseball, he'd said. It was the South, after all.* "*But he's so small.*" *Mom couldn't help herself. She was worried. Should have been. He'd stayed hurt, played hurt most of the time. She never knew, or that's what he'd believed.*

Trask felt the car slowing as it left the highway.

They reached the ME's office, introduced themselves to the Maryland State Police officers working the case, and watched as the doc cut into the tattooed bodies. One spent round came out of the head of one of the victims; another had been killed by a shot that had gone all the way through his torso.

The doc handed the bullet to the Maryland guys, who looked at it before passing it to Carter.

"7.62 round," Dix said.

"Everybody loves an AK," one of the troopers said.

"It wasn't an AK." Carter had the round under a microscope on a counter that ran along the side of the examining room.

"Yeah, yeah. Not a true Russian AK-47," the trooper shot back, pissed at being corrected. "The usual cheap-ass Chinese knock-off. A Norinco SKS."

"It wasn't an SKS, either." Carter still had the round under the scope.

"*Sure* it was," the trooper shot back. "Both the vics were MS-13. Our most probable perps are M-18 types. We've had intel they were trying to move into the area. They hate each other, and the gang weapon of choice is the AK—excuse me—the *Norinco SKS*. They can get one for twenty bucks from the underground dealers, and we have fits matching the round to the rifle—"

"Because you don't get the usual lands and grooves on the round that you'd see in a good American rifle," Carter interrupted. "The reason being that the SKS is a Chinese assault rifle, made to stand up in the worst combat environments imaginable, with little or no maintenance. It never jams because the rifle bore is oversized compared to the round. The slug just rattles around on its way down and out of the barrel. It's accurate at short range, but shit after a couple hundred yards." He pointed to the microscope. "Not an SKS."

The troopers, then Wisniewski, then Trask, took turns looking at the bullet, which bore very distinctive rifling marks.

"Big deal." The same trooper spoke up. "The gooks happened to get one of their barrels right."

Carter looked at him with a hard glare that made it clear the debate was over. "NOT an SKS."

He nodded toward the ME.

"Thanks for letting us sit in on your exam."

Trask and Wisniewski followed him back to the Buick and their assigned seats. The trip back to DC was a repeat performance. No conversation, no radio. Complete silence. Trask nodded off again.

First day of Little League. Not actually Little League. The minor league for Little League. The ones the small kids had to go through to make it to a real Little League team. "Anyone here a catcher?" No hands up. Just mine. If nobody else wants to do it, I'll get to play. I'll put on the "tools of ignorance." Ignore the bat swinging in front of you. Just concentrate on the ball. Focus. Good. Eyes stay open. The bat's just a distraction. Feel the ball hitting the mitt. What's that pain? My knees? Another doctor. "Osgood-Schlatter disease, I'm afraid. Best thing to do is limit any sports activity..." "It doesn't hurt that bad, Mom. Just a little." The only lie I remember ever telling her. The pain's just another distraction. Like the bat. Focus on the ball. Ignore the bat, ignore the pain. Concentrate.

The car pulled back into the parking lot at the FBI field office.

After they parked and returned to the squad room, Trask heard Carter speaking to Barry Doroz.

"The Maryland guys think we have a gang war about to break out. Thirteen versus Eighteen. Both the dead kids were certainly MS-13, and the round they dug out of one body was a 7.62, but it wasn't the usual cheap ammo. It looked like a higher-quality round to me, and it was marked up pretty good. I don't think it was fired by an SKS."

"That could just mean that one of the gangbangers got his hands on a better rifle, couldn't it, Dix?" Doroz had asked.

"It could. I don't think that's what happened. I'd like you to have Frank Wilkes take a look at it."

Trask remembered Wilkes poring over the evidence in the Reid case. He was the best criminologist in DC, an expert in all things forensics, the Merlin of the local crime lab.

"Sure," Doroz said. "I'll make the call."

He reached down for the phone, but it started ringing, and after Doroz answered it, they were off to another ME's office, the medical examiner for the District of Columbia. Three more gangbangers blown away, this time on DC turf. Trask had a late hearing in the district court, so he drove himself in case the exams took longer than expected.

He watched as Kathy Davis began the autopsy on one of the three newest victims. Doroz and Carter were looking under the sheets covering the other two. Wisniewski stood back, looking over Carter's shoulder. Frank Wilkes had answered Doroz' call and was standing at the head of the exam table with Commander Sivella. Wilkes was a thin, studious little man with graying hair and coal-black eyes that peered from behind a thick set of glasses.

"They're all MS-13," Carter said. "Found lying on the back porch of a place in Northwest. Georgia Avenue just north of Columbia, about the 3100 block. The tat across this one's back says *Salvatrucha*. It's fresh. He probably got it within the last day or two. The other one has that Horns of the Devil sign on his right bicep. That one," he pointed to the body on the examining table, "seems to have been a Latin scholar."

Trask looked at the right side of the dead man's neck. The Roman numerals XIII stared back at him.

"Here's your cause of death for this guy." Kathy's raised forceps held a bullet extracted from the body on the table. "Looks like a 7.62. Right through the heart, back entry. A front rib stopped it, or it would have gone through him."

She handed the bullet to Wilkes, who held it up to the light as a narrow ribbon of blood trickled down the white plastic glove on his hand. He put the round under one of the lab's microscopes.

"SKS?" Carter asked.

"No SKS fired this."

"How can you tell, Frank?" Sivella asked.

"I'll have to take it to the lab to be sure, put it into the computer, but the markings don't look like SKS markings to me. Some newer Norincos will leave fairly sharp lands and grooves, but most of the street guns we see don't. The marks on this round are more consistent with a very high-quality weapon. Like a sniper rifle. A good one."

"That's certainly consistent with what I'm seeing here." Kathy was looking at the wounds on the other two bodies. "Somebody hit what he was aiming for. Two heart shots and a head shot. Three shots, three kills. Not the usual spray of automatic drive-by fire."

"Excuse my ignorance," Trask said. "Are there high-quality sniper rifles that fire AK ammo?" *It's good to have some real experts around to rely upon. I should actually know this already, need to read more ballistics lab bulletins.*

"I wouldn't call this AK or SKS ammo, either," Wilkes answered. "The usual stuff we see in the SKS 7.62 x 39 ammunition is the steel core bullet. This looks more like a NATO round, 7.62 x 51 maybe."

"What's the 39 and 51 difference?" Trask asked.

"The 7.62 is the metric diameter of the cartridge. The 39 and 51 measurements are for the length of the cartridge," Carter said. "Bigger cartridge, better range. More powder behind the round, right, Frank?"

"Yes. I don't have the cartridge here, of course, just the spent round. I'm just guessing that if we're dealing with a NATO country sniper rifle—something indicated by the type of bullet and the ballistics markings—we'd see a longer range, sniper type of ammunition. Probably the 7.62 x 51."

"Gangbanger snipers?" Sivella asked.

"As I said earlier today in Baltimore, I don't think so," Carter said.

"What *are* you thinking, Dix?" Doroz asked.

"We know *somebody's* at war with this gang. If the MS-13 *thinks* it's Barrio 18, then regardless of who starts the war, then they *will* be at war with the 18th Street crew. That's a fact. I'm just not convinced that a gang shooter is good for these hits."

"Food for thought, then," Sivella said. "Both for all my new homicide cases, and for the federal gang task force that's supposed to be taking these things off my hands. If it's not a gang sniper, I might have to pull you back to Homicide, Dix."

Carter nodded, then turned and walked out of the morgue. He didn't return.

"I guess I need a ride back to the office," Wisniewski said.

"I'll take you, Tim," Doroz chuckled.

"Cold shoulder?" Sivella asked.

"Not exactly," Wisniewski answered. "I'm not sure exactly what to call it. He's sharp as hell on the case, as you can see, but it's like he doesn't really exist away from it. Jeff and I rode for two hours with him today—Baltimore and back—without hearing a word from him. It was like he didn't know we were even there."

That's why I was floating, Trask thought. *No conversation. Just the road noise and the wind.*

"Keep an eye on him," Sivella said. "And keep me posted.

Trask's hearing that afternoon was a nightmare. Any time a prosecutor drew Senior Judge Richard Scott for a guilty plea at 4:00 p.m., the attorney knew to call home and tell his wife not to hold dinner. Most federal district judges could handle a routine plea in well under an hour, some in half that time. Judge Scott, on the other hand, was very proud that in more than twenty years on the bench, he had never had a guilty plea that had subsequently been set aside by the Court of Appeals because of an inadequate plea inquiry. Federal Rule of Criminal Procedure 11 required the judge to make sure that the defendant indicated on the record that he knew what he was doing, knew the rights he was waiving, and had, in fact, committed the crime to which he was pleading guilty. Judge Scott's Rule 11 inquisitions went far beyond the requirements of the rule; in fact, most Assistant United States Attorneys (AUSAs for short) worried as much about Scott talking the defendant *out* of the plea as the length of the process.

The defendant *du jour* was an ugly little troll who had been shipping ecstasy tablets—the rave party drug of the moment—to the nation's capital from his home in Phoenix. Trask thought he might actually get out of the proceedings in less than two hours, but then the judge asked the accused whether he was under the influence of any medications that might affect his mental clarity. The laundry list of maladies and medications that came spewing from the defendant marked him to be a hypochondriac of the highest order, and Trask cringed at the answer, since he was familiar with "Richard's Ritual," the judge's tortuous inquiry into the effects of every drug on the list.

While the pointless script was playing out, Trask was present in body only. He glanced from one portrait to another. Dead judges who had ruled the courthouse in the past. His eyes remained open but glazed over—he couldn't close them for fear of being accused of sleeping through the hearing—as he recalled significant cases decided by each late jurist. Some decisions had withstood the tests of time and appellate review. Several had not.

Back with Mom and the doc again. "You like music, Jeff?""He loves it," she said. "We got him a radio with an earpiece and he listens to the thing all night when he's supposed to be asleep. Hides it under his pillow." How did she know? She always knew. "Pick out a song, then, and play it in your head when you get bored." It had worked for him ever since; the order when the chaos started to crowd in. No more talk of medication. "Music is the Doctor" from The Doobie Brothers started playing on his mental jukebox.

Two hours later, after finally asking the perp whether the aspirin he took daily for cardiac therapy had any effect on his ability to understand the gravity of the plea he was about to enter, the judge finally got into the actual details of the offense. It was seven-thirty before Trask started the forty-five-minute drive home to Waldorf, Maryland, a bedroom suburb at about five-thirty on the beltway "clock."

Lynn met him at the door with a kiss and the appropriate amount of spousal sympathy. "Put on something comfortable. I ate already, chicken and dumplings. I'll heat you a bowl, and then I've got some more info for you."

"About what?"

"Our case, of course. Eat first and give your mind a rest. I know you need a break after that marathon with Judge Gollum."

Trask smiled at Lynn's nickname for Judge Scott. The diminutive and bald jurist did bear a strong physical resemblance to the character from *Lord of the Rings.* He changed, wolfed down the meal while watching the news on the big screen in the living room, and then sat back in his chair. He yawned, and then yawned again.

"No naps yet. Not until I tell you about *my* afternoon," she said.

"OK. Shoot." He yawned again.

"You going to stay awake for this?"

"I'll try to. Five autopsies, two silent rides with Dixon Carter, and then Judge Gollum. No guarantees."

She sat down on his lap and started to unbutton her blouse.

"That's not fair." *It isn't. I can't concentrate on anything else, even if I want to, and I don't want to. Pick a song—yep, that one's appropriate.*

"Stay awake then. Barry brought back some of the personal papers on the vics from the local shootings. One was a kid named Diego Morales, the one with the new tattoo. I'll tell you what I think that means in a minute. He had his ID in his wallet, and also a pay stub from a delicatessen in Langley Park."

"Nice work. We'll go by and talk to the owner tomorrow after they open up."

He yawned again. She unbuttoned two more buttons.

"Stop that," he said. The music in his head started his fingers tapping on the chair arm.

"You really don't want me to stop, and you really don't want to go to that deli tomorrow."

"Why not?"

"I drove by it on the way home after work. It burned down yesterday, and the fire flared again today in the rubble. The firefighters were still hosing down the ashes. I talked to one of the guys on the scene. After I showed him my creds, he told me it was an arson job."

Trask closed his eyes and shook his head. When he opened them, her blouse was on the coffee table. He smiled.

She saw his fingers hitting the chair arm.

"Now? What song?" she demanded.

"'Night Moves.' Bob Seger. 1976."

"Why that one?"

"Oh, I don't know. Something about points sitting way up firm and high."

"You wish! They used to be." She shook her head and laughed. "Anyway, I think Diego Morales may be your killer of the ambassador's kid," she said, leaning over to kiss him.

"How do you figure that?"

"In addition to the bullet hole, Barry said he had a lot of bruises, about two days old. That means he just got 'jumped in.' That's the term MS-13 uses for an initiation. The new recruit has to carry out some special mission first—like murdering a rival gang member—then he gets the shit kicked out of him for thirteen seconds. It's only after completing his assignment and getting 'jumped in' that he's allowed to get his tattoos as a full-fledged *Mara* member."

"Makes sense," Trask said. "Fresh bruising, new tat. Timing lines up. We'll need a lot more to make the case, of course, find out who ordered the hit on the ambassador's kid and why, but those are excellent leads, babe." He yawned again.

"Thanks. Barry thought so, too. He wants you to go with him to see the ambassador Monday, with a photo spread. See if he can pick out Diego."

"OK. I'll need to get some sleep then."

He leaned back, closed his eyes and tried to keep a straight face. He couldn't. When he opened his eyes, the bra was gone. She kissed him again.

"Not so fast, hotshot. In case you hadn't noticed, I'm amped up about this case. I need one of those physical sleeping pills you're so good at, or I'll be up all night."

Chapter Six

August 15

Trask reached his office at 8:00. He checked his e-mails and the court docket to make sure no emergency hearings had popped up. His schedule was clear, so he crossed the street to the FBI field office. Barry Doroz was not alone. Michael Crawford was in Doroz' office, and a man in a well-tailored suit with flaming red hair and a matching moustache stood from his chair and turned when Trask entered the room.

"Morning, Jeff. This is Tom Murphy; he's with the State Department," Doroz said.

"Very glad to meet you, Jeff," Murphy said.

Trask thought that Murphy's smile was a bit too wide, his manner too friendly. *This guy reminds me of some used car salesmen I've met in the past. Must be the State Department emphasis on diplomacy—a professional glad-hander.*

"Jeff Trask, Tom. Nice to meet you, too, I hope. What part of the State Department?"

Murphy smiled at Doroz.

"You're right, Bear, smart *and* careful. I'm from the Diplomatic Affairs Division, Jeff. We're responsible for all sorts of things regarding foreign ambassadors to the US. We oversee the accreditation of the ambassadors and their staffs, deal with issues involving diplomatic immunity for the embassy staff and their families, and we handle any problems arising with any of the personnel in any of the foreign missions. El Salvador is one of the nations I monitor. My boss just wanted me to ride along with you guys today to see if there was anything that State could do to facilitate your investigation."

"To make sure that this is really an FBI case, not a State case, and that some bungling AUSA didn't start an international incident?"

"Barry's already assured me that I don't have to worry about that, but yes, that too, if something should come up."

"Do you know something that we should be worried about?" Trask asked.

"I'll give you some background on the way over to the embassy."

It was a nice day, and it made no sense to drive with the Metro stop as close as it was. They walked through the Law Enforcement Memorial to the Red Line entrance in Judiciary Square and got on the down escalator leading to the subway.

"Barry tells me you've been briefed on the civil war in El Salvador, and on the gangs that sprang up in the refugee *barrios* in LA?"

"Yes." Trask looked around to see if anyone else was within earshot.

"Nothing I'm going to say is classified," Murphy said. "You could get it all on the web in about fifteen minutes."

"OK."

"The pertinent facts for today are these. The war was basically between two political factions. On the conservative, pro-American side, you had the ARENA group, which was backed by the military, the National Civilian Police, and our CIA."

"Hard-line, right-wing bastards like myself and these agents here?" Trask asked.

"Much harder, I'm afraid," chuckled Murphy. "Some of us in State believe that they *had* to be hard to survive. Others disagree. At any rate, the opposition was aligned with the FMLN."

"The Liberation Front?"

"Yes, a more radical group, and in the recent elections, the winners by a narrow margin. The new regime has done and said all the right things publically—that their priorities are to maintain the good relations between El Salvador and the US—I really don't think there's much reason to worry about them. The new ambassador comes from that group. It's the first time the FMLN has been in power, and that's a matter of concern, especially given the tensions between the new government and some of the other Salvadoran national agencies. The ARENA candidate who lost was, after all, the former director of the national police."

"And what does this have to do with our murder case?" Trask was looking around again to see if anyone was eavesdropping.

"It has to do with the *Maras*. The ARENA administrations were very tough on the gangs. The Salvadoran cops were known to meet gang members at the airport in San Salvador when they arrived after being deported from this country. If the cops saw a banger with the usual tattoos, they'd haul him straight to one of their infamous prisons just for being a member. Tattoo equals guilt equals jail, or worse. Some of the gang members never made it to prison. It wasn't unusual for their bodies to be found alongside a country road somewhere. Before 9/11, some *Mara* members were trying to cut their tats off with razorblades on the flights back to the home country. The airlines were forced to rehab the lavatories to clean up all the blood."

"What's the relationship between the gangs and the new administration?" Doroz asked.

"The new president won because he portrayed himself as a moderate," Murphy continued, "not just another Marxist financed by Hugo Chavez. He held out some olive branches, tried to persuade gang members to leave the *Maras*, and called many of the inmates in his country 'political prisoners.' The problem is that he's now got the same troubles Castro faced before he hit us with that Mariel boat lift in the seventies. Even Communist workers' paradises and liberation fronts have real thugs and criminals to deal with, psychopaths who don't give a damn about which side of a political argument you're on before they rob you and cut your head off. When their gang soldiers weren't *all* immediately freed, the *Mara* hard-liners—especially those from MS-13—felt like the new 'moderates' in the FMLN sold them out, and they declared war on the new regime just like they did with the old one."

"You think that's the reason the ambassador's kid got whacked?" Crawford asked.

That's what he wants us to think, Trask thought. *Murphy's already trying to paint the case as a politically motivated assassination. If he's successful, special agents from the State Department will be calling the shots over Doroz' head, and the main justice hall-crawlers will be passing notes to me at the trial table.*

"It's certainly possible," Murphy said. "I just thought you guys investigating the case needed to hear that side of the story before interviewing the ambassador again. I know you have rules regarding what information can be released and when, but we'd like to be kept in the loop as much as possible. The Secretary is personally interested in the case, and called your US Attorney last night."

"The Secretary of State?" Trask asked. "I'm surprised I wasn't in Eastman's office first thing this morning."

"Ross called *me* this morning, Jeff," Doroz said. "I told him that Murph here was briefing us, and that I'd keep you from embarrassing him."

"Wonderful."

"Seriously," Doroz laughed, "he said he had complete confidence in us, but he wanted an update after our meeting with the ambassador. He thinks a lot of you. I think he called me because I've been around longer."

"I think he called *you* because it's a subtle way of telling *me* that he's going to be checking on this from every angle possible," Trask said. "Complete confidence aside, my direct and personal updates aren't going to be enough where ambassadors and the State Department are concerned."

Murphy was chuckling again. "I don't know how long you've been in the capital, Jeff, but you've certainly learned some of the games."

The train pulled to a stop at the Dupont Circle Station. They rode the escalator back up into the sunlight.

"Dupont Circle. This is where that Georgian diplomat Makharadze killed that kid during a DWI isn't it?" Trask thought aloud. "Georgia waived his diplomatic immunity, and we actually got to prosecute him, as I recall."

"A very rare event," Murphy said. "I wouldn't count on seeing that again in your lifetime."

A very weird thing to say, Trask thought. *Wonder where that came from? Diplomats all over this city getting away with everything from serial traffic violations to rape, and he acts like the waiver was something that shouldn't have been pursued. He must be concerned about his own status when he's overseas.*

They walked a few blocks east to the embassy.

Murphy presented his credentials first, which got a knowing nod at the reception desk. They were almost immediately ushered into the waiting room outside the ambassador's office, where they sat on a couch. A dark-haired secretary smiled at them from her desk. She was twenty-something and stunning, at least a fourteen on the proverbial ten-scale.

"That didn't take long," Doroz said, returning the secretary's smile.

Trask noticed that the girl's glance lingered on Crawford, who was smiling back at her and blushing.

You may need oven mitts for that one, Puddin'.

"About a quarter of the country's income comes from money mailed home by Salvadorans still living and working in the US," Murphy whispered to Trask. "They like to keep us happy, so we won't be waiting long."

"Please come in, gentlemen."

The distinguished figure of Ambassador Juan Carlos Lopez-Portilla stood in an open doorway in front of the couch. After introductions, they followed him into the ambassador's office, but instead of sitting behind his desk, he joined them around a coffee table in front of it. A steaming pitcher and five cups had already been arranged on the table.

"One of El Salvador's specialties, of course," the ambassador said. "I always take my coffee black, but I can have cream and sugar brought in if anyone requires it."

"Black is fine, Mr. Ambassador," Trask said. "I wouldn't want to ruin the flavor of excellent coffee with cream and sugar any more than I'd want to ruin a good Canadian whiskey by mixing it with soda."

"I'll accept that, Mr. Trask," the ambassador said, "with the qualification that the sugar is also excellent, having also been grown in El Salvador."

"My mistake," Trask said. "Perhaps I should try a cup sweetened with Salvadoran sugar."

"You may have a career ahead of you in diplomacy," the ambassador replied. His smile was brief. "You are here, of course, on much sadder business."

"I'm afraid so, sir. Mr. Doroz has some photographs for you to look at, if you don't mind. We'd like to know if you recognize any of these individuals."

Doroz removed the spread from a manila envelope and handed it to the ambassador. Six photographs of young Hispanic males, three above three, were arranged on an 8x10 sheet of paper. The face of the late Diego Morales appeared in the fourth photograph.

"I'm afraid I do not know these people," Lopez said after looking hard at the spread. "There is a member of my staff who might, however. Do you mind if I ask him to look at them?"

"Of course not," Trask replied.

"Excellent. I'll show the photos to him later, then, and—"

"Mr. Ambassador, our courts have rules of evidence which require that we witness any identification which your staff member might make. We would need him to sign and initial any photograph he recognizes. We can't just leave this with you."

"I see."

The ambassador was silent for a moment. He rose from his chair and opened the door to the waiting room.

"Marissa, please have Señor Rios join us."

The ambassador returned to his chair. He did not speak, and stared vacantly at the photo spread on the table until the door opened again. A man dressed in a black suit and wearing a black patch over his left eye entered the room.

Trask had always heard cops talking about their antennae, their investigative intuition or sixth sense that let them know when somebody was just "wrong." *If I've actually managed to grow a pair of the things, they're about to overheat with this guy.*

"Gentlemen, may I present José Rios-García, my deputy chief of mission?" the ambassador said. "I'm afraid he may have been more familiar with my son's activities than I have been lately, with the pressing duties of my office. Much to my regret, as I'm sure you understand."

"Of course," Trask said.

Rios merely nodded to them, not offering a handshake. The ambassador handed him the photo spread. Rios scanned it and looked at it again. Trask noticed a small hesitation on both passes, at the point where the man's good eye was focusing on the fourth photo. Rios handed the sheet back to the ambassador.

"No, Señor. Lo siento mucho." Rios gave a nod to Trask and turned and left without another word. Trask had the feeling he had just been x-rayed.

I need to ask the ambassador the hard question. No sense in sugarcoating it.

"There was an eighteen tattooed on your son's right shoulder, Mr. Ambassador," Trask said. "Was he involved in Barrio 18?"

Lopez-Portilla shook his head. "Not really. Ten years ago, I was working on my master's degree at UCLA. Armando was eight years old. We didn't live in the *barrios*, but my son naturally gravitated to others from our home country. His mother and I were not happy with the tattoo, of course, but it was my impression that Armando got it simply out of desire to identify with the other boys. If he was actually involved in any gang activities, I never knew it. Perhaps I was too busy."

"I'm sure you did your best, sir," Trask said.

"I am sorry, gentlemen," the ambassador rose, signaling they were being dismissed. "We do not seem to have been of much assistance."

"Thanks for trying, Mr. Ambassador," Trask said. "We'll keep you posted. Would you have a set of your son's records from school on hand? There may be something there that gives us some leads."

"I have some papers at home. I'll have them brought in today. Leave your contact information with my secretary, and she'll see that you get them. Let me know if there is anything else you think might be of assistance."

They left the way they had entered, each leaving a business card with the ambassador's secretary on the way out. Trask noticed that the lovely Marissa's smile lingered twice as long on the face of Special Agent Michael Crawford as it did for either Doroz or himself.

"I think old eye patch recognized one of those photos," Trask said as they walked back toward Dupont Circle.

"How do you figure that?" Murphy asked.

"Just a feeling. Don't you guys keep some sort of roster of personnel for foreign embassies?"

"Yes. It's called the Diplomatic List. Why?"

"I'd be interested in seeing whatever information you have about the deputy chief of mission," Trask said.

"And why is that?"

"Call it a feeling again, Murph. Call it whatever you want to. Is there a problem furnishing us that info?"

"Probably not, but I may have to get the Secretary's approval. It's on a need-to-know basis, that sort of thing."

"See what you can do, please." Trask looked at Murphy and smiled. "Tell the Secretary that my US Attorney is personally interested in the matter, and that we'd appreciate being kept 'in the loop' on our own investigation."

"Of course." Murphy was not smiling now. The train slowed. "This is my stop. I'm heading back to State. You fellows have a nice day."

"I'm with you, Jeff," Doroz said after the doors closed again. "Darth Vader recognized that photo. The fourth one, Morales."

"What's up with the State Department wanting to guard this Diplomatic List?" Crawford asked.

"State has always operated under the theory of 'don't make waves.'" Doroz said. "When you have to try and solve problems by talking them to death, you don't want to see the problem in the first place. A lot of times, the messenger who brings the problem in gets shot—figuratively, of course. State hates real bullets.

"Murphy was probably hoping it would be either a quick solution—photo recognized, case closed—or a case of random violence with no repercussions for anyone. The last thing he wants is complications, especially complications over which State has no control. Don't sweat the info, though. We'll get it. If not from State, then through some of our other sources."

Meaning CIA, Trask said to himself. *That'll stir the pot.*

"Speaking of sources," Doroz continued, "it seems that our man Puddin' here was really cultivating one in the embassy. Think you can handle her, Mr. Crawford?"

Crawford was blushing again.

"Just remember to register her on the appropriate official Bureau forms when she starts providing you information," Doroz prodded. "You did have your cell phone number written on the back of your business card, didn't you, Mike?"

"You told me to put it on *all* my cards," Crawford protested.

"Good man," Doroz said as the cell phone on Crawford's belt began to chime. "Wonder who that could be."

"I better stop and take it here," Crawford said as they neared the down escalator to the Metro.

"Yep, wouldn't want to lose *that* signal," Doroz agreed.

Trask started humming a song.

"What's that?" Crawford asked, holding the Blackberry to his ear.

"*Hot Child in the City*. Nick Gilder. 1978. Before your time." Trask's fingers drummed the beat on the handrail as he descended into the Metro.

Trask and Doroz walked back through Judiciary Square, reached the FBI field office, and took the elevator to the squad room. Trask saw Lynn at her computer terminal.

"Hi, babe. Violate any international protocol this morning?" she asked.

"He did fine, as usual," Doroz said, slapping him on the back. "The ambassador said he ought to go into the foreign service."

"Not without me," she said.

"No worries there," Trask said. "But with the permission of the squad supervisor, I'd like the squad analyst to see what she can find out about a couple of things."

"Granted," Doroz said.

"Give me a rundown on anti-gang initiatives undertaken by the ARENA party before they lost the election in El Salvador. See what you can find out about any internal conflicts within the FMLN. And finally, since Very Special Agent Doroz assures me he can get some documentation from somewhere, I need to know all you can find out about one José Rios-García, the deputy chief of mission who doesn't seem to want to extend the courtesy of speaking English to American visitors to his embassy."

Lynn looked up at Doroz.

"Again, granted," he said.

"Did you recognize any of the photographs?" asked Juan Carlos Lopez-Portillo.

"The one who killed Armando was the fourth on the sheet," Rios said. "We have already dealt with him."

"And the one who ordered it?"

"My information is that it was ordered locally by the head of a *Mara* clique here in Washington, Esteban Ortega. He probably got orders from someone in *La Esperanza*."

"How reliable is your information?"

"The parasite who gave it to us thought he was saving his life by doing so. He was also wrong about thinking he would be allowed to live. I believe the information is accurate. The Americans seem to have arrived at the same conclusion, otherwise the photograph of Armando's killer would not have been on their page of photographs."

"How long do you think it will take to deal with Ortega?" the ambassador asked.

"Not long."

"Good. But José," the ambassador continued, "use your English when we have American visitors."

The man with the eye patch grunted, then turned away.

Crawford paced nervously in front of the red panda exhibit at the National Zoo. She had told him to meet her there, but she had only said "after work" with no time specified. He had already been around the exhibit twice, had stayed there long enough for one of the keepers to remark that he "must really like red pandas." He still wore the suit he'd worn to the ambassador's office, not wanting to miss her by taking the time to change. He'd already sweated enough to require another dry cleaning despite the two snow cones he'd gulped down trying to fight the heat.

Her call had been just to inform him that she would meet him here to deliver Armando's school records. *Or had it been just that?* She had seemed eager to see him again after the glances exchanged in the embassy. He recalled the smile...*and those eyes!*

When he saw her coming down the walk from the visitor center entrance he noticed that she *had* changed clothes. The skirt and blouse from the office had been replaced with a sundress that did nothing to hide the shape that wore it. He knew he was staring but couldn't help it, although he managed to close his mouth after a moment. She giggled as she reached him and handed him the large envelope.

"Am I that funny looking?"

"That thought never entered my mind," he said.

"A penny, then, for the ones that did. As long as they're not *too* evil."

"N…nothing evil at all," he stammered. He looked at her, summoning all the composure he could muster. "There are some women a guy looks at because they're flaunting it. He thinks the way she *makes* him think by how she dresses, how she carries herself. Then—I hope you won't mind me saying this—there are the true beauties, like you. My thoughts had only to do with appreciation of what I saw. Like when I saw the Grand Canyon for the first time, or a beautiful car like a Ferrari."

"I'm like a canyon and a car?"

"Only the awe-inspiring ones."

She laughed again. Her laughter calmed him, made him feel more confident. They walked through the other exhibits, not really looking at the animals.

"You should have changed clothes into something cooler," she said.

"I didn't know exactly when you'd be here."

"I didn't know myself," she said. "I finished my work and locked up when it was done—no set time. I come here a lot after work, almost every day. I feel like I know some of the animals. Do you like them?"

"I like them more in the spring and fall. They smell a little worse this time of year."

She laughed again. He loved her laugh. He had decided some time ago that if he didn't like a woman's laugh, there was no future in the relationship.

"Which ones are your favorites?" he asked.

"Probably the pandas—the ones from China. They're like big stuffed toys, and they always seem to be playing, just rolling around, even when they're eating. How about you?"

"The big cats, I guess."

"So you're a predator?"

Crawford paused and thought for a second. Should he give a macho yes or…

"I like to study them, like I study the predators we hunt. The criminal predators."

"I see."

She was nodding.

I think I made the right call there, he thought.

"Should we go see them then?" she asked.

"Who?"

"Your big cats, silly." She was laughing again.

"Oh, sorry," he said. "Sure."

They walked at a relaxed pace to the zoo's great cat exhibit. A solitary Sumatran tiger paced back and forth at the front of his cage. They stared at the huge animal for a moment, and then walked to the next exhibit, which held a couple of African lions.

"Which one would you bet on?"

He thought for a moment. "The lions."

She was laughing harder now.

"What?" he asked, laughing himself.

"I asked which *one*, and you said, 'The lions.' The tiger is bigger."

"That's why I'd bet on the lions. There are two of them."

She laughed again, and she turned and held his hand for a moment.

"This was fun," she said. "Let me know if I can help with anything else."

"Of course."

He watched while she walked toward the entrance, not moving until she was out of sight.

Chapter Seven

August 16, 2:00 a.m.

As the two vans pulled into the rear of the Qwik Shine Car Wash in northeast Washington, DC, a small army of Hispanic males emerged from the building and began removing crates from the truck beds. As each worker entered the building, he was directed up the pull-down stairs by another man. After climbing the stairs with his load, the *Mara* soldier was met by Esteban Ortega, who looked at each crate and then told the worker where to place it.

Ortega was pleased with himself. The car wash was the perfect front. It was a defensible structure, solidly built, and the long, cavernous attic—covering the building's office, wash track, and waiting area—was big enough for the grow operation. Best of all, the legitimate commercial purpose of the building was the perfect cover, both for the massive amounts of electricity and water that would be consumed, and for the laundering of some of the profits that would be generated by the hydroponic marijuana.

He had plenty of seeds for the "white widows": high-yield, hybrid marijuana plants with an extraordinarily high THC content, the product of years of experimentation and grafting by some of Amsterdam's most dedicated disciples of horticulture.

The *Mara* commanders in *La Esperanza,* El Salvador's largest prison, had suggested the switch to the marijuana from cocaine. The seeds were easily concealed and transported across the border from Mexico, the "white" was now selling in the United States for between $4,000 and $7,000 a pound, and it didn't carry the heavy penalties that coke or crack did if the workers were arrested. Five kilos of cocaine powder, or just an ounce of crack, meant a ten-year mandatory sentence in an American federal prison, followed by deportation back to El Salvador and even more time in *La Esperanza.* To get a ten-year mandatory sentence for marijuana trafficking, the feds had to put 1,000 kilos on a defendant—a whole metric ton of weed—or find him with a thousand plants. Accordingly, Ortega's grow would only contain eight hundred plants at any one time.

Ortega wasn't concerned about deportation himself. Like several members of his *Mara* chapter, he had been born in Los Angeles and was an American citizen by birth, even though both his parents had been Salvadoran immigrants. He had spent enough time in El Salvador with the *Mara* chieftains learning his trade and fighting the ARENA government's forces, but his US citizenship had been a factor in the commanders choosing him to head the Washington clique. The less jeopardy a subordinate faced, either in jail time or through other government leverage, the less likely he was to fold under the pressure of a federal prosecution if caught.

The crates were all unloaded. Ortega barked an order, and the worker bees began lugging the lengths of copper tubing off the trucks and into the building.

From the green Buick parked behind a strip mall about one hundred yards to the south, Detective Dixon Carter raised his eyes just above the bottom edge of the driver's window and focused his binoculars on the activity in the rear of the car wash. He was alone.

Pipes? Makes sense, I guess...It's supposed to be a car wash, after all. Helluva lot of them, though. They could redo the plumbing in my whole subdivision with that much copper...What the hell?

Carter felt the cell phone vibrating in the pouch on his belt. He always had it set to vibrate. Surveillances like this, court appearances, movies...all required silence. Judges hated it if your phone rang during a trial or hearing, and Carter hated it more when a cell gave away his position on a stakeout. He sank back down in his seat and answered the call.

"Carter."

"Dix, turn your dome light off and don't shoot me. I'm about to open your passenger door."

Carter turned to his right and saw the face looking over the edge of the passenger side window. He flipped the switch so the light would not activate, then nodded. Tim Wisniewski, dressed in black from head to foot and wearing a black stocking cap, climbed in and sank down into the reclined bucket seat.

"What the hell are you doing here?" Carter demanded. "And where'd you get that outfit? Ninjas-R-Us?"

"I'm supposed to follow you around, partner. Orders of the triumvirate," Wisniewski said.

"The what?"

"Your masters. Sivella, Doroz, and Trask."

"Never say 'master' to a black man."

"Sorry. Massa then."

"You're asking for it tonight, aren't you?"

"Give it a rest. I'm half Pole, half Irish. If it weren't for you black guys, I'd still be a member of two oppressed minorities myself. You ever hear the one about the Polish fighter pilots in World War II?"

"You don't expect me to tell a step-and-fetch-it joke after it, do you?"

"Nope. Anyway, there were these three Polish fighter pilots stuck in a Warsaw ghetto, their planes had been blown to hell by the Blitzkrieg, and they're sitting there in their little apartment feeling all depressed and guzzling vodka. They got drunk and figured they needed to whip somebody's butt. They saw a rat run across the floor and into a rat hole, so they drew up a formal declaration of war on the rats, rolled it up, and crammed it into the rat hole. They figured they'd identified an enemy they could whip. By the next morning, two of 'em were POWs and the other one had a war bride."

Carter didn't want to, but he couldn't help laughing.

"I know all the best Polish jokes," Wisniewski said. "Just let me know when you're ready for another one. What and who are we watching?"

"*I*," Carter corrected, "have been watching the local clique of MS-13 in their relocation efforts following the fiery demise of the deli they used to run. *You* should be watching the insides of your eyelids. I don't recall inviting you."

"Like I said, the triumvirate commands, and I obey. No surveillance van tonight? Might be more comfortable."

"I wasn't expecting company. How'd you know where to find me?"

"Didn't. I had to follow your ass out here. You don't check your six very often do you? Traffic was awful light, and I'm sure you would have noticed my tail if you'd looked for one. I'm parked around the block."

"Great. Now I'm a Polish surveillance joke."

"That's funny," Wisniewski laughed. "Hadn't thought of that."

He glanced over the window edge toward the car wash. The silhouettes of several men carrying lengths of copper tubing were outlined in front of a security light on the corner of the building.

"What's with all the pipe?"

"At first I thought they might be refitting the car wash system," Carter said. "But that's way more than they need for that job."

"How'd you track these guys here?"

"Lynn Trask did some research on the guy who was on paper for the deli. Ortega's his name. He put in a claim with his insurance company after the fire. They smelled an inside arson job and called ATF. ATF had Ortega listed as an MS-13 member and called Barry Doroz. He had Lynn run some financial screens on Ortega, and she found out he'd just filed a purchase deed on this car wash. I heard them talking about it in Bear's office, and I found the reports on Bear's desk after they left today."

"So you snooped the boss's office and assigned yourself some overtime?"

Carter looked at him hard. "I decided to check it out on my own time."

"You've got some weird recreation hours." Wisniewski glanced at his watch. "Two-thirty a.m."

"I'm a dangerous man. Haven't you heard? You're lucky you called before popping up at that door, otherwise I probably would have killed my second partner."

"You're gonna be *real* dangerous if you never sleep. To everybody, including yourself. I'm more worried about becoming the partner who got 'the best cop on the force' killed than I am about getting whacked myself."

"I don't need a damned babysitter, *junior*."

"Nope, but you need a partner, *pops*, so just let me do my job while you do yours. I could have snuck up on you and blown your ass away just now."

Carter kept his binoculars trained on the car wash.

"You were following me in a black Dodge Charger. Nice wheels, so I assume they're yours and not the department's. Before you called my cell you'd been crouching beside the dumpster in the alley between this store and the Office Max for about ten minutes, and despite that wardrobe from *The Guns of Navarone,* your white face sticks out like a neon sign. Use some camouflage grease next time you want to hide in the hood. I was actually worried that I'd have to bail you out of some ambush, but you do pretty good surveillance for an Anglo from Santa Fe."

Wisniewski whistled. "Very impressive. What's *The Guns of Navarone?*"

"An excellent film. World War II period piece. Rent it sometime."

Carter shook his head in disbelief. Even more copper tubing was being offloaded. Wisniewski noticed the silhouettes, too.

"That, my senior partner, is either going to be a very large marijuana grow, or they're going to be counterfeiting pennies."

Carter nodded. "My conclusion as well."

He put the binoculars back in the case and started the car, leaving the lights off. He backed the Buick into the alley, circled around the end of the strip mall, and pulled up beside the Charger.

"You're lucky. The wheel covers and tires are still there. Follow me out, if you can."

Wisniewski followed as Carter pulled into a convenience store four blocks away. The Charger parked beside the Buick.

"I need some coffee before I head home for my nap," Carter said. "Get what you want. This one's on me."

He poured a large cup of black coffee from the customer urn's spigot and headed for the counter, nodding to the large black man behind it. "How's things, Marv?"

"Been better, been worse. Who's the midnight skulker with you, Dix?" He nodded toward Wisniewski, who was approaching them.

"New partner. I'll get his stuff tonight."

Carter looked down at his wallet to pull out a bill. When he looked back at the counter, he saw his coffee, a coke, six individually wrapped condoms, and seven Tootsie Roll Pops.

"You did say the usual, didn't you?" Wisniewski asked.

Carter arrived at his townhouse at 3:27 a.m. He poured a half glass of red wine to help himself fall asleep. The light on his answering machine was blinking. It was Melody, saying she was just calling to check on him, that she still cared about him and wanted to make sure he was all right.

If you cared that much you'd still be here, Mel. You'd understand. I expect the divorce papers any day now. Hell, YOU left ME; I didn't desert you. Maybe I ought to file the damn things myself and serve you with them. . .I miss you, Mel.

He hit the delete button on the machine, which politely informed him that he had no more messages, and sank into the recliner facing the television without picking up the remote. He downed the last sip of the pinot noir, staring vacantly at the dark screen.

Six condoms and seven Tootsie Pops. What was the extra one for? Carter laughed out loud, remembering Marv's face. *"The usual." The kid got me good with that one. Polish fighter pilots. Two POWs and a war bride.*

He laughed again, then immediately began sobbing. He stopped crying only when the wine and exhaustion finally numbed his mind. He spent the brief remainder of the darkness sleeping in the chair.

Chapter Eight

August 16, 8:30 a.m.

"Good morning, Jeff," Doroz said, looking up from a stack of papers on his desk.

"For some of us. I just walked through your bullpen. Dix looks like shit."

"Yeah, I know. He and Tim pulled some late surveillance last night on the MS-13 clique's new car wash. I didn't OK it in advance, had to fill out the forms and back date 'em this morning so they can get paid for the OT. If I'd known about it beforehand, I'd have said, 'Hell, no.' I don't think Carter's been sleeping lately."

Trask sank into a chair facing the desk. "I thought you never wanted a supervisory job."

"Didn't, and still don't." Doroz shoved the completed forms into his out basket. "It's a pain in the ass, but they gave me the choice of running this squad, one of those antiterrorist jobs where I'd be chasing ghosts all day without ever putting the cuffs on 'em, or a desk at headquarters. This was the only option that left me doing active crim' work." He shoved a pile of forms from one side of the desk to the other, next to three other similar stacks. "I even hate being in this office. I usually hang out in the bullpen with the guys on the squad, or in the conference room."

Trask saw lines on Doroz' face that he hadn't noticed before.

"I'm glad you're around for this case, Bear."

"Thanks, but my brain's so mushed out with all this paperwork, Dixon Carter's still thinking rings around me with less than four hours sleep per night.

I might get half a day of real work in between the department's precious forms and holding the hand of whatever staff employee needs a father figure for a day."

Trask glanced out the door to see Lynn blowing him a kiss from her desk. Doroz followed his eyes and saw it, too.

"At least you can handle that one for me."

"I'll give it my best shot," Trask said, chuckling.

"She's a hell of an analyst, Jeff. I point her and she takes off."

Trask nodded in agreement. "She was a hell of an agent, too."

"Too bad I can't partner her up with Dixon Carter and have her kick his ass out of this depression. They won't let me put analysts on the street." Doroz waved at the door. "Shut that thing, will you?"

Trask reached over and pushed the door shut. "What's up?"

"I think," Doroz said, "that Dix and Tim didn't go out *together* last night on that surveillance. They left here at about the same time—Dixon first, Tim a few minutes later—but I don't think it's like Tim to pull something like this surveillance without prior authorization and no backup."

"You're right; it's not," Trask nodded. "Think he's covering for Dix?"

Doroz smiled. "Why don't you take this job for me? It took you ten seconds to get where I got in thirty minutes, and you didn't have to grill Tim like I did."

"Did Tim admit it?"

"Hell, no. He's playing the good and faithful junior partner. Said they met up after he parked his car at his house and then left together. They came up with the idea to stake out the car wash after dinner and just did it on a whim. They saw a bunch of pipe being unloaded and think that the *Mara* boys are starting a marijuana hydro-grow."

"Good, Bear. Let *Tim* try to pull Carter out of his funk. It might happen, once Dix starts trusting him." Trask paused for a moment. "From what I've seen, despite his problems, he isn't missing anything in this case."

"Right again." Doroz rose from his chair and stared out the window. "That's the other weird part about this. With the fatigue, which we can all see in his face, you'd think he'd be overlooking things, getting sloppy, but he's not. It's like having a damned detective *savant* around. None of his old humor, no life away from the job. Just a zombie version of Sherlock Holmes who looks like he could collapse at any second."

"You're worried about what might happen if the lead starts flying again."

"Of course I am. If he doesn't snap out of this pretty damned quickly, I'm going to have to send him back to Willie Sivella."

"You've talked to Dix about this?"

"Sure. He says all the right things. He's working on it, just needs time. I just don't know how much more I can give him. Any suggestions?"

"Give him the time that you can. I don't have any magic wand to wave."

"We'll ride the storm out a little longer, then. I just don't want him or anyone else getting hurt in the process."

"Don't say that to him."

"I don't have to. He's wearing Juan Ramirez around his neck like an albatross." Doroz checked his watch. "It's time for your lovely wife's briefing. She took those ideas of yours and found some stuff."

They left the office and walked out into the bullpen, where Puddin' Crawford, five other FBI agents, and four task force officers, including Carter and Wisniewski, were staring at their respective computer terminals behind low cubicle walls.

"You ready, Lynn?" Doroz asked. When she nodded, he said, "Conference room, folks."

When they were assembled, Lynn pushed a button and the screen dropped again. Trask, standing at the back of the room, glanced at Mike Crawford to see if he resented being replaced.

Nope. Looks like he's glad to have a true analyst on the squad. Frees him up to be a full-time G-man again. Good.

Lynn hit a key on a laptop, and the image of a prison flashed across the screen.

"This is an assignment presented to me by our prosecutor," she began.

"Before you continue," Doroz turned and faced the room, "I'd like to say something about that. Some of you guys, both agents and cops, have never worked a case with a prosecutor closely involved in the investigation process. It's essential in a long-term conspiracy investigation to have a prosecutor on board early. It helps focus the investigation. When you have the best prosecutor in the district, a former military guy who's a helluva tactician and not afraid to get his hands dirty, it's a big advantage. I've worked with Jeff before, and so have Dix and Mike."

Mike? He must be serious about this, Trask thought. *He's using Puddin's real name.*

"Jeff's also your co-supervisor as far as I'm concerned. When he tells you to do something, consider it an order from me. If you don't like it, come see me and I'll tell you to do it anyway. Questions?"

There weren't any.

"Sorry for the interruption, Lynn."

Doroz took his seat. Trask caught the smile that Lynn flashed him before resuming.

Thanks, I think, Bear. No pressure, as usual. He smiled back at Lynn. *If I screw this up, babe, we'll be canoeing out of a satellite office in Idaho.*

"This is *La Esperanza,*" she said pointing toward the screen, "the largest prison in El Salvador. It's a prison from the outside, usually surrounded by the army and a lot of Salvadoran cops. Inside, the inmates often run the asylum. It used to be controlled inside the walls by members of the 18th Street gang, otherwise known as Barrio 18 or M-18."

She clicked forward to the next image, showing bloody bodies lined up against one of the prison walls.

"This is following the prison riots of 2004, when 216 inmates were decapitated, hacked, shot to death, or burned by M-18 prisoners. The riots caused the ARENA government to spread the gang members throughout the country's prison system. One of the results was a drastic reduction in the M-18 forces within *La Esperanza,* and the ranks of *Mara Salvatrucha-13* members grew to the point where MS-13 now controls the prison population. We think the warden and other government officials equalized the gang ranks intentionally inside the prisons to punish M-18 for the riots. They increased the MS-13 population for 'balance,' but the pendulum has now swung too far in the other direction.

"The MS-13 bosses inside the prison have their own cell phones and are in constant contact with their cliques throughout the hemisphere. They're the smart ones, the ones who keep lower profiles. Their more violent soldiers and some of the mouthier leaders get transferred to a more maximum security prison at Zacatecoluca. They call it Zacatraz after our Alcatraz. Inmates there are kept pretty isolated. Our intel is that a lot of the *Mara* prisoners—both M-18 and MS-13—expected to be freed after the FMLN took the reins of the Salvadoran government, but they weren't, and so the word may have been passed to the various MS-13 cliques to attack those who have betrayed them. That may be the motive behind the murder of the Salvadoran ambassador's kid…"

———

Trask held the door for her as she joined him in the parking lot. They'd driven to work together for once. He pulled the Jeep into traffic and headed southeast toward Waldorf.

"So how'd I do, co-boss?"

"Very nicely," he said.

"But I missed something?"

"I don't know that you did." *That did a fat lot of good. She knows you too well.*

"What did I miss?"

Way to go, ace. She DID do a good job, but you had to have it perfect, and she feels that. Now she's upset.

"Lynn, it really was exceptional work—but I put my case hat on when you ask me case questions."

"OK, fair enough. What did I miss?"

"You covered all of the journalism school basics very well except for one. The what, why, when, and how. . .you nailed all of those. I just didn't get enough who."

"I said the ARENA government. I know you want some info on the eye patch character at the embassy. I'm working on that."

"You're right. You did say the ARENA guys." *Let her figure it out. Be quiet for a minute.*

She was looking out her window now. "You wanted to know *who* in the ARENA government."

"*That's* the analyst at work. The one who knows what I'm thinking before I do."

She turned back toward him and kissed him on the cheek. "That," she said, "is impossible. But I'll work on it. I'll get you your who."

"I know you will. Thanks."

———

August 17, 2:16 a.m.

José Rios-García, deputy chief of mission for the United States Embassy of El Salvador, pulled the bolt back on the Norinco SKS, AK-47 knockoff. The assault rifle and its twin in the front seat of the stolen black Cadillac Escalade were loaded with banana-clip magazines filled with steel-core 7.62 x 39 ammunition.

"Turn here, Hugo. A quick right past the back of the building. Get ready, Mateo."

The Escalade went dark as its headlights were switched off. It left the street and crept slowly around the side of the car wash until it cleared the left rear corner. The tires screamed as they bit hard into the concrete. The two men standing outside the rear door threw down their cigarettes and lunged for the safety of the concrete walls on the other side of the door, but they were too late. The deep chatter of the automatic rifles was the last sound they ever heard.

It was also the sound that woke Detective Dixon Carter, who had dozed off in the front seat of the Green Buick, which was parked again behind the strip mall to the south of the car wash.

What the hell?! Wonderful. Now I have to call this in, and Willie and Bear'll have my ass for being out here alone again. Shit, can't ignore it.

"Dispatch. Detective Carter, Homicide."

"Dispatch. Go ahead."

"Shots fired. Rear of the Qwik Shine Car Wash, 2110 Bladensburg Road, Northeast. Send two ambulances."

"Roger. Any description on the suspects?"

No, goddammit. I slept through it.

"No, dispatch. I was in the area and heard the shots. No description. I'll meet the ambulances and crime scene behind the car wash."

"Roger."

Chapter Nine

August 17, 3:47 p.m.

Trask started the two-block walk north toward the United States Attorney's office from the courthouse where he'd covered an arraignment for Bill Patrick, who was out sick. His first thought was to drop the thick case file in his office so he wouldn't have to carry it across the street to the FBI field office. Two things changed his mind. He figured that Ross Eastman, the United States Attorney for the District of Columbia, had probably left a message to see him immediately about the shootings at the car wash. The problem there was that Trask hadn't had a chance, thanks to the morning hearing, to get the info Eastman wanted, and the last thing he wanted to do was to sit in Eastman's office without the details.

The other consideration was the weather. It was one of those August steamers, a hundred degrees in the shade with 100 percent humidity to match, thanks to those who had picked the confluence of the Potomac and Anacostia Rivers as the site for the nation's capital. Trask was already having to wipe his forehead with his handkerchief, and he didn't want to appear in Eastman's doorway looking like he'd been stoking coal in a packet steamer's engine room.

It was still early enough so there were shadows along the east side of 4th Street. He crossed the street to take advantage of the shade, which provided about four degrees of relief from the heat of the sun, walked past the entrance to the Triple-nickle, and crossed the street to the FBI field office. An hour in the squad room would give him the necessary facts for the briefing of the boss, and a chance to cool down a little.

Dixon Carter was in Doroz' office when Trask arrived.

"You're a little late for the execution, Jeff." Carter looked as sheepish as Trask had ever seen him.

"Willie Sivella stopped in to ream him a new one," Doroz said, still sitting with his feet propped up on his desk.

"I was told," Carter said, "that if the Cap found me out on the street again without my youthful partner and mole, it would probably be my last day on the job."

"Sorry I missed it." Trask sank into the chair beside Carter. "I'm sure it was entertaining. You deserved whatever was said, Dix, but do I understand that you're still with us?"

"Kinda like the fraternity in *Animal House*," Doroz said. "Double-secret probation, except it's not secret. And I get to be Dean Wormer. Thanks for putting me in that position, Detective Carter. Nothing I like better than having to write extra report cards on my senior task force officer."

"Sorry, Bear."

"So what exactly happened out there, Dix?" Trask asked. "I'm probably late for a meeting with my US Attorney."

"The official word, both for the press and anyone outside this office," Doroz said, "is that Detective Carter just happened to be in the area when he heard shots fired, rushed to the scene, and found two dead Hispanic employees of the car wash lying by the back door. Perforated by AK-47 rounds, fired fully automatic."

"The truth, Jeff, is that I was staking the place out again from the parking lot in back of the strip mall. I dozed off and didn't even get the plates on the shooters' vehicle, or even the type of vehicle for that matter. The AKs woke me up, and all I saw were muzzle flashes and headlights." Carter shook his head. "Sorry."

"Let's look at the positives," Trask replied. "You were on the scene and got something out of it. You're sure the weapons were AKs and not some sniper rifle this time?"

"Yeah. Fully automatic fire. AK-47s or clones. Unmistakable sound, even for a half-awake idiot like me. The ME did the autopsies early this morning. Kathy dug the usual cheap 7.62 bullets out of the vics' bodies, and I saw the crime scene guys prying the same kind of rounds out of the back door of the car wash. No NATO rounds this time."

"And our victims?"

"MS-13, no doubt about that, either," Carter said. "Both of 'em were fully tattooed with the trappings of their fraternal association."

"So our theory is what?" Trask asked. "A drive-by ambush by M-18 members?"

"That's how it looks." Carter shook his head again. "But that's not how it feels."

"Why not?"

"Ask your bride to step in, Jeff." Doroz nodded toward the open doorway.

Trask walked to the door. Lynn was already looking up from her cubicle. He tilted his head toward the office, and she nodded.

"We were knocking this around this morning while I was waiting to be filleted," Carter said. "Willie was a little late getting here. I said then that it didn't feel right, that it felt like a set-up. I was too tired to figure it out, but Lynn wasn't."

"Figure what out?" Trask asked.

"That it would be stupid and suicidal for M-18 to pull this kind of attack right now," Lynn said as she entered the office.

"Because...?"

"It's the numbers, Jeff." Lynn held up some papers. "You remember the initial briefing on MS-13? Ten thousand members locally, maybe twenty. I ran everything I could think of this morning on the M-18 numbers in and around DC. There was a murder of an MS-13 member on January 18 by four local M-18 types. Apparently the date was significant to them, and they went looking for an MS-13 rival to whack. They butchered him and left his body by one of the local streams. All four of the killers were arrested. The significant thing is that this murder's the only recent M-18 incident I could locate that's amounted to anything. All the intel estimates conclude there are only a couple of hundred 18ers in the metro, and they usually keep their heads down because the MS-13 troops outnumber them about fifty to one. The Maryland State Police wrote reports on four suspected homicides in the week after January 18. All of the vics were M-18 members. Probably retaliation in kind by MS-13 for the one they lost."

"Four in custody and four more dead. Where were those 18ers living—the ones picked up for the January murder?" Trask asked.

Lynn picked through her stack of papers until she found what she was looking for.

"Two from Bladensburg, Maryland. One in Reston, Virginia. One with no known address."

"You thinking they'll try another retaliation raid, Jeff?" Doroz asked.

"Exactly. You're the big bully on the local Central American gang block. Even if it's not really an organized M-18 group tugging on Superman's cape, you can't ignore it. You can't let your main rival start to move into turf that you own. You have to respond. The question is, where?" Trask turned back to Lynn. "Any demographics on where the largest concentration of 18th Street members is in the metro?"

"I anticipated that question," she said, smiling proudly. "To the extent there is one, I'd say upper Prince George's County, Maryland."

"Bladensburg, again?" Trask asked, smiling back. *It's nice to have some common sense to add to the data collection.*

"It's a reach, but yes. That's the only place I could find with any recent, multiple arrests of M-18 types."

"Bear, can you—"

"I'm on it," Doroz said, reaching for the phone. "We'll warn the locals and set up out there tonight." He looked up at Carter. "Dix, you and Tim will be riding with me."

Carter rolled his eyes skyward, then nodded.

"I'd like to come," Trask began, but he caught the warning glance that Lynn was shooting at him and shifted gears, "but it's out of my jurisdiction, and Ross Eastman is certainly going to order me to keep my impetuous young ass away from the scene. I'll be at home, with our lovely and talented squad analyst, waiting by the phone. Keep me posted as soon as anything happens. Ross will be calling his counterpart in Baltimore within the hour, and he'll want real-time information."

"Will do," Doroz said.

"I had one other reason for thinking it's not the 18ers," Lynn said. "I just found out about the car wash a couple of days ago by tracing the money from the deli insurance settlement. This Ortega character claimed that someone had burned down his business, and he just signed the settlement check over when he bought the car wash. How'd the 18 crew know about the MS-13 move to the car wash so soon?"

"Where's Puddin'?" Doroz asked. "Anybody seen Crawford?"

Special Agent Michael Crawford, wearing shorts and a polo shirt that his mother had told him made his eyes stand out, waited a short distance *away* from the panda exhibit. *Don't want her to think I'm stalking her,* he thought. *I'm not, actually. Or am I? She's a source, or a potential source, for now.* He asked himself what would happen if she wanted to be more than that. What would win? The Bureau's restrictions on dealing with a potential witness, or the other thoughts of her that had dominated his mind now for the past three days? Rather than answer, he chose to ignore the question.

She came around the walkway looking at the animals. She was wearing another sundress, blue and white. He tried to walk up behind her, to surprise her.

"How long have you been waiting?" she asked before he could say anything or touch her.

"About thirty minutes," he confessed.

"I was waiting for you by the lions."

"You're kidding."

"No."

She looked up at him, and then kissed him. He almost fell backward.

"I'm sorry," he stammered. "I just hadn't expected that."

"It's the twenty-first century in El Salvador, too," she said. "I'm not required to have a chaperone when I leave my apartment, and I'm not even *in* El Salvador. Does that bother you?"

"No. Not at all."

He thought of that priorities question again...and ignored it again. Another question replaced it. "Do you think it's completely safe for you to be seen with me like this?" he asked her.

She laughed again. "Give me your address, then. That way I can come see you where it's safe and cool. I'll make sure I am not followed."

"Let me know when you're coming so I can clean the place up."

"No!" She laughed again as she walked backward away from him. "I want to see how you really live. I'll surprise you!"

He watched her turn and walk back toward the entrance. His apartment would be immaculate for the foreseeable future.

At 11:47 p.m., Esteban Ortega and seven other members of the Washington, DC, east-side clique of the *Mara Salvatrucha* checked their weapons and headed northeast on Bladensburg Road in two vehicles, a stolen Chevy Cavalier and a Ford minivan.

Chapter Ten

August 18

Ross Eastman was looking out the window of his very large corner office on the fifth floor of the Triple-nickle, his back to Trask, Doroz, and Bill Patrick, the Criminal Division chief and Trask's immediate superior. Eastman was the epitome of a Washington political appointee. His manner, grooming, dress, and credentials were impeccable. He was average in height, average in weight, and average in actual legal ability, which made him a danger to no one—especially not to those in the halls of Congress where he had formerly been employed as counsel to the House Judiciary Committee. He had, accordingly, been a smashing success there and had been granted his appointment of choice, which turned out to be United States Attorney for the District of Columbia.

Eastman's strength, however, was actually one of *character*. He was the Washington anomaly, the public servant who actually wished to serve the public, even if it meant that his own interests might not be best served. He had learned he could best serve the nation in his current position by making sure that the most talented assets in his office got the assignments that required the most talent, and he provided those assets with any support at his disposal. Their successes then became his own.

"This isn't the end of this thing, is it, Jeff?"

"I really doubt it," Trask said. "Bear and the local guys were only able to pick off the van that had the MS-13 shooting team. Our guys rolled in on them while they were stopped at a light before they crossed the line into Maryland. There was a small Chevy with the van. The Chevy was on the hot sheet; the van wasn't. Whoever was in the car peeled out and went through the light and around the squad car that blocked the van. The Maryland cops found the Cavalier abandoned about a mile away, nobody in sight."

"We concentrated on the van because we figured it had the shooters, Ross."

Doroz was completely comfortable using the US Attorney's first name. He'd worked cases with Eastman years before, when the latter had been just a line prosecutor. That history and his own reputation in the FBI gave Doroz the freedom to speak his mind. Besides, someone else wrote *his* report card, so he'd decided to deflect the harder issues away from Trask.

"The gangbangers like to roll by and slide the side doors open on those things, then light their targets up with the AKs."

"I can't fault your decision there, Barry," Eastman said. "And it's good that you got them before they killed somebody. Plus, you got them before they crossed into Maryland, so we get to control the case, for now. We've got venue, District of Maryland doesn't. What charges do you have, Jeff?"

"Illegal possession of machine guns. Four shooters in the back of the van, four fully automatic AKs. We don't want to charge a conspiracy yet—might give us double-jeopardy issues for what we anticipate will be an overall conspiracy indictment later. The driver gets charged as an aider and abetter, and he's already on paper: probation for a tax case. They're all MS-13 troops. Tats and colors, the works. Two from El Salvador and two from Honduras. The driver is a US citizen, born in LA."

"Did you serve the Vienna Convention notices?"

"Yes, sir. We had the initial appearances this morning, and I put the consul notification forms, in Spanish, in front of each defendant. Not one opted for the notification."

"That's a little strange, isn't it? Not wanting your home government to know you've been arrested and locked up?"

"I really don't think so," Doroz intervened again. "Our analysis on the *Maras* right now shows that they have nothing but contempt for the new government in El Salvador, and the gangs are *really* at war with the new military regime in Honduras."

Eastman turned back toward the window again. "I got a call from the White House this morning, guys," he said when he finally turned back toward them. "Not the Attorney General, the *White House.* The president's chief of staff told me that he wanted to make sure I had my best team on this. They don't want an international gang war breaking out in our capital city."

"Do you have any suggestions other than what we're already doing, Ross?" Patrick asked. The question was an honest one, not a suck-up. There was no deception in Bill Patrick, a great walrus of a man well over both six feet and three hundred pounds with a large moustache that curled down around the corners of his mouth. He had moved into the criminal division chief's office when Robert Lassiter died.

"No, I don't," Eastman responded quickly. "I *do* think we have our best people on it, both from our office and the Bureau. I just have a bad feeling about this."

"If it's any consolation—and I know it's not—so do we, Ross." Doroz was standing and pacing about the room as if it were his own office. "Dix Carter is convinced that the car wash double homicide was just meant to *look* like a gang drive-by, with the purpose of starting a local firefight between the MS-13 and M-18 cliques."

"I hear that Detective Carter has been a bit off the reservation lately."

Damn. I thought we had a lid on that, Trask thought. *Ross has his own sources watching us.*

"A bit." Doroz knew not to try to minimize the problem, which was now exposed. "I think we've addressed that, and he's still the best detective the Metro Police can give us. You did say that's what you wanted?"

"Of course, and I know he's a fine detective," Eastman retreated. "Just as long as you think he's still contributing to the investigation."

"He's contributing a lot," Doroz said. "Despite the personal problems, he sees things the rest of us miss. His instincts are still flawless."

"I hope so. If this thing gets out of control, gentlemen, people with agendas that have nothing to do with justice or law enforcement are going to start playing in our little sandbox, and I'll have no shot at controlling things at that point. Each and every problem with the case will be viewed through the political microscopes, fair or not."

"We know that, too, Ross," Doroz responded, "and the last thing *I* want is my own headquarters breathing down the back of my neck while we try to get some real work done."

"Then we're all on the same page," Eastman said. "Bill, this is Jeff's only priority for now. I want you to reassign every other case on his calendar to somebody else. Give him whatever extra bodies he needs."

"Understood," Patrick said.

"Can I pass on the extra bodies for now?" Trask asked.

Eastman looked surprised. "Why is that?"

"Too many cooks in the kitchen, for one thing," Trask replied, "and like you said, it will probably come to more if this gets worse. Right now, Ross, this is an investigation, not a prosecution, except for my five new friends and their assault rifles. That's an easy case and won't require any legal genius. I think we need to minimize the possibility of any leaks right now, and frankly, I'd like to know how you found out about our problems with Dixon Carter."

"A point well taken." Eastman smiled. "My info comes from Willie Sivella. I had lunch with him yesterday."

"That's reassuring then, I think," Trask said. "Anyway, I promise to come running for help if I think I'm getting over my head."

"Good. Then go fix this thing. I know we're in a reactive business, but if you guys have ever had luck with crystal balls, now's the time to pull them out. I need to convince the freaking White House that we're on top of this."

The intercom on Eastman's phone buzzed. "Yes?"

"It's the Attorney General for you, Mr. Eastman."

"See?" Eastman said. He waved them out as he reached for the phone.

August 19

It was 2:27 a.m. in the house at the end of Amwich Court in the Saint Charles neighborhood of Waldorf, Maryland. Trask stared at the ceiling, unable to stop his mind from racing.

They'd gone back to the squad room after the meeting with Eastman, and he'd listened to Doroz, Carter, Lynn, Tim, Puddin', and everyone else thinking out loud for the better part of the afternoon. None of it made sense. Spinning wheels going nowhere. Theory after theory, each one without a firm foundation, crumbling into sand when subjected to any real analysis. A sniper, a gang raid that may not have been a gang raid. A dead ambassador's son. White House interest.

What the hell was going on?

He drifted off. The dream was not a good one.

Mom's reading the thermometer. She's worried. Talking to Dad. A hundred and seven. Doc Huddleston said to get me to the ER. I'm four, I think. Four or five. Burning up with fever. They throw me in a tub of ice water. I'm screaming.

He forced himself to wake up again. The sheets on his side of the bed were soaked in his sweat. He sat up.

He looked at Lynn sleeping peacefully beside him, the dry side of the top sheet draped across her bare shoulders. She'd struck out so far in finding out anything at all about José Rios-García, old Mr. Eye Patch. There'd been nothing on the web. A complete blank slate in the information avalanche of the digital age.

That doesn't make sense. Public figures can't hide from the web.

He was glad they'd transferred the master bedroom downstairs into the newly finished basement level. They had more room, and it was cooler. Even so, it was still too warm. A ceiling fan for the bedroom might be the next order of business.

You're still sweating, even down here. Go to the den. There's a fan in there. Watch a little tube. Get a drink. Get your mind off of it. Close the files.

He tried to bring the music into his mind, something peaceful to settle the agitation. The jukebox wouldn't start. He sat up on the bed.

This isn't good. Every time the music won't play something is really screwed up. FUBAR, in fact.

He was reaching for the handle on the bedroom door when he heard it. A faint sound from outside the room like the brush of clothing against the dry-wall. He pulled his hand back and froze.

Did you really hear something, or is your head working triple-overtime?

He considered waking Lynn, but decided against it after listening and hearing nothing more outside the room.

Be quiet just to make sure. The door hinges! No, they're OK now. She had me WD-40 'em last week. They won't squeak. Probably nothing to worry about, anyway.

He turned the handle slowly, silently, opening the door a crack.

Your imagination's running wild, idiot.

His heart was racing anyway. He opened the door slowly and began to stick his head out to look to the left, up the stairs. The adrenaline and the last-second glimpse of a shadow enabled him to duck under the machete as it sliced the air above his head and dug into the doorframe, sticking there.

"LYNN!" Trask screamed her name as he bull-rushed the figure in front of him. He drove his assailant back hard against the edge of the wet bar across the room and pounded his fist into the man's face as hard as he could. The punch seemed to have no effect, and the guy retaliated with an uppercut that caught Trask square in the gut. He felt the air leave his body and the weakness hit his legs, dropping him to the floor.

Shit! There's another one behind me!

He rolled instinctively to his left, grabbing the first attacker's foot with his right hand and pulling it out from under the man, who came down on top of him. The second shadow had to halt his own machete stroke in midair as he waited for an open swing. The first man pushed off Trask, who was still on the floor.

I still can't breathe!

He looked up as machete number two was rising in preparation for the downswing.

Got to get the left arm up, shield my head and neck!

The first shot from the Smith and Wesson .45 entered the back of the skull of machete-man number two and exited his head just below the left eye, depositing an impressive amount of blood and brain matter on the wall behind the bar. The machete hit the floor just before the lifeless hand that had dropped it.

The second round entered the *front* of the skull of machete-man number one, who had started his own rush toward the shooter, dropping him eight inches from her feet. Since number one had dropped into a crouch before his rush toward Lynn, the blood and brains from *his* exit wound sprayed all over her husband.

Trask caught his breath and scrambled over to her, kicking both corpses as hard as he could. "You killed 'em both, babe. They're both dead," he babbled, shaking.

"I had to," she said, pointing the gun at the corpse lying at her feet. "That one saw me naked."

Trask stumbled to the light switch across the room. The two bodies lay oozing blood onto the new carpet. He picked up the phone and dialed 911. After alerting the locals, Patrick, Eastman, and Doroz, he sank down in a corner of the rec room, staring vacantly at the corpses.

Lynn came out of the bedroom wearing jeans and a T-shirt. Trask thought he heard a siren screaming from the mouth of the cul-de-sac.

"You better get dressed," she said. "Crime scene and everybody in the free world will be here in about a minute."

"I need a shower." He stood up, looking at the red and gray stains splattered on his chest.

"Later, Jeff. They'll need to take some pictures. Just throw something over your underwear for now."

"I'll have to redo the whole damned room. Carpet's ruined."

"It's OK. We have insurance."

"I need to call them."

"Just sit down for now." She put her arm around his shoulders and kissed his cheek. He was shuddering involuntarily, as if a large spider had just crawled up his leg. "You gave me time to get the gun," she said. "You did good."

"I'm glad we bought that gun."

"So am I."

"I'm glad you can shoot it."

"Me, too. I love you."

His breathing was slowing. "I love you, too." He kissed her on the forehead.

She held his face. He pulled her close and held her as tightly as he could. Swirling red lights were coming through the bedroom window. The doorbell rang. The adrenaline and fury were leaving him. He was back in the present now.

"Can you answer the door while I find some pants?" he asked.

Chapter Eleven

August 19, 8:15 a.m.

Lynn made it a point to be early to the office, even after the long night in Waldorf. She'd been through it all once before, and beating the crowd to the office would mean avoiding the grand entrance. There'd be those like Barry and Carter—the ones who'd been through it themselves. Just a pat on the back or even a hug. *Way to go lady, you did your job when you had to. We understand.* But there would also be the looks from the new kids, the question on all their faces about the event that would turn them all into stupid TV reporters wanting to ask the same stupid question. "How did it *feel* to kill someone?" None of them would ever really ask it that way, of course, unless he or she truly *was* an idiot. They'd try to mask it, try to paraphrase it. "You OK?" would be the usual version, but they'd want more answers than the one that responded to their question. They'd want the sordid details. Over and over and over again.

Yeah, I'm the LIVE one. I'm OK. The guys I shot and killed are not OK. That's how this works. Maybe I should feel guilty about whacking those assholes, but they came into my house—MY HOUSE—hell-bent on killing my husband and probably me with him. The truth is that I'll never lose a minute of sleep over them or even their souls. Maybe I should, but I won't. They gave me no choice. It's all on them.

Dixon Carter was already there when she walked in. Otherwise, the squad room was empty. He saw her, stood up, and came over to her desk. He offered her his hand. She shook it, and he put his other huge dark hand over hers.

"You OK?" he asked, raising an eyebrow and grinning slyly.

She cracked up giggling. "Yeah, Dix, I'm fine."

"Jeff?"

"He's got a bruise on his abdomen the size of a cantaloupe. Other than that, he's good."

"Great. Nice work. Maybe not nice, but good work. Necessary work."

"I know. It's cool, really."

"We're all glad you were there. Otherwise we might have lost our favorite prosecutor."

"He's a lot more than that to me, but I know what you mean. We did some cases together, once upon a time."

"That's what I heard."

"You know, when I saw him fighting those guys, I had the weirdest thoughts. I mean, I know I was protecting the guy I love, but I also thought about what he means to you guys. Like you said, your favorite prosecutor. I remember working cases before I met him, busting my ass on an investigation and then handing it to some jerk who treated it like just another file. He's never done that."

Carter nodded. "He cares, he's good in court, and he's a hell of an investigator himself. Smart as a whip."

"You have no idea." She regretted saying it for a moment, but then she didn't. She was talking to Dix, the lead detective on Jeff's case. He needed to know. There could be a time when it mattered.

"How's that?"

"When I first met Jeff's mom after we got married, we talked about what kind of kid he'd been. You know, just girl talk. She said he was always two things as a boy: sick and smart. Nearly died a couple of times from fevers. Pulled through, of course."

She looked at Carter and put a finger over her lips. She read his eyes, and he understood. Don't pass this on to anyone else.

"They had his IQ tested a couple of times when he was a kid. One test came back over 200. The other one couldn't even be scored it was so high. They never told him, and they made me swear not to ever tell him. She thought it might me too much of a burden on him. She wanted me to know because we really hit it off…anyway, she said my biggest challenge would be to keep him from getting bored. She was right. I've seen it happen."

"With you?"

"No, not yet. Not that I could tell, anyway. We used to be in a winter bowling league. Just something we decided to try for fun. He studied the hell out of the game, like he does everything else. He figured out the right ball to buy for the lane surfaces, the oil patterns, and he practiced like crazy. He got really good. Averaged 210 in one league, then he finally rolled a perfect game and just walked away from it. We've never been back."

"Maybe he's found the perfect job then," Carter said. "Every case a new sport?"

"I think so," she said. "It's the people problems that seem to interest him. He always hated math, even though he can do it all when he needs it. I think he's bored to death by the fact that two and two always equal four."

"Not when you're dealing with the devious human elements."

"Exactly. He loves the human variables, thinks of them as puzzles. It makes him great at his work."

"That all makes sense," Carter said. "When I did my first stint in Homicide, I got real interested in profiling. You know, serial killers, criminal masterminds, that sort of thing. Went to a couple of seminars put on by the leading profilers. I cornered one guy after one of the lectures and asked if he had any tips on how to get started. He told me just to read a lot—biographies as well as case files."

Lynn wrinkled her forehead. "OK...and this has to do with Jeff...?

Carter laughed. "I know he's not a serial killer. No, what interested me is the sickly kid and fever part tied to the super-smart adult. When I was reading all the bios, that was a very common theme, for both the suspects and for some very famous non-crooks."

"Really, like who?"

"Let's see. Scientists and math wizards? Isaac Newton, James Watt the steam engine inventor, Edison, Nikola Tesla. Writers? Robert Louis Stevenson. Politicians? Teddy Roosevelt. Even athletes like Bobby Jones, the great golf pro. Several more, but I wasn't a sickly kid, so I can't remember 'em all."

She smiled. "Who were some of the killers?"

"John Wayne Gacy, Patrick Kearney, the LA freeway killer, a serial killer from Cleveland named Eric Olson, Adolf Hitler."

"Gacy and Hitler?"

"Yeah. The health battles seemed to make them more determined to succeed in something later in life, good or bad. Anyway, they were all sickly kids with amazing minds in one way or another. Tesla said he kept seeing images in his mind throughout his lifetime; he called it 'picture thinking.' I'm no doctor or shrink, but I always had a theory that some of those with the childhood fevers may have had their brains locked open in some fashion by the high temps. Maybe they kept a creative or memory function that the rest of us lost as we got older. I do know that some of the literature on super-memories said that some children who have it seem to lose it as they mature. It also said that some kids get diagnosed with autism or other problems."

"Jeff's mom said the shrinks wanted to medicate him while he was in grade school. She wouldn't let them."

"I love her for that. I also love the fact that he's on this case, and I love the fact that his wife can shoot like Annie Oakley."

Doroz walked in and was surprised to see he was not the first in the office.

"You—" he said, pointing to Carter, "ought to still be asleep. And *you*—" he pointed at Lynn. "What the hell are you doing here at all?" He paused. "You OK?"

"I'm good, Bear," she said, laughing. "Really."

"Here's your vest." The deputy United States marshal handed Trask the new black body armor, still wrapped in plastic. "Wear it to and from the building, and while driving. You're required to go through our firearms training course in order to carry a weapon on your person."

"We've got a .45 at home," Trask said.

"Can't use it. The regs say you have to carry what we carry. We'll issue you a Glock .40 cal after you go through the training."

"We've done the paperwork on that already, Jeff," Patrick said from behind his desk. "Main Justice has the application, and it's approved."

"Am I still on the case?" Trask asked, wincing as he shifted in the chair. The bruise on his abdomen made sitting uncomfortable.

"Yep. I had a long talk with Ross this morning. I'm not sure he's gotten used to you and your bride whacking bad guys on an annual basis, but he said he'd rather see *them* in the morgue than you, and he's not sure any other of his assistants would have survived the attack. We also agree with FBI's assessment that this wasn't an attempted gang hit, so no conflict of interest."

"I'm still sorting all this out myself."

"That's natural," the marshal said. "I'm on our SWAT and fugitive apprehension teams. I've had to take subjects down the hard way three times. You wonder why you were the one who had to deal with it at all. You didn't ask for the dirty work. You have to realize that they gave you no choice."

"I figured *that* out last night about the time I ducked under a machete."

"Two recommendations," the marshal continued. "One, get a house alarm."

"OK."

"And get a dog."

"That sounds redundant, and expensive."

"They *are* redundant to a point, but alarms don't have incredible senses of smell, hearing, and loyalty, and dogs can't get taken out with one snip of a pair of wire cutters. If you have to pick one, get the dog. A big one, preferably."

"Right. Anything else?"

"We don't have the manpower to watch your residence 24/7, but between our guys, the FBI, the Maryland State Police, and the Saint Charles County Sheriff's Office, we'll be doing enough spot checks on your house to make people *think* we're there all the time." He handed Trask a sheet of paper. "Here's a list of all the phone numbers you need. Call the Saint Charles County guys first if there's any more trouble. It's their beat, and they're closer."

Trask nodded.

"Now get out of here," Patrick said. "Take the rest of the day off, and don't argue about it."

Same orders Lynn got from Barry this morning. She'll be home when I get there.

Trask went back to his office to get his sport coat, but sat down at his computer before leaving. He remembered seeing the website for a pet rescue center in southern Maryland. He also remembered the conversations he'd had with Lynn on the dog issue. She'd always had them, loved them, wanted one. Make that two. *"Separation anxiety," she'd called it. "Make sure there are two so they'll have company while we're at work. They won't tear too many things up that way. And no expensive breeds from some puppy mill. Give a couple of pound puppies a good home."*

He found the website and wrote down the phone and address. He made the call and said he'd be there in twenty minutes or so. After fiddling with what seemed like five square yards of Velcro and straps, he got the vest on and headed for the Jeep.

The drive down the Indian Head Highway was wide open since it was the middle of the day and between rush hours. He turned east on 227 and found the farmhouse, which was surrounded by a grassy field with a wire fence to keep in the pack of dogs that followed the Jeep up the gravel road drive. A woman with a weathered face came out of the house and walked toward the gate as he parked and shed the body armor.

He told her that he and his wife had been talking about adopting a couple of dogs for weeks and that he wanted to surprise her.

"I just have mixed breed rescues here," the woman said. "No purebreds."

"That's what we want," Trask said. "My wife wanted rescues. She said they're the best dogs she's had. What do I do, just pick a couple out?"

The woman pointed to a wooden picnic table and benches a few yards away. "Go sit over there a spell. Let *them* pick *you* out."

He did as instructed, and watched as the pack—about twenty-five in all, ranging from a litter of tiny Jack Russell puppies to a couple of very large dogs—milled about in the grass.

Lynn wanted a "cuddle puppy." The marshal told me to get a big one.

He was admiring a shepherd-mix pup when he noticed that one strange-looking little dog was slowly walking toward him.

She was small—about twenty-five pounds—and reddish blond, with a small white spot on her chest and a face that reminded him of a fox. She seemed to have an excess of long hair about her shoulders, and a long, bushy tail that curved up and over her back. She hopped up on the bench beside him and held up her paw like she was waving at him.

"This is Nikki," the old woman said. "She's half Shiba Inu and half Whippet. I knew when you called that she would pick you. She's been waiting for you."

Shiba Inu, Trask thought, trying to ignore the supernatural implications of being pre-selected, sight unseen, by an animal. An old Redbone song started playing in his head. "The Witch Queen of New Orleans." The pages of a book he'd read on dog breeds flashed through his memory. *Shiba Inu: a Japanese breed, like a smaller version of an Akita, but a lot smarter.*

"There's a special condition with Nikki, though, if you want her."

"Is she sick or something?" Trask asked.

"Oh no. Healthy as can be. She's one of a pair."

Trask scanned the other dogs and saw none that looked like the little dog that was now sitting beside him on the bench, leaning in so her head was resting on his shoulder. He patted her head, and she licked his face.

Oh yeah, you'll do fine. Lynn's going to love you, squirt, even if you do have funny long hairs growing out of your back.

"I don't see any others like this one," he said, still stroking Nikki's head.

"Oh, it's not another Shiba." The woman pointed to the edge of the pack where a dark, very large dog with piercing, light blue eyes was sitting and watching Trask and Nikki with keen interest. "Barbie!"

Barbie?

The big dog trotted over to them. Trask felt himself stiffen a little. The dog certainly *looked* menacing.

"This is Nikki's little sister. The local police found them tied to two ends of some wire wrapped around a gas meter in a trailer park. No food, no water. The cops brought them here when they were both puppies. She's a couple of months younger, but as you can see, she kind of outgrew Nikki. They're inseparable."

"What kind of dog is she?" Trask asked.

"Not sure. My best guess is a shepherd mix—probably with a Huskie. That's where she gets those eyes."

"Is she dangerous at all?"

The woman laughed. "No, she's really a big creampuff. Follows Nikki around like she's her mother. Nikki's the boss."

"I'll take 'em."

"Good. I have a good feeling about you, and so does Nikki. They're both housebroken and spayed. Except for a registration fee, they're also free."

Trask paid the nominal registration fee required by the rescue association and tried to throw in an extra twenty for the woman's expenses, but she declined it.

"I just want my kids to get good homes," she said.

Trask loaded the dogs in the back of the Jeep and headed toward Waldorf. Nikki didn't stay in the backseat for long, climbing precariously onto the center console where she sat and again rested her head on his shoulder. He felt himself giggling.

"Nikki, my girl, your new mama's going to love you."

He looked at the rearview mirror and into the back seat, where Barbie was stretched out and sleeping. Trask suddenly smelled an odor so strong it made him want to gag, and he pulled the Jeep to the side of the road, thankful it was a rural area. He coaxed them both out with the leashes and watched in horror as Barbie unloaded a massive pile of foul-smelling waste on the shoulder. He leaned down and glanced at her rump to make sure it had avoided the deluge before putting both dogs back in the car.

Barbie, huh? That name is changing tonight, big dog. I should have asked what they've been feeding you. Might want to change it very soon.

He turned the Jeep into the driveway and pulled the dogs out of the back on their leashes. Lynn met him at the door. She smiled when she saw them, and then stopped in mock horror.

"I tell you I want some dogs, and you drag home a hyena and a wolf?"

"Just sit there on the stairs."

She did, and Nikki obliged by offering her paw, then jumping into Lynn's lap. Lynn looked at Trask, her eyes moist.

"Her name's Nikki," he said.

"She looks a little funny, but she's home now. What's the big one's name?"

"It's changing. They called her Barbie, believe it or not. The woman I got them from said they're both housebroken. They better be. Barbie there shits large quantities of nuclear waste."

"She's big enough and looks kind of scary. Come here, girl."

The big dog bounded up to the stairs in one stride and tried to imitate Nikki by sitting in Lynn's lap. Lynn laughed aloud as the beast licked her face and lay across her legs.

"Look at those blue eyes!" She smiled down at Trask. "Just like her daddy's."

"I didn't father that thing."

"Don't listen to him, baby," she said, rubbing the great black head and ears. "I can tell he already loves you. Put 'em in the backyard for a while, Jeff. We need to go find a pet store."

Two hours and six hundred dollars later, Trask told himself how lucky he was that the dogs had been "free." A large plastic doghouse with metal, fabric-covered beds inside now occupied a corner of the patio behind the house. There were food and water dishes inside and out, large pillows in the den and master bedroom, big bags of dog food stacked in the laundry room, and a variety of veterinary meds—heartworm pills and flea repellants—sitting on top of one of his prized Klipsch stereo speakers. He turned in his chair at the computer desk and looked around the rec room. Lynn was on the couch watching TV. Nikki was lying with her head in Lynn's lap, fast asleep. He smiled.

Where's that big—

"WOOF!" The deep bass tone came out of nowhere.

"Ow!" Trask yelled as his knees jerked reflexively, cracking into the underside of the desk.

Lynn doubled over on the couch laughing. "She snuck up on you! That big wolf of a dog snuck up on you!"

Trask turned, rubbing his knees. The monster was sitting right behind him, tongue out and tail wagging as if to say, "I got you, bud."

"Wonderful. A black, blue-eyed wolf with a sense of humor. You just named yourself. Boo it is."

The big dog lay down and rolled over, the blue eyes still fixed on him.

"I think Boo needs a belly rub," Lynn said.

———

In the upstairs bedroom of a row house in Alexandria, Virginia, Special Agent Michael Crawford looked down as the olive-skinned hand of the most beautiful creature he'd ever seen slowly stroked *his* naked belly, her head resting on his shoulder. He wanted to pinch himself, but didn't want the dream—if it was one—to end.

She looked up at him and saw the question in his eyes. "What is it, Michael?"

"I just have to ask you, Marissa, why me?"

"Why not you? In my country, a girl looks for stability and safety. A good man. A gentle man. I knew you were a good man when I first saw you. I could tell it in your eyes. Now that we have made love, I know that you are a gentle man, too." She kissed him. "Now, your turn."

"My turn for what?"

"You know, silly! Why me?"

"In my country," he said, "a man doesn't look for a girl like you."

She sat up on the bed revealing the most perfect body he could ever imagine. "And why not?"

"Because girls like you don't exist in this country."

Chapter Twelve

August 22, 10:40 a.m.

"The good news," Carter said as the squad sat around the conference table, "is that it wasn't the MS-13 crew who tried to take you out. That's also the bad news, since we don't know who did. Neither of the machete slingers had any tats, and both of them were about ten years too old for the part. Still, to the extent we can tell at this point, they do appear to have been Central American, although that's a guess, too. The bad guys weren't carrying any ID, and their prints don't match anything we have on file."

Trask shrugged. He looked up at Doroz. "So we have zilch?"

"Just their machetes," Doroz said, reaching into a box by his chair and sliding an eighteen-inch-long blade down the table to Trask. "The ones used in the attack at your place are in evidence for processing. This is a duplicate. According to one of our weapons geeks at headquarters, they were all made by a company called Imacasa in El Salvador. The problem is that Imacasa now has a major North American market, and you can buy these things anywhere. I got this one at my friendly neighborhood hardware store. They're supposed to be great for clearing brush."

"Or tearing up carefully stained doorframes or decapitating unsuspecting prosecutors," Trask said.

Doroz shrugged. "Yes and yes. The bottom line is that the weapons don't really give us anything, either."

"They *have* been the weapon of choice for the *Maras* in the past," Lynn noted.

"And for revolts in Cuba, Mexico, Africa, and the Philippines," Trask said. He saw that Lynn was giving him a mild glare. "Sorry. I'm as sure as you are that our would-be assassins were probably Salvadorans. After all, we've been jacking up MS-13 lately, and even if these guys weren't full-fledged *Mara* types, it feels connected. But Bear's right; evidence-wise, we have nothing."

"You do have this." Doroz tossed a newspaper toward Trask. "Front page of the metro section, below the fold."

Trask opened the morning edition of the *Washington Post.*

"I hadn't seen this yet, or yesterday's for that matter. I was out adopting a hyena and a wolf." He scanned the page.

Federal Prosecutor and Wife Kill Intruders;
AUSA and Spouse Involved In Prior Deaths

Waldorf, Md. An Assistant United States Attorney and his spouse, an employee of the Federal Bureau of Investigation, were apparently the victims of an attempted home invasion robbery three nights ago, according to the Saint Charles County Sheriff's Department. Two armed intruders allegedly broke into the home of Jeffrey Trask, a federal prosecutor employed by the Office of the United States Attorney for the District of Columbia. Investigators report that Trask fought off the assailants until his wife, an analyst with the Washington field office of the FBI, was able to reach a handgun kept by the couple for protection. Lynn Trask, a former special agent with the Air Force's Office of Special Investigations, then shot and killed both intruders. Trask was involved last year in the prosecution of serial killer Demetrius Reid, who died during his trial in a freak courtroom scuffle. Following the trial, Robert Lassiter, Trask's supervisor, was murdered on the steps of the federal courthouse by an assassin alleged to have been hired by Reid. The gunman was then shot and killed by Lynn Trask and Washington Police Officer Timothy Wisniewski.

Investigators were unable to provide a motive for the break-in and attack. It is unknown whether associates of Reid, the former leader of a local cell of a Jamaican drug cartel, are suspects. Reid was charged with conspiracy to distribute cocaine and with several drug-related homicides at the time of his death. One of his alleged victims was Juan Ramirez, a District of Columbia police detective who was found buried in a shallow grave in Prince George's County, Maryland.

A spokesman for Ross Eastman, United States Attorney for the District of Columbia, said that Mr. Eastman considers Trask to be a surviving victim of an attempted homicide, and that no actions are contemplated against Trask at this time.

"Wonderful," Trask said. "At least our friends at the *Post* don't have a freakin' clue that this might be tied to our current investigation. Of course, neither do *we*." Trask glanced at the article again, but another, smaller story caught his eye. He slid the paper back toward Doroz. "Look at the story on the left edge."

"'Local defense attorney found murdered'?" Doroz asked.

"Yep. Darren Regan. It says he was found in his office, handcuffed, sitting in a chair, and shot in the back of the head."

"Disgruntled client?" Lynn asked.

"Could be," Trask said. "Of course, the last client I saw him with in federal court was the driver of the MS-13 van we pulled over."

"*Godammit!*" Doroz said, exasperated. "I'd like to get a handle on one part of this thing before three other bricks fall on my head. Dix, can you—"

"Call Commander Sivella and get the reports on the Regan murder?" Carter asked. "Got it. If he's still talking to me."

"Thanks. Anybody else got any thoughts?"

"We're lucky to be ahead of the press on this, for now," Trask observed. "If they had any inkling that the machete guys at my place or this murder of Regan even *might* be related to the killing of the ambassador's kid, some beat writer would be smelling a Pulitzer, and we'd have the press and every worrywart and glory hound in DOJ *and* FBI headquarters down here. We don't *know* they're related for sure, so there's no point in speculating about it yet, even to our respective bosses. What I'm saying is we need to keep a very tight lid on this mess for now, please."

"Hell, yes," echoed Doroz. "We need to keep the headquarters weenies out of this mess until we know what the mess is. Everybody here is now a clam, got it?"

August 22, 5:50 p.m.

Dixon Carter pulled the green Buick into the driveway of his town home and sat for a moment. The meeting with Sivella had been about what he had expected:

cool and very official. Carter had copies of the homicide file Doroz had asked for; that hadn't taken long. Neither had the follow-on ass-chewing. The initial confrontation at the FBI office had taken place while the commander was merely mad. Sivella had now had two full days to think about it, had gotten even madder, and had taken plenty of time to prepare his remarks. Carter's ears were still burning with them.

"I don't care who you are, how many commendations you've earned, how long you've been around. You still take orders, goddammit. And don't try to hide behind your partner, who's trying to cover for you. This better not happen again, and believe me, I'll know if it does. Got it?"

"I'll know if it does." How is he going to know? Does he think he could have one of those new kids tail me without me knowing about it? Fat chance. He'd have to—WAIT A MINUTE!

Carter got out and walked to the rear of the Buick. He bent down and ran his hand along the underside of the frame in front of the bumper.

Nothing yet...smooth...nothing...nothing...THERE!

He stood up and went inside to change, returning a short time later in sweats. He pulled a creeper out from under his tool bench and grabbed a flashlight before lying down and wheeling alongside the rear of the car. The flashlight's beam found the device where he had felt it.

Is it hard-wired or a slap-on? No wires. A slap-on. Battery-powered.

Carter pulled the device from the frame and examined it.

One of the Department's newest and best. A GPS set to ping every five minutes. Enough battery power to last four months at that setting. You wouldn't have to follow me with this, would you, Cap? Never thought I'd suspect you would waste one of these expensive little gizmo's checking on your own guy. Pretty clever. Sit at your desk and check on my whereabouts without having to leave the building. Probably have the software to monitor it on your laptop. Check on me from your home after dinner or before you go to bed.

He put the GPS unit on the garage shelf.

Check away, boss. Your little bug will tell you that I'm all tucked in tonight.

Carter went for what appeared to be a jog through the neighborhood, the real purpose of which was to determine if he was under any *human* surveillance sent to double-check the electronic rat he'd found on the car. After circling the blocks in front of and behind his residence and finding nothing out of the ordinary, he returned to the garage, started the Buick, and drove away.

August 22, 9:30 p.m.

Lynn entered the code on the electronic alarm, activating it. The little box chirped three times, indicating that all was now secure at Castle Trask. They'd had one of the control units installed in the den and the other in the bedroom, so that if the power was cut, they'd know from the lack of the monitor lights on the box. She glanced over at the couch across the den, where Boo lay stretched out over the lap of her husband, who was stroking the big dog's head. Trask saw the amusement on her face.

"Why did this one decide to adopt me?" he asked. "You get the twenty-pound shadow, I get this monster."

"She loves her daddy, and he loves her."

"I think my whole lower half's asleep. No blood flow. Where's Nikki?"

"Asleep on the pillow at the foot of our bed."

"OK. Where's the gun?"

"Loaded and ready in the headboard. You expecting another attack?"

"We have to be ready for one. I have to admit I don't know *what* to expect at this point."

"What are you thinking?" she asked.

"That whoever sent those guys was more concerned about having us killed with machetes than having us killed."

"You lost me on that one."

"Think about it. If your primary goal is to whack somebody, there are a hundred ways more certain to achieve that purpose than a machete attack. Guns are great, car bombs are, too. Chemical agents, poisons. . .Don't get me wrong. I think we were supposed to die that night. I just think that the message was more in the machetes than in the success of the attack."

"So the fact that it failed doesn't necessarily mean that they—whoever 'they' are—will be back?"

"I don't know. As long as we're supposed to think we were attacked by members of one of the *Maras,* then the message has been received, even if we're still alive and kicking. Or maybe they were trying to either kill us, or if we survived, get us thrown off the case as potential victim witnesses. You know, build in a conflict of interest."

"You're saying that someone else wants us to think the *Maras* are after us, but they really aren't?"

"Look at all your research, Lynn. When MS-13 hits somebody, they leave calling cards all over the damn place. They wrapped the ambassador's kid in a 76er's jersey and carved every variety of the number thirteen into his flesh before they cut his head off. You drive into their turf, and they've spray-painted their little blue slogans on every wall in the hood. Don't you think they would have tried to take public credit for this, even though it failed?"

"Maybe they were planning to tag our house after we were killed."

"And maybe their new pledge class is made up of middle-aged goons who were going to get jumped in after this big assignment—a new cure for a midlife crisis. I don't buy it. Maybe they *did* intend to graffiti the place up after they killed us. Who knows?" He shook his head. "Maybe I'll never walk again after I lose the use of both legs because this moose thinks I'm nesting material. Boo, wake up and move."

The big dog climbed down from the couch, then sprawled at Trask's feet, gazing up at him with powder blue eyes with a look that questioned why she'd been so cruelly banished.

"You're so mean," Lynn said.

"Shit," he said, reaching down and stroking Boo's back. "You're OK, Boo, you just don't realize that you're not a puppy anymore."

"Actually, she still is. She could grow a bit bigger, as young as she is."

"Great. I'll have to dig a septic tank in the backyard just for the Boo-poo. Have you seen the size of those mounds she drops?"

"They're both wonderful dogs, Jeff, and worth every little bit of trouble they bring with them."

He reached down and scratched the big black head again. "Come on, sentry," he said. "I'm tired, and it's time for you to take your post." He headed for the bedroom, mentally humming a song by Lobo. "Me and You and a Dog Named Boo." *Way to go, genius. Try getting that one out of your head now.*

———

August 23

At 2:45 a.m., Carter parked the Buick in the garage. He pulled the creeper out and reattached the GPS onto the car's frame. His stakeout of the car wash had been a waste of time for once. *All quiet on the Eastern Front,* he told himself as he sank into the recliner.

———

At 3:17 a.m., Esteban Ortega lowered the handgun and sneered at the man writhing in pain on the floor of the car wash before him. Blood was running from the gunshot wound in the man's left thigh down into the track slots between the brushes on either side of the wash area. Ortega bent down close to the man, whose forehead bore a "666" tattoo. Seven other members of the MS-13 stood by, grinning, insulting the victim, urging their leader on.

"You know you will die tonight, amigo," Ortega said. "It is your misfortune that you are the only coward from Barrio 18 that we could find on the street. No matter; you are only the first, and there will be more. Two of my soldiers died here last week as the result of your attack. More were arrested and are sitting in jail. I will kill four of you for each one of us that falls." Ortega pulled his shirt off, revealing a torso covered with the inked insignia of the MS-13. "This is what a *man's* chest looks like. And I don't want your worthless blood staining my shirt.

"I do have one offer to make you tonight," Ortega continued as he pulled a large hunting knife from a scabbard on his belt. He held the knife in his left hand; the gun was still in his right. "You can tell us who ordered the raid that killed my soldiers last week, and where we can find the *putas* who did it. In that case," he raised the gun, "you can die quickly. If you do not talk," the hand with the knife went up, "you will scream instead."

"I do not know who hit your men." The man moaned, clutching his wounded leg. He looked up into Ortega's face. "If I did I would not tell you. I will not help you kill my brothers."

"A brave choice," Ortega nodded, "but one with consequences." He nodded to the others. "Hold him."

The man screamed in agony as the knife began to carve.

"He makes too much noise," Ortega shook his head. "We need something to silence him, and I do not want to waste one of our washrags. Remove his pants."

Twenty minutes later, the body lay motionless.

"Put him in the truck," Ortega said. "We will make a delivery later tonight."

Two of the group dragged the body away by its feet leaving a wide trail of blood through the wash area.

"We need to clean this place up," Ortega ordered. "Turn on the wash. My car is dirty. Bring it around."

Chapter Thirteen

August 23, 9:00 a.m.

Trask sat at the table in the courtroom and read the file that Crawford had provided him regarding the school life of Armando Lopez-Mendez. There was nothing in it to amount to a lead in the murder. An average student doing average high-school stuff. No steady girlfriends or even close friends. Predictable. Kid gets jerked back and forth between the US and El Salvador every three or four years. Probably had no real idea who he was or where he belonged.

He closed the file and picked up another. *The van from the retaliation raid.* He was looking at the computer trace on the van's vehicle identification number. Vincente Santos was the registered owner. He had also been the driver.

The MS-13 boys wanted a van for the raid on Bladensburg—needed it for the shooters in the back. Slide the door open and fire. You can steal a damned Cavalier anywhere, but vans are harder to come by. They're not parked on every street like cheap compacts. Mr. Santos happened to have one, and he was in the club. Born in Los Angeles to Salvadoran parents. Tenth-grade dropout. Two fairly old prior convictions from California: one for burglary, one for dope. Served almost no time. The LA jails are like Lorton, too crowded. No one does the time they're sentenced to serve. Verified MS-13 banger. Tats to prove he's proud of it.

Trask picked up a copy of the daily court docket and looked at his watch. *Almost time.* The nine o'clock hearing was a probation revocation case in front of Senior District Judge Waymon Dean. The original case, the tax case, had been filed when Santos had gotten lucky with a lottery ticket, but had filed a fraudulent return in an attempt to get a refund on the sizeable withholding amount. The case had not been one of Trask's, but he had volunteered to handle the revocation matter. That matter had become even easier when an FBI agent from the property crimes squad had handed him a CD with a recording on it.

"ALL RISE."

The clerk's call and gavel crack shook him out of his musings, and Trask stood as the old man entered the courtroom. Unlike some of the other senior judges, all of whom seemed to be pushing eighty, Judge Dean was still mentally alert and as physically fit as many men thirty years his junior. A tall, thin man with completely white hair and a matching, bushy moustache, he spoke with a pronounced Virginia drawl.

"Case 00425-01. United States v. Vincente Santos. Counsel, please state your appearances."

"Jeffrey Trask for the United States, Your Honor. With me at counsel table is Special Agent Driscoll of the FBI."

"Mitchell Clark for Vincente Santos, who appears in person and with counsel."

Trask glanced over at his opposing counsel.

Haven't seen this guy before. Looks like he just passed the bar. I wonder if he knows what he's getting into with this client. Darren Regan had him at the initial hearing, and he's in the morgue now.

"This is a final hearing on a probation revocation for Mr. Santos," Judge Dean declared sternly. "My records, and my memory, reflect that Mr. Santos here is one of those who believe that the United States government doesn't have the Constitutional authority to collect income taxes. Mr. Trask, I sentenced this defendant to probation, didn't I?"

"Yes, Your Honor. I was not originally assigned to this matter, but that's what the record reflects." *I could try and respectfully bust your chops for not locking him up when you had the chance, Judge, but there's no point in doing that now, especially when the defendant's going to push those buttons for me.*

"My file," Judge Dean said, "shows that despite that leniency, and some stern warnings to Mr. Santos, the probation office now alleges that the defendant has violated the conditions of that probation by associating with other felons and by refusing to report to his probation officer for scheduled appointments."

The judge nodded in the direction of a woman in her forties, seated at a side table. Trask recognized her as Ruth Deavers, one of the probation office supervisors.

"There is a new and supplementary violation report, Your Honor," Trask said. "The defendant is being charged in a new matter with aiding and abetting others in the possession of illegal machine guns, which we believe were about to be used in some local gang warfare."

"What does your client have to say for himself, Mr. Clark?" The judge's piercing blue eyes peered over the top of a pair of wire-rimmed glasses.

"Mi…Mister Santos admits he…he acknowledges having had some contact wi…with others who have criminal records, Your Honor…" Clark stammered nervously.

"Take it easy, son. Is this your first hearing?"

Trask felt himself smiling as the judge glanced at him and winked.

The old guy does have a soft side—for this rookie, for the moment.

"Yes it is, Judge." Clark managed to get the answer out without stuttering.

"Well, you're doing fine. Were you appointed or retained for this case?"

"I've been hired by Mr. Santos."

Getting a chunk of that lottery money yourself, Clark? Trask thought.

"Good, good." The judge was smiling. "Now, what does Mr. Santos want to do here? Is he contesting these violations?"

"We *are* contesting the violations, Judge, although we are conceding…we are admitting some of the *conduct* in the probation report, but we…we just don't think that they are really…we don't think that they can fairly be called violations."

The judge took off his glasses and started polishing the lens with a sleeve of his robe.

"Why don't you tell me, Mister Clark…and take your time. But I need to understand how you think your client here can admit violative conduct without admitting violations. Did he, or didn't he, have contact with other convicted felons?"

"Yes, he did judge, but—"

Good, kid. Admit what you have to admit.

"OK, just hold it there. And did he fail to report to the probation office as he had been ordered to do?"

"Yes, sir, but—"

"Hold it again. So now you tell me why you think those actions are not violations of his probation."

This better be good.

"Judge, my client asserts that he has the right to associate with those who share his heritage under his constitutional rights of assembly and association—"

"As long as they are not convicted felons, Mr. Clark."

The judge isn't smiling now. Wait till he hears the recording.

"We are asserting, Your Honor—"

That's an awful lot of asserting, kid. A bad buzzword to throw out too often. Especially to an old lion like Waymon Dean.

"We are asserting that the convictions of some of these individuals with whom Mr. Santos was associating were unfairly adjudged and that they may have been the products of ineffective assistance of counsel."

"That's for them and their defense attorneys to litigate, Clark, not you. Let's cut to the chase here, son." The judge turned his eyes toward Trask. "Does the evidence, Mr. Trask, show that these contacts were with other convicted felons?"

"Yes, Your Honor," Trask answered.

"Felons who weren't just tax cheats?" The white eyebrows arched high over the glasses.

Here's my trump card. Sorry, Clark.

"Your Honor, in addition to being the driver in what we believe was to be an attempt to murder members of a rival street gang, and in addition to chauffeuring four convicted felons in his van who were at the time in possession of fully automatic weapons, Mr. Santos seems to have been involved in the distribution of some stolen property. The FBI had a wiretap on the office telephone of one Richard Stevens in another investigation. That investigation targeted the fencing of stolen property. Mr. Stevens is *yet another* convicted felon, with convictions for receiving stolen property. We have a recording of an intercepted conversation between the defendant and Mr. Stevens. My file shows that a copy of this recording was provided to Mr. Clark last week."

"What about that, Clark?" the judge asked.

No "Mister Clark" now. Grandpa's about to break out the hickory switch, kid.

"I did get the disc, judge, but I haven't had the time to listen to all of it yet—"

WHAT!? Clark, you dummy, you're dead meat.

"And my client asserts that these conversations have been misconstrued—"

Again with that asserts stuff; you took your client at his word, Clark, and you'll never do that again after today.

"Your Honor," Trask said, fixing his gaze on the face of Vincente Santos, who was sneering at him. "I suggest that the Court allow me to play the recording of that conversation. I *have* listened to the entire conversation and think that the Court will have no difficulty ascertaining its true nature. It's about five minutes long. Agent Driscoll can authenticate the tape."

"Do you want Agent Driscoll to have to testify on that, Clark?" the judge asked pointedly. "Seems to me you said that your client has admitted talking to this Stevens."

"We'll stipulate to the authenticity of the recording, Judge."

Clark, you'll never forget this.

"Let's hear your evidence, Mr. Trask." Judge Dean leaned back in the leather chair and started polishing his glasses again.

Trask cued the disc in the laptop on the table in front of him, and the voices of Vincente Santos and Richard Stevens began to resonate over the courtroom's audio system. The first four minutes of the recording *did* concern the redistribution of certain personal property at a fraction of its retail value, but then neither of the speakers had actually purchased the property in question. It was the last portion of the conversation that caused Mitchell Clark to turn pale, Vincente Santos to start looking at his shoes, and smoke to appear from every orifice in the white-haired head of Judge Waymon Dean.

> "How's your probation goin' Vincente?"
>
> "That whole thing's a crock, Rich."
>
> "Yeah, I know."
>
> "You bet your ass. Same motherfuckers who think they can grab all my money think they can tell me how to live my life, what I can do, what I can't do."
>
> "Yeah, I had to go through the same shit on my parole."

"Right. This old judge I got, Mean Dean they call 'im, he's a cranky, stupid old bastard. Thinks he's king of the country. Goddamn feds. And this PO I got, Mizz Deavers, what a dried-up old bitch. Wants to screw up my schedule just so she can talk down to me every damn month. Fuck 'em. They're not gonna tell me how to live my life."

"You tell 'em, Vincente."

Trask hit the stop button. He looked over at Clark.

I think the kid's gonna hurl. He's looking really green.

"Ruth, how much time can I give this guy?" The judge's voice had dropped to a measured growl. The probation officer stood at her table.

"Your Honor, since there was no imprisonment time adjudged at the initial sentencing, all five years remain available to the Court."

"Probation is revoked, and five years it is, Mr. Santos. You're remanded to the custody of the Bureau of Prisons. You'll have plenty of time to help prepare your defense for your next case. Court's adjourned."

Judge Dean started to step down from the bench, but then he turned back. "One more thing, Mr. Santos."

The defendant's sneer was gone. He looked weakly up at the bench while a deputy marshal was locking his wrists in handcuffs.

"They say in the law that sometimes truth is a defense," the judge said. He smiled. "Not this time."

The judge nodded to the deputy, who turned his prisoner back toward the door.

Trask headed for the FBI field office.

August 23, 10:30 a.m.

"The body, our latest one," Doroz explained, "was dropped on the corner on the front of this building—the field office of the FBI in Washington, DC, for

God's sake—just before dawn this morning. An 18er. Three sixes tattooed on his face. One bullet hole in a thigh, about a hundred knife tracks in his chest, and his severed privates stuffed in his mouth. Throat cut to finish him off. Surveillance cameras only saw a dark pickup stop, and someone threw him over the bed wall. No plates on the car. Retaliation both for the hits at the car wash and for our arrests of their compadres. In my opinion, clearly the work of a very pissed-off MS-13 crew. The body's on the way to the ME now."

"This, on the other hand, was professional." Trask flipped the file on the Regan murder across the table to Doroz. "No prints anywhere in the guy's house that weren't his own. No signs of forced entry or a struggle. None of the neighbors heard anything, so a silencer was probably used. One small-caliber shot to the back of the head. Victim seated in a chair with his hands tied behind his back. *And,*" he continued, looking at Carter and then back again at Doroz, "no gang graffiti or machetes. Any ideas?"

"He was a defense attorney. You talk for the scumbags long enough, sooner or later they talk back when they don't like the results," Carter said matter-of-factly.

"That's kind of cold, Dix." Doroz thumbed through the case file. "Any recent significant losses in court for Mr. Regan?"

"Just the usual bottom-feeders," Carter said. "I got his calendar for the past few months from his secretary. The guy didn't take on many power players. Hookers, shoplifters, low-level pushers. Mostly in superior court."

"He didn't do much federal court work," Doroz agreed. "I wonder how he ended up with one of our MS-13 guys."

"He was still on the federal appointment list," Trask said. "I saw him in district court from time to time, usually when the bigger defense attorneys had a conflict and the court needed somebody to represent an indigent. He actually wasn't a bad guy, knew how to get the best deals for his clients."

"Meaning he would have suggested to his new client that he cooperate with us?" Doroz asked.

"Yes. Especially when it looked like a certain conviction," Trask said.

"So maybe one of the *Mara* bosses didn't like that suggestion. They didn't want any extra heat, so they changed their murder method," Carter offered.

Trask leaned back in his chair and looked at Carter for long seconds before he spoke again. "Dix, from the get-go on this thing you've been saying that you didn't think it was the *Maras* who were pulling all this off. Wrong guns, wrong ammo, no tattoos on the visitors to my house. Why do you think that they're good for *this* hit?"

"I don't know that they are," Carter said. "Just a theory. The murder seems connected to the arrests of that shooting team we interrupted."

"Then why this one defense counsel? Any of the rest of them threatened or attacked? Has anybody asked them?"

"I'll get on that now." Carter stood up and left the room.

Trask looked at Doroz, who shrugged.

"Bear, did Murphy ever get us that personnel roster we asked for? The one for the embassy?" Trask asked.

"Not yet. Want me to call him?"

"Yeah. But tell him—ask him nicely—to bring it over *here*. I'd like him to think we've just been checking our notes and it's a simple loose end.

"It's not?"

"No," Trask said. "It's not."

August 23, 2:49 p.m.

The man with the eye patch climbed the stairs to a second-floor apartment in the aging apartment building. He wrinkled his nose in disgust at the odor. The place reeked of refuse and neglect. He found the number and knocked on the door.

"One hundred thousand, as agreed," he said when the door opened. He handed the briefcase to a shorter, thicker, and younger man with the number "18" tattooed into the left side of his neck. "Also as agreed, your brother has been released from *La Esperanza*, and will join you and your wife in Ecuador. Your plane ticket is inside the case. If I ever see you in this country or in El Salvador again, I will kill you. I will also hunt your family down and exterminate them. *Comprende?*"

The younger man nodded, and then closed the door.

The man with the eye patch returned to his car and motioned his driver out of the vehicle. "Hugo, see that he does not make his flight and that the case is returned to me. I'll circle the block and return for you. Make it quick. We've been busy today, and I'm hungry."

He watched as Hugo entered the building, then he spat on the sidewalk. *Fucking Mara scum.* He opened the driver's door to the limo and slid behind the wheel. The light at the first corner was turning red as he reached the intersection. Seeing no other vehicles approaching, he ignored the signal and turned left. Three more left turns later, he pulled to the curb in front of the building. Hugo was there, carrying the briefcase. He got into the passenger's seat, and the car pulled away from the curb.

4:10 p.m.

Frank Wilkes waited for the officers to stand aside and give him room to work. The apartment, a small one-bedroom in the Northeast project facing Rhode Island Avenue, was in order except for the corpse lying on the floor in the center of the room, just inside the doorway. There was a small-caliber bullet wound in the center of the dead man's forehead. Wilkes took dozens of digital photographs of the scene, and then returned the camera to his bag.

Cause of death is not a mystery in this case, he thought.

He nevertheless dutifully took a swab and ran it through the pool of blood beside the dead man's head, placed the swab in an evidence bag, and repeated the procedure with a swab he scraped along the inside of the corpse's mouth.

"Jeez, Frank, any doubt that's his blood?" asked one of the patrolmen standing in the doorway.

"Probably not. No doubt at all that we won't know unless I check it." Wilkes glanced at the cop with a look that ensured he would not be interrupted again. "Turn that light off, will you?"

The room darkened, Wilkes took a can of luminol spray from his bag and stepped around the corpse. He sprayed the floor, a small table, and a wooden armless chair that were several feet away from the corpse. He looked back at the cop in the doorway. More questions were written on the man's face, but he was not asking them.

Wilkes waited a few seconds, and then noticed a faint blue glow on the chair at the joints where the vertical bars forming the rear legs and sides of the back passed through the seat. He took more swabs, wiped them along the blue lines, and placed the swabs in evidence bags. He walked past the cop in the doorway.

"It may mean nothing, may mean everything," he said as he left.

———

4:45 p.m.

Murphy was smiling as he knocked on Doroz' office door. He had a manila folder in his left hand while he extended his right to Trask.

Another song flashed through Trask's memory. "The Backstabbers" by the O'Jays.

"How's my new favorite prosecutor?" Murphy sank into one of the chairs facing Doroz' desk.

"I'll let you know in a minute, Agent Murphy, as soon as I see what is, or isn't, in that folder," Trask said. He was standing, and not smiling.

"The personnel roster for the embassy of El Salvador, just as you asked."

"Just a lot later than I expected it," Trask said, thumbing through the papers. "And regarding one official, pure bullshit." He handed three pages back to Murphy. The first page bore the photograph of the man with the eye patch. "I do not believe for a microsecond that this apparently non-English-speaking deputy chief of mission is a career diplomat, or for that matter, that his name is José Rios-García. I would like to know, Agent Murphy, who the hell he really is, why he lied to us about not recognizing one of the photographs we showed him, and what his purpose is in this country."

Murphy stopped smiling and leaned backward in his chair. "Hypothetically speaking," he said, "what do you think would happen to a junior Assistant United States Attorney if he attempted to press an investigation, unsupported by anything other than speculation, into a high-ranking official of a foreign government who enjoys full diplomatic immunity? I'm trying to help you out as best I can, Jeff, and I'd hate to see you put yourself in a no-win situation."

Trask nodded, pacing about the room before turning back toward Murphy. He felt his blood start to boil, and he waited until he could speak with some control.

"I appreciate your concern, Murph. I really do, and I assure you that I have no intention of starting some international incident *without* just cause. But *hypothetically speaking*, let's say that a junior Assistant United States Attorney—*and his wife*—had to fight off a couple of hired goons with machetes who attempted to decapitate this attorney and his wife with the said machetes. Do you wonder just how pissed off that guy might be? Do you wonder if that guy would hesitate at all to charge anyone on this planet, *anyone*, with obstruction of justice if he could show that this *anyone*—being an American citizen and maybe even another government employee and therefore *not* enjoying diplomatic immunity—was concealing evidence in a related homicide investigation?"

"I gave you what we have on file."

"And I'm telling you that it's bullshit. And I'm also telling you that if the time comes when I can prove it's bullshit, and that you knew it was bullshit when you gave it to me, you can expect to spend about half a year's salary paying some defense mouthpiece to wait outside a grand jury room while you're inside explaining yourself. Or do you think that your friends at State are actually going to stand behind you and provide counsel for you in that situation?"

Trask saw Murphy's eyes look away for a split second.

"That's what I thought. You know as well as I do they'll promise you full support and then cut you free like a kite caught on a power line. Come back when you can tell me who this pirate really is."

Murphy stormed out the door.

"Wheeew," Doroz whistled. "Thanks for inviting me to that little party. Here I was thinking I had a shot at retirement in a year or two."

"It's all on me, Bear," Trask said. "I just needed a witness. Let's see if Murphy still knows which country he works for."

Doroz was suddenly looking past him. Trask turned and saw Dixon Carter and Tim Wisniewski standing in the doorway.

"We have another dead defense counsel," Carter said.

6:20 p.m.

Sivella's homicide team and the crime scene crew were still at it when they arrived. The law office of William T. Boydston looked undisturbed, a sharp contrast to the body seated in the chair behind the desk. The office had the usual impress-the-clients collection of treatises and published law reporters perfectly arranged in a rosewood shelf directly behind the matching desk. The file cabinets to the side of the bookcase remained closed.

Trask's eyes scanned the titles for a moment: *Black's Law Dictionary, Corbin on Contracts, Prosser on Torts.*

The usual collection of law school texts. Books he hasn't opened since law school. The same for the Atlantic and Federal Reporters. All for show, for the clients. We all use the web now. The computer search engines are ten times faster than thumbing through the books.

He stepped around to the side of the desk, seeing that the crime scene guys were working behind it.

The obese body of Boydston sat tilted back in a leather swivel chair, his hands tied behind him. A large wad of paper had been stuffed in his mouth, and blood trails fell from two small holes in his head, one at the base of his skull in the rear, one between the eyes. The body of a woman in her fifties lay at his feet. There was a single hole in the back of her head.

"His secretary, Lynette Morris," Sivella said. "Was this guy on the list for our MS-13 crew?"

"He represented one of the shooters in the back of the van," Trask answered.

"Would he have told his client to cooperate, like the last one?" Doroz asked.

"No, not Big Pink," Trask said. He saw the question on Doroz' face. "We called him that because he *was* big, and when he had blood in his head he had a very pink complexion. Not the pale gray you see now. He was a meter-runner: he'd rather tell a client to go to trial just to pad his bill. He really didn't give a shit if the guy lost and served more time, as long as he could get paid for going to court."

"What's our best guess on the time of death, Cap?" Carter asked Sivella.

"Lunch hour, probably. He had a one-thirty appointment, and the client came in and found the bodies. We checked the secretary's appointment book and called the last client he'd seen before lunch. Divorce case. The gal said she left at 11:45 and all was well. She said no other clients were waiting."

Trask walked out while the CSI troops were shooting the rest of their digital photos. Boydston's office opened onto a short hallway that led to the waiting room.

Shooter comes in before Big Pink and Lynette can leave for lunch, waiting until the future Mrs. Ex-whatever clears the area. He orders the secretary into the back with her boss and then does the dirty work. Nothing's ransacked, no filing cabinets open. Her purse, his wallet are still where they should be. Not a robbery. Just like with Regan. A hit, pure and simple.

He opened the front door from the lobby, looking out onto K Street, NW.

Parking lane, parking meters. Four lanes of traffic. Another parking lane on the opposite side of the street. Clothing stores, a Starbucks of course, and a bank. A BANK, with an ATM directly across the street.

Trask walked hurriedly back into the office and grabbed Doroz, who followed him outside. Trask pointed toward the bank. "Think it would be worthwhile getting the camera tape from the money machine?"

Doroz looked at him and shook his head. "For a lawyer, you don't miss much."

"I read a lot. That's how you guys got McVeigh in Oklahoma City, wasn't it?"

"Yep. The ATM camera caught the truck and survived the blast, too. I'll go pull the tape."

Trask went back inside and found Sivella. "I think we need to call the other defense attorneys and give 'em a heads-up."

"Agreed."

"Bear's pulling the camera tape from an ATM across the street. Probably had the office entry in its frame of view."

"Good. Let's all sit down to look at that. The FBI gang squad room in an hour?"

"Sure. How long before we can see if there's a ballistics match with the rounds from the Regan shooting?"

"If Kathy can get to the autopsy tonight, we could have a preliminary tomorrow. I'll ask Frank Wilkes to expedite the ballistics."

Lynn had set up the squad briefing room so that a machine fed the ATM camera tape into some computer software, which in turn fed the running images onto the drop-down movie screen.

"This way, I don't have twelve guys looking over my shoulder at my computer monitor," she said.

"Start it at 11:40, please," Trask said.

The film was the usual grainy, black-and-white product of a device designed only to identify the faces of those who would attempt to defraud or make off with the ATM machine. The time counter marched past 11:44 a.m.

"We should see our divorcee any time now, if she was telling us the truth," Sivella said.

At 11:46 a.m., the head of a woman exiting the law office was visible over the tops of the passing cars. Then the screen went black.

"What the hell?!" Doroz exclaimed.

"The timer's still running," Trask pointed out, "which means the camera's still rolling. Let it run, Lynn. Better yet, fast-forward please."

At 11:58 a.m., the camera resumed its surveillance of K Street NW, unobstructed.

"Somebody else apparently reads a lot—enough to know to block off an ATM camera when they're about to commit a homicide or two," Doroz said, looking at Trask.

Trask looked at Sivella. "Commander, does that look like the degree of planning one would expect from a bunch of street-gang thugs?"

"Hell, no. It smells more like a damned spook operation."

"That's what I've been trying to say all along, Cap," Carter said. "I don't know what we're into here, but it isn't simple gang warfare."

"I agree," Wisniewski said.

"What a surprise." Sivella snorted, shaking his head. Wisniewski was playing the junior partner role with an eye on an Oscar.

"What's our next step, Jeff?" Sivella asked Trask.

"Bear, please set up another meeting with the ambassador. Don't bother going through Murphy. Tell the ambassador that we just want to give him an update on our progress, such as it is. Then get somebody in the know over here from CIA and DEA. Somebody who's been on the ground in El Salvador, if possible. In the same room and at the same time. And again, don't invite Murphy."

"You want to see the ambassador before or after this meeting?"

"After, if we can get CIA and DEA together any time soon."

"What's my police department's role in this for now?" Sivella asked.

"In my career-suicidal opinion," Trask said, "it should probably be playing dumb, and being very ready to throw a rash and impetuous prosecutor under the bus. In other words, you don't know what the hell I'm doing or why. If we catch anything on this fishing expedition, we'll let you know."

"When you say 'we' do you mean...?" Doroz asked.

"Yep, you and me, Bear. You're a bullet-proof hero just trying to keep me under control, and if asked, you had no idea what I was doing, either."

"We have our assignments," Doroz said, looking at the rest of the group.

10:41 p.m.

"Sorry. It's been an insane day," Crawford said, collapsing into the couch beside her.

"Anyone see you leaving your place?"

"I don't think so." She kissed him on the cheek.

He took her hand. "It's important that they don't."

"Are you that ashamed of me?"

"God, Marissa, there's nothing I want more than to show you off in every restaurant, club, and concert in town. Every office party, charity ball, ballgame, everything. It's just dangerous for you right now with all this going on, and we don't know who all the players are yet."

"It's the *Maras*. I have always hated them."

"I'm not fond of them either. Vicious crew. Can't even join up without getting the hell beat out of you."

"That's the easy initiation, the one the guys get."

"What?"

"It's worse for the girls. If a girl agrees to join them, she doesn't get beat up for thirteen seconds, she gets raped by the six biggest guys in the gang."

Crawford paused, stunned. The question on his face was clear.

"No," she said, tears forming in her eyes. "Not me. My little cousin, Carolina. They made her do it. She grabbed one of her father's guns after it was over and shot herself. She was fifteen. I used to babysit her."

She started sobbing. He held her and kissed her forehead.

"I'm so sorry. I had no idea."

"I know I must be careful for now," she said wiping her eyes on her sleeve. "I understand. And you must understand, I will do anything, help anyone, to erase the *Maras*. I know that's what you are doing now. If you need anything from me, just ask."

Chapter Fourteen

August 24, 9:10 a.m.

"Who'd you pull in?" Trask asked, cradling the phone on his left shoulder while looking at his computer screen.

"A past DEA station chief from San Salvador and a CIA field officer who was down there about five years ago," Doroz said. "Actually they were in-country at about the same time. Both before the current regime took power, so their contacts were probably with the old ARENA government, but they were all I could find in the local area on short notice, and on the QT."

"I'm sure they'll do for now. Thanks, Bear. When did you tell them I'd be there?"

"Nine-thirty."

"Then I'll be there at nine-thirty-five."

"We'll see you then," Doroz said, chuckling.

Trask checked his e-mail for the fourth time, including his court docket, which remained conspicuously empty. *Your only assignment,* he reminded himself, *is to solve about ten murders, keep from getting your US Attorney fired, and keep your own head, and Lynn's, attached at the neck.* He opened the e-copy of the homicide blotter—Sivella had agreed to put him on the distribution list—and scanned the list of the last three days' violent deaths.

Eight more autopsies for the MEs to do. Let's see...I'll be, somebody finally finished off Calvin Hart. It's that time of year. He gets shot every fall. Bookies who don't pay their bettors run that risk. Calvin always did better with basketball than football. Two dead in Anacostia; shot each other and died on the scene. One dead hooker. What's this? An M-18 member whacked in Northeast?

He jotted down the date and time—there was no name yet for the victim—and grabbed his briefcase before heading for the gang squad. As he passed through the bullpen on the way to the conference room, he dropped the note on Carter's desk.

"Pull that one for me, will you, Dix?"

"Sure. I'm starting a collection. Tomorrow OK?"

"Yeah. I won't have time to read it today anyway."

"What's the interest?"

"M-18 victim, shot to death. May not be related, but I'm taking no chances."

Carter nodded.

Doroz and the other two were waiting in the conference room. Trask made his apologies for being late as he closed the door and Doroz made the introductions. There was Steve McDonald from CIA, a stout man with gray eyes and matching hair in a badly fitting sport coat. Kevin Hall was from DEA: taller, leaner. His glasses gave him the look of a college professor, a prof wearing a blue and white camp shirt. Trask noted that they had positioned themselves on opposite sides of the conference table.

"I have a problem, gentlemen," Trask began. "I have a dead ambassador's kid, several dead MS-13 troops, counting some on the Maryland side, at least one dead member of Barrio 18, and two dead defense attorneys who were scheduled to represent some other *Mara Salvatrucha* pawns who were probably on their way to plunk some 18ers when they got pulled over. I also have a State Department agent who, it is my strong belief, is not giving me the whole story about what's going on."

"State pukes!" snorted McDonald at the exact same moment that Hall rolled his eyes skyward. Trask told himself there was at least one small piece of common ground between the two: their contempt for things officially diplomatic.

"I know your agencies probably have different perspectives on what may be going down here," Trask said. "I'd like them both. Who wants to start?"

"I've seen the papers and thought some about this. I'll give it a shot," Hall said.

"This should be good." McDonald snorted again.

"You can provide your own poisoned perspective when I'm done," Hall replied, staring coldly across the table. He turned his eyes to Trask. "DEA's mission, as you know, is to try and put a damper on dope flowing through Central

America on its way to the US. My station worked El Salvador. We worked closely with our contacts in Guatemala, Honduras, Panama, Nicaragua."

"Who was moving most of the dope while you were there?" Trask asked.

"Who wasn't?" Hall said. "Your MS-13 and Barrio 18 gangs, cartels from Colombia, Mexico, and Jamaica, Mr. McDonald's buddies in the Salvadoran government…"

McDonald snorted again.

"Sounds like it was the accepted fundraising technique for everybody," Trask said.

"Exactly," said McDonald. "So you picked a side."

"Not every side was in the business of using government death squads," Hall snapped back.

"Excuse me?" Trask asked.

"We started noticing them back in 1980," Hall said, "during the civil war down there. Four Maryknoll nuns were raped and murdered by some government guardsman. It caused a big stink up here that lasted for all of fifteen minutes. It was the ARENA group's not-so-secret response to the leftist gangs. Pick 'em up off the street and have a few summary executions. The official policy from the government toward the gangs was something they called *Super Mano Duro*. It means 'super-hard hand.' The policy was to kill or imprison every gang member or associate they could find."

"It worked," interjected McDonald. "You want death squads that like us and kill gangbangers, or communist death squads who hate us and shoot innocents?"

"I'd prefer neither, of course," Hall replied.

"Dream on, Kevin," McDonald said. "You always thought you could ride in on your white horse, clean up the drug trade, and everyone would love one another. Were you at Woodstock, for Christ's sake?"

"Continue, please, Mr. Hall." Trask was playing referee.

"The real nasty group was *La Sombra Negra*, The Black Shadow. Trained, I believe, with some help from our very own CIA." He shot a look at McDonald. "Hitler would have loved them. Targeted assassinations of opposition leaders, gang members, church officials, anyone who posed a threat to the status quo, all justified in the name of *reducing violence*."

"The Salvadorans put *La Sombra Negra* out of business in 1995," McDonald interjected. "The ARENA government prosecuted them."

"A show trial to cover their tracks and get the international press off their backs," Hall responded. "The killings slowed for a while, then picked back up again. Gang members were jerked off the street by guys in vans with darkened windows, found shot in isolated places. All killed in the fashion of *tiros de gracia.*"

"Indulge me, please," Trask said. "My high-school Spanish didn't cover that phrase."

"Sorry. It means 'shots of grace.' The victims' hands were tied behind their backs and each got a round in the back of the head: base of the skull. That and the way the hands were tied was the signature of *La Sombra Negra.*"

"What was unique about the hands?" Trask asked, shooting a look at Doroz.

"Man operates with his opposing thumbs," McDonald responded. "The Black Shadow guys always bound the thumbs together to make sure the gang-bangers couldn't free themselves."

Trask opened his briefcase and pulled one of the crime scene photos from the case file marked "Murder of Attorney Darren Regan." The print showed the lawyer's hands bound behind his back. The thumbs were tightly bound together with two loops of the cord. He handed the photograph to McDonald. "Look familiar?"

"Yes, it does." McDonald passed the photo across the table to Hall.

"How was this guy killed?" Hall asked.

Trask pulled another photo out of the file. It was an autopsy photograph showing the entry wound low on the back of Regan's head. He handed it to Hall.

"Textbook," Hall said. "A *Sombra* execution, or a damned good copy of one." He passed the print to McDonald. "Can we at least agree on that?"

"Yes," McDonald said after a moment. "We can. Who was this guy?"

"A local defense attorney assigned to represent one of the MS-13 types we arrested,"

Doroz said.

"Then you should know," Hall said, "that in the early nineties, one of *La Sombra Negra's* contributions to the *Super Mano Duro* was the murder of attorneys in San Salvador who tried to represent the *Mara* members in court."

"You're not aware of any connection between the *new* government and the death squads, are you?" Trask asked.

"No. They hate each other's guts," McDonald said. "Kinda like me and Hall."

Trask reached into the briefcase and pulled out the photo of the man with the eye patch. "Do either of you recognize him?"

"No," Hall said. "I've never seen him before."

McDonald paused. "The face *seems* familiar, but I can't place him at the moment."

"Thanks for trying," Trask said. "Can we agree, gentlemen, that whatever side of the debate you're on regarding the relative merits of the conflict in El Salvador, we do *not* want death squads from *either* side prowling the streets in this country?"

Both nodded.

"Good. Then please keep this under your hats for now, but get back to me with anything else relevant that might come to mind."

Trask shook hands with them before Doroz escorted them out. When he returned, Doroz handed an envelope to Trask. It had been opened.

"From Frank Wilkes," Doroz said. "The ballistics on the murders of the two defense attorneys and the secretary. All killed by the same weapon. Small-caliber handgun, probably using a silencer. He ran the rounds from the Langley Park and Georgia Avenue sniper shootings, too. Different sniper rifles. Same kind of ammo, but no matches with the rifling on the rounds."

"So we're kind of batting .500 on the tests," Trask said. "For now, on this case I'll take that."

August 25

At 1:47 a.m., a black male of less than medium height and much greater than medium weight opened the back door and stepped out of the Qwik Shine Car Wash. He nodded to the guards, who were now posted on the inside of the building, behind the steel door that had replaced the wooden one. He tossed the duffel bag into the rear of a dark blue Ford Explorer and backed away from the building to the left.

Thank you very much, thought Dixon Carter as he peered through the binoculars, *for backing toward me and for keeping the light above your license plate in working order.* He jotted down the plate number, then activated the computer mounted on the dash of the Buick and ran the numbers. The screen blinked back at him about a second later, indicating the recorded registration data for the license plate. *Yeah, I thought I recognized you, Peewee. We'll have a talk tomorrow.*

Carter backed into the alley and headed home. After pulling the car into the garage, he retrieved the GPS from the shelf and returned it to the rear frame of the Buick. He walked inside and collapsed into the recliner. It was 3:30 a.m. before he fell asleep.

He wished he hadn't. The nightmare was there again, replaying the scene. Juan Ramirez standing on the stairs, saying, "I got this, Dix. Go rest your leg."

Carter twisted in the chair, reliving the pain in his leg from the healing gunshot wound. He had nodded to Juan and then left the townhome, leaving his partner to deal with the snitch they were moving to a safe house. There had been a couple of uniforms out front. He was home and in bed before they'd gone in to check on the delay. No Juan, no snitch. Just the suitcase at the bottom of the stairs and the badge tossed on the hallway floor like a piece of trash.

He imagined the scene in the hallway after he left. Juan following procedure, following the snitch down the stairs. Reid had to have made his move at the bottom of the staircase, getting the jump on Ramirez. The Jamaican outweighed his partner by a good eighty pounds, and none of it was fat. One sucker punch would have done it. One sucker punch he could have prevented if he'd stayed.

The dream shifted to the farm in Maryland. The dig. The duct tape wrapped around Juan's head. His partner's body in the same shallow grave with the snitch. Carter jerked awake and looked at his watch.

Four-thirty.

He got up and headed for the shower.

Time to get ready for work.

Chapter Fifteen

August 26

Trask sat on the right side of the pine-framed couch in the den, his feet on a matching ottoman. The History Channel, or the "Hitler Channel" as Lynn called it, droned at low volume on the TV across the room. It was a bit past midnight, and Lynn was in bed with Nikki asleep beside her. Trask had to lean a little to his right so his right hand could access the notepad that rested on the end table, since the massive head of Boowulf—her now official, veterinarian-registered name—lay squarely in the middle of his lap. She was snoring, so Trask bumped up the TV volume a notch with the remote.

It had been a relatively calm day. The only real development had been a call from Chief Magistrate Judge Noble informing him that the remaining three defense attorneys from the MS-13 bust had all asked to withdraw from the case, not wishing to join the ranks of the newly dearly departed. Noble had granted their requests and told Trask that the court would be asking for volunteers from the defense bar to represent the five defendants. If there were no takers in the next couple of weeks, other appointments would be made by the court. Trask had assured Noble that they were running down every lead possible to prevent a further winnowing of the defense bar.

He thought about the few pieces of his current jigsaw puzzle, the most suitable metaphor for almost every criminal case, especially homicides.

He closed his eyes and made mental notes, cataloging the facts as he remembered them. He usually had no trouble doing this. The file cabinet in his head opened, and he pulled the images out of the files. He had trained himself to store them there, each page mentally photographed and recorded. The files spread across his mind, he returned to the puzzle.

In the center, he usually started with a big splash of color. Fit all the blood-red pieces together so that the crime scene was complete. Then he started defining the rim, the limits of the case. He tried to weed out any false suspects so he wasn't distracted by all the collateral stuff. As the investigation team collected the various pieces, he could usually fit them together, and the whole picture would begin to take shape in his head, to make sense. A few pieces in one corner showing a motive, a few more showing the manner and cause of death, all hopefully leading to the final collection of pieces showing the killer. The big disadvantage with the process was that he was working without a box with a big, full color photo of the puzzle on the front showing the completed scene. He had to work from logic, from experience, sometimes from hunches.

He had several problems with the current puzzle. First, he didn't have one crime scene, he had several. He hadn't even decided they all actually belonged in the same puzzle, although his gut told them that they did. Until that was determined, defining the limits of the case was impossible. Did he have one, self-contained murder case with the ambassador's kid? Were the various gang shootings just part of a war between the *Maras?* Was the embassy murder only related to the other shootings through an MS-13 connection, if in fact the ambassador's son had been killed by MS-13? Was MS-13 responsible for the murders of the defense lawyers, or was some Salvadoran vigilante group now operating in DC? It was if someone had burned the boxes and thrown thousands of pieces of several puzzles together in one pile.

There was one thing of which he was certain. He didn't have *all* the pieces yet, so there was no way of telling how related the cases were, how many distinct puzzles he was dealing with. He turned the page on his mental notepad so a fresh one appeared.

The only two incidents that were now conclusively part of the same criminal scheme were the murders of Boydston, his secretary, and Darren Regan, the other defense counsel. They'd all been shot with the same gun. Trask drew a rectangle in one corner of the page and put all three victims' names inside the box. He drew another box, writing inside it the names of the five defendants from the thwarted MS-13 shooting mission. He then drew a line connecting the two boxes, writing "possible" above the connector. The victims had represented the defendants, after all, and he found it unlikely to be a coincidence, given the way the victims had been executed.

He drew another box, writing the names of Diego Morales and the two other victims from the Georgia Avenue sniper shootings inside it, and then another for the two other MS-13 casualties from the Langley Park convenience store murders. He thought a moment, and then drew another box for the two MS-13 bangers who'd been mowed down at the back of the car wash. A line between the Langley Park and Georgia Avenue boxes was labeled "sniper." Even though ballistics said it was a different rifle, it was the same *modus operandi*. Lines were drawn between all the boxes having to do with MS-13, which were simply labeled "13."

The next box was simply labeled "Armando" for the ambassador's son. Trask thought for a moment. He drew a line from this box to the one containing the name of Diego Morales, marking the line "probable." Lynn's analysis had made sense. Fresh tats and bruises and a new *Salvatrucha*, initiated shortly after the body of the ambassador's son was dumped in front of the embassy. Bad blood between the *Maras* and the new government, and an MS-13 signature killing. He decided to concentrate his focus on the ambassador's kid and his probable killer for now. That puzzle seemed to have more clarity than the others. If he got lucky at all, if there were in fact connections to the other boxes, some of the pieces in Armando's jigsaw would point the way to pieces in the other puzzles.

As an afterthought, he drew a final box at the bottom of the page and wrote "M-18 victim" inside it. The single victim found in the project in Northeast. He drew an arrow pointing toward the other boxes above it, with a question mark just above the arrow.

Maybe unrelated. Make a note. Check the ballistics.

The clock on the DVR beneath the TV indicated 1:15 a.m. Trask switched off the TV and the lamp on the end table and headed for the bedroom with a large dark shadow trotting dutifully behind him.

It was 7:00 a.m. when Trask left the house. Saturday morning. He took 301 North out of Waldorf toward Brandywine until he reached Surratt's Road.

The good old Surratt family. Co-conspirators with Booth in the Lincoln assassination, or so the verdict read. Old Mary Surratt hanged with the rest of them.

He made the first left onto Dangerfield Road.

Dangerfield, huh? Am I here because I don't get no respect, or is a "dangerfield" really what I'm wading into now?

At a stop sign, he took another right, and another turn took him to the main gate of the Cheltenham Federal Law Enforcement Training Center, FLETC, or "fletcee" for short. Junior Walker's *Shotgun* started playing in his head.

He spent two hours under the tutelage of a US marshal firearms instructor, becoming acquainted with the weight, feel, and shooting characteristics of the Glock on the firing range. It was not the hand cannon that his .45 at home was, but it had some kick to it.

Enough to stop somebody if I actually hit them. The Post *would love that.*

His target was pulled back up from down-range.

"Nice shooting. Very tight pattern." The instructor nodded with approval.

"I always qualified expert with the pistol at the Academy," Trask said. "Had fits with the M-16. Funkiest balance I ever saw on a rifle."

"We're not giving you one of those. Just sign here, and you're good to go with the Glock."

He signed the forms and left with the pistol in a shoulder holster.

He drove into the District but did not stop at the Triple-nickel. There was no rush hour gridlock, and he made respectable time as he pointed the Jeep up Wisconsin Avenue, NW , toward Bethesda. He saw a sign for the turn to Fort Reno Park.

July 1864. Lookouts on the highest point in town—all of four hundred feet—see some of Jubal Early's Rebs prowling around and notify Fort Stevens in time to turn back the only Confederate attack on Washington. May 2008. Some alleged scientist with the Geological Survey thinks he finds arsenic in the dirt and they close the park. The city fathers panic, build a fence around the whole damned thing, at the cost of a pretty penny to the taxpayers. Park opens two weeks later after they conclude that the first tests were a false positive. Fence is still there.

Trask looked at his image in the rearview mirror.

Why do I remember all this stuff?

He kept left and passed the turn to the right for 41st Street. Two blocks later, he turned into the parking lot. He got out and walked up to the storefront.

The brick façade bore a brass plate: "The Law Offices of Victor Scarborough." As he had expected, the place was locked down tight. No lights inside.

Nor would there be, Trask thought.

He turned and looked to the other side of the street.

No bank this time.

He returned to the Jeep and headed back to the FBI field office. Saturday or not, there was plenty of work to do.

———

"His name is Brian James," Carter began, "but he goes by Peewee. The citizen's tip I got this morning said that he was buying lots of high-dollar weed from a car wash in Northeast. I figured it might be our MS-13 crew's dope, so I stopped by Peewee's place, picked him up, and brought him in. We've got some history. I've arrested him twice before for dope, once for weed, once for crack. He took felonies on each one."

"Which means career offender status and a boatload of time if he takes another hit," Trask said. "So we have some leverage to encourage cooperation."

"Finally. A break." Doroz leaned back in the tilt chair at the head of the conference table. "Did he flip?"

"Yes, he said he's seen the error of his ways and is ready to join the forces of truth and light," Carter said. "Tim and Puddin' are downstairs printing him now."

"Good catch, Dix," Trask said, trying to mask his suspicion. "You say this was a tip you got?"

"Came in on the hotline early this morning. Shortly after 2 a.m. Anonymous call on a throwaway cell, unlisted. I've had Peewee flagged for years, so the tip-line guys called me on *my* cell. Turned out to be good information. He was firing up a big blunt of weed when I knocked on the door. No denying the smell. He tried to tell me he'd just bought a dime bag to smoke, but I bluffed him, told him I had a team with a dog on the way, and he could tell me the truth now or later. He caved and showed me a duffle bag of the stuff. Had to be at least fifty pounds of high-grade kush."

Trask nodded. "Kush" was the generic street name for superior-quality marijuana. He thought that he remembered reading somewhere that the name had originated in Afghanistan.

I've got it now, the purple Indica marijuana from the Hindu Kush mountains. Grand Daddy Purple, GDP, or Purple Kush. That's it.

"Was Tim with you when you pitched him?" Trask asked.

"No. Like I said, I stopped at Peewee's place on the way in this morning, and he knows me. Tim sat in on the interview, though, after I brought him in."

"What did Peewee say about how he bought it?" Doroz asked.

"He told us he got it from 'those damn wets' at our car wash. Apparently, he has some contempt for those who violate the law by entering our country illegally, although he likes the quality of their weed. No phone contact in advance. He said they won't give out any numbers. He knocked on the back door and flashed his roll, and they ushered him back into the office. That's where they're doing their business."

"They haven't had time to grow their own yet," Trask observed. "Even if they planted the same night that you and Tim saw the pipe going in, the plants would just barely have sprouted."

"My conclusion also," Carter agreed. "They had to import some product, and in the meantime they're cultivating a customer base as well as their crops."

"Any objection if we sign him up?" Doroz asked Trask. FBI policy required that an AUSA sign off on the recruitment of a source if the cooperator faced potential charges of his own.

"No. Just make sure he understands that he's still getting charged. He'll just be working his sentence down if he follows directions." Trask looked at Carter. "When can he buy again without it looking like it's too soon?"

"He told us he sells the whole load twice a week," Carter said. "Today's Saturday, and he was due to go back in on Wednesday."

"Good," Trask said. "Wire him up. Transmitter and a recorder. I need some hard confirmation of the location, in case he can work it into the conversation. Have him say something innocuous about the office once he gets in. It'll help with the T3."

"T3?" Doroz asked. "He said no phones..." Doroz stopped himself. "Oh, you're not talking a phone tap, you're talking a bug!"

"Exactly," Trask said. "Think we can get it in?"

"Get us the court order, we'll get it inside," Doroz said. He paused for a minute. "And I think we can tickle the hell out of it."

"How so?" Trask asked. "Tickling" was the Bureau word for generating relevant conversation on a wiretap or bug.

"Think about it, Jeff. We've got reason to send ATF in on the arson at the convenience store. We can send the locals in because they've had a tip about the weed, and we can even go in as our big bad FBI selves to ask about the ambassador's kid, the shooters we grabbed, whatever. Odds are they'll lie to us in the office, then talk about what really went down after we leave. It's worked before."

"Excellent." Trask nodded. "Something that will probably lead us somewhere and make one Ross Eastman a bit more comfortable." He looked at Carter. "Good going, Dix."

"Thanks," Carter said. "I better go help Tim. We've got some work to do explaining the rules to Peewee." He walked to the door of the conference room. "Open or shut, Bear?"

"Shut for now, thanks Dix."

Doroz looked at Trask with the question on his face. Trask answered it.

"No, Bear, I don't want to hear the tip call. I do want to verify that there *was* one, otherwise we'll have perjured testimony when he says one came in. But no, I don't want to hear Carter's voice on the damned tape calling in his own tip. Hopefully, he thought far enough ahead to mask it or have someone read the script for him and use a throwaway cell phone. For now, I want the bug. If we have to manufacture our luck to get it, so what? If Dix is camping out at the car wash again, he's not violating the Constitution, just Willie Sivella's order."

"Willie slapped a GPS on his car. I have no idea how he got around that."

Trask froze in disbelief for a moment, then shook his head and laughed out loud. "I'm very glad that Dixon Carter is on our side," he said. "One more thing." He handed Doroz a slip of paper. An address was written on it. "Have your tech guys put a pole cam on this place for a few days, please."

"OK. Where is this?"

"Northwest, up toward Bethesda. It's Victor Scarborough's office."

"Skippy Turner's old defense lawyer? I heard that Vic died last night."

Scarborough had represented Turner, one of Doroz and Trask's former defendants. Turner was a low-level heroin dealer who had sold his poison at local sporting events such as unsanctioned boxing matches and cockfights before being sent away for twenty years.

"Yep. Cancer. He did all his own work, was too cheap even to hire a secretary. Didn't have many friends. There wasn't even an obit in the *Post.* I was up there this morning. There are some streetlamp poles on the other side of Wisconsin. Have the techies aim the cam at the office, if that's possible. "

"And why is it we're watching this dead guy's joint?"

"We aren't. Not yet, anyway. I'll get us the bug, you get me the pole cam. And once it's set up, we'll go see our friend the ambassador."

"There's that 'we' again."

Trask walked out of the conference room into the squad area, stopping long enough to bend over Lynn's shoulder and give her a peck on the cheek. "Do me a favor?" he said.

"Sure."

"Give this a read and see what you think." He dropped the file on her desk. "Eighteenth Street gangbanger got shot in Northeast. See if you see anything that the homicide guys missed."

"Will do, sir."

"'Sir,' huh? I could get used to that."

"In your dreams."

Trask returned to the conference room. He saw that Doroz was signing some overtime sheets for the task force officers. "Not even doing that in your office anymore, Bear?"

"Nope. I like it better in here."

———

Crawford looked at the photo on the bookshelf. A pretty little girl who would grow up to be the gorgeous woman who was now cooking dinner for him in her apartment was being held by a man who would become the ambassador of his country to the United States. "How long have you known the ambassador?" he asked her.

"All my life, as you can see. I call him my Tio Juan. My uncle. He and my family are very close."

"Did you come here with him after the elections in your country?"

"This last time, yes. I have lived in America before, when my father and my uncle Luis went to college in California with Tio Juan. I went to elementary school there."

"Which is why your English is so good."

"Thank you."

"You're welcome. What's that you're cooking? It smells wonderful."

She giggled. "After three nights of fast food at your place, I thought you might like to try some Salvadoran dishes. We are having *bistec encebollado,* a beef steak simmered in onions, and *popusas.* They're like tortillas, only thicker and stuffed with cheese. Sometime they are stuffed with meat, but we're already having the *bistec,* so I thought the cheese would be better."

"It smells great." Crawford looked at another of the photos on the shelf. He could see the same girl, a teenager this time, standing with another girl and four adults. "Your family?"

"Yes." She put a dish on the dining table, removed the oven mitts from her hands, and placed one on his shoulder. "That's my father there, my mother, her brother and his wife, my Tío Luis and Tía Anna and Carolina, my cousin. The one I told you about." She wiped tears from her eyes with the sleeve of her blouse. "I miss them."

"I'm sorry," he said. "I should have figured that out." He decided to change the subject.

"How long has Mr. Rios-García been with the embassy?"

She hesitated a brief moment before answering. "He got here just after Armando, the ambassador's son, was killed."

"Did you know him in El Salvador?"

"Yes," she said. "Very well."

She smiled and kissed him.

"Sit down. Dinner's ready."

Chapter Sixteen

August 28, 11:00 a.m.

Trask and Doroz sat in the waiting room outside the office of the ambassador. Trask had decided to risk not notifying Murphy. Their excuse would be that it was a routine call, just a status report.

The pretty secretary with the long, dark hair offered them coffee again, which they both politely declined. The Eagles' "Witchy Woman" started playing in Trask's head.

He turned to Doroz. "With all the defense counsel running away from the case, our MS-13 friends might have to wait a bit for their trials."

"First time I've been around that kind of problem," Doroz said. "How does the court handle something like that?"

"Judge Noble's first move was to ask for volunteers," Trask replied. "He's looking for the brave champions of civil rights, the ones who aren't all speeches and no substance. The hypocrites will keep their heads down or claim schedule conflicts. These appointments will take some guts."

"Any takers so far?"

"Just one that I know of," Trask said. "Victor Scarborough. Solo practitioner. He has an office on Wisconsin, up toward Bethesda."

The warning glance that Trask shot him caused the obvious question to freeze in Doroz' throat. He paused for a second, and then gave a slight nod.

Good, Trask thought. *He understood the play. We'll see if it works now. Nobody's neck's on the line.* He thought for a moment. *Just mine.*

"The ambassador will see you now, gentlemen." The secretary opened the door into the inner office.

As before, Lopez-Portillo joined them around the low table. He waved the secretary out after the handshakes. "How can I be of assistance today, gentlemen?" he asked.

"Just some routine questions, sir." Doroz took the lead, as they had agreed. "We find that it often helps to reflect on a tragedy like this after some time has passed, after the initial shock wears off."

"Of course." The ambassador nodded.

"Things that may not have seemed significant when they happened can take on a new meaning, make more sense later. A remark Armando may have made to you or his mother, a new friend who seemed to have popped up just before your son's disappearance. Have you thought of anything like that?"

"No."

Trask saw that the ambassador appeared to have lost a considerable amount of sleep. There were lines around the man's eyes that had not been there before. He seemed to have aged five years in a week.

He's starting to look like Dixon Carter. The reflection on a lost life always brings guilt. There's the notion that something could have, should have been done. The weight's a lot heavier when that's true.

"Are you making any progress at all?" Lopez-Portillo asked.

"We think we are," Doroz said. "Unfortunately, we have to ask you to bear with us a while on that. If we fill you in on everything—especially since you haven't been able to supply any facts yourself—your grief might cause you to start creating things to go along with whatever patterns we think we've seen. It's only natural, but it can throw us onto some false trails. We need whatever evidence you might have to come from *you*, without us suggesting it to you. It's a one-way street, for now. I hope you understand."

"Yes. Of course," the ambassador said quietly.

"The minute we have something firm, you'll be the first to know." Doroz nodded sympathetically.

The ambassador looked up at them. "Would additional investigative resources be of any help to you?" he asked. "I can always call in some favors from my friends at the State Department, and I have met your Attorney General on several occasions."

Trask forced himself to reply in a natural tone of voice, at what seemed to be a normal pace. "I work for the Attorney General, Mr. Ambassador, as does

Agent Doroz. We've already been assured that the full resources of the Justice Department are at our disposal, if needed, and we've assured our superiors that we will not hesitate to ask for that assistance if and when it appears to be needed. As Agent Doroz has said, we feel that we're making some very good progress in the investigation, and when the time comes, we'll lay everything out for you."

"Will that be before, or after an arrest is made?" the ambassador asked.

"Probably afterward, sir," Trask said, making a mental note of the strange question. "The warrants are not generally issued until the grand jury returns an indictment, and the arrests are then made immediately. That's done in order to keep the defendant from fleeing when news of the indictment gets out." *Unless we do a complaint first. But I'm going to keep that a secret, too. I'd like to get a live defendant to trial in this mess, and somebody seems to be shooting them at a pretty good clip.* "I hope you understand."

"Yes, I believe so. We have always admired your Justice Department and," he nodded toward Doroz, "the FBI as well. We hope to model some new systems in El Salvador after many of your institutions."

"Thank you again for your time, Mr. Ambassador," Doroz said, standing.

After the departing handshakes, they headed back out past the secretary's desk. Trask saw that Doroz couldn't help but glance at her just a bit longer than was diplomatically required.

"They do grow them pretty down there, Bear," he said when they hit the sidewalk.

"There's no denying that. Good idea to leave Puddin' at the office today. He's in a lovesick daze lately, and I can see why."

"Did he actually register her as a source?"

"He gave me the form like I told him to. I threw it in the bottom of my desk, never put it in the system. Headquarters frowns on agents sleeping with sources, and I kind of saw this one coming. Whatever she gives us will be raw intel and corroborated by some other set of eyes before it lands on any reports."

Trask laughed. "Our young Mr. Crawford is lucky that his boss has his back."

"He's a good kid. I may need him to have my back some day. I'll put him on the pole-cam tapes after we get it installed, see if anything shows up."

"Not a word to anyone else, please," Trask said. "That's our control on this little experiment."

"For once, I hope you're wrong, Jeff."

"Why?"

"Because if you're right, some very dangerous people are going to be very pissed at us."

"I've got an alarm, a gun, a vest, a wolf, a very dangerous wife, and all the protection that the FBI and the Commonwealth of Maryland can provide."

"Yeah," Doroz said. "We're from the government. We're here to help."

———

7:15 p.m.

"That was wonderful, Michael," she said as she dabbed the corners of her mouth with her napkin. She looked around and shook her head. "Your apartment is spotless and your lasagna is amazing. You tell me that I'm too good to be true, but I think it is you who are too perfect. Do you have bodies hidden in your closet?"

"No," Crawford said, laughing. "I'm just trying very hard to impress you, to not screw this up. The only thing hidden away is all my normal clutter." He opened the closet in the entryway and took out a large box that had been concealed under the bottom of an overcoat. He tilted the box toward her so she could see the contents. "See? All these papers and magazines and bulletins would normally be spread all over the living room where I could just grab them, read and sort them, put them in stacks until I got tired of looking at them, and finally purge or file them. For you, I filed them already. Kind of."

"When I come back tomorrow night, I want them spread out all over the place. I don't want to change you. I like what I see already."

"I think that's supposed to be my line."

She got up from the table and walked over to him. "The dishes can wait for now. Let's go mess up your bedroom again."

Chapter Seventeen

Tuesday, August 29

"He's inside." Carter spoke into the hand-held as he kept his binoculars trained on the rear door to the car wash. The Buick was parked in what had become its customary place. The *Maras* were used to seeing it there, a fixture in the back of the shop a block away, probably owned by a shopkeeper who always worked late or who even lived in the back of his store. Tim Wisniewski sat on the passenger side. He, like Carter, had reclined his bucket seat and had binoculars fixed on the car wash.

Inside the surveillance van, parked behind Carter's Buick along the wall of the store in the strip mall and out of sight of the car wash, Doroz and Crawford adjusted the volume on their headsets. Doroz checked his watch: 11:36 p.m. He made a note on a pad; the time would be used later for the surveillance report.

"We've got him loud and clear, Dix," Crawford said. "The transmitter's working fine."

The voice of Peewee James filled their ears and several bytes of digital memory on the recorder that was running inside the van.

"You boys been busy in here," Peewee was saying. "Yeah, I like what you done to the place, know what I'm sayin'? Waitin' room's all cleaned up, new service desk...Place is lookin' *gooood*."

"Esteban is in the office," another voice said. This one had a Spanish accent to it.

"Definitely not Peewee." Doroz nodded toward Crawford.

The bad guys didn't suspect anything, and they'd already confirmed where Peewee was heading. Probable cause in progress.

"Whollaa ameeego." Peewee's Spanish was atrocious. "Damn, you been remodelin' in here, too. Office looks like a professional place of biz-ness. New panelin' and a nice desk. Uptown."

"What do you want, my friend?" Esteban Ortega asked.

"I wuz wantin' to get some more of that fine kush that you sold me on Wednesday," Peewee answered.

"How much did you want?"

"Just enough to get me through to the weekend. . .maybe a couple a pounds? I got a late order from a new buyer."

"The ticket for that is twelve thousand, since you are a regular customer."

Doroz and Crawford heard the crinkling of the paper bag as the money was dumped on the desk. They'd given Peewee the sack of cash prior to sending him in, after recording all the serial numbers. If the *Maras* were foolish enough to hold the cash, and if it was recovered later, the recorded bills would be further evidence of the dope purchase. Crawford and Doroz heard the rustling of plastic.

"Probably a grocery sack," Doroz observed. Crawford nodded again.

"Two pounds," Ortega said.

"I'll probably see you again next week," Peewee said. The sound of rustling plastic indicated that Peewee was checking to see that the bag was appropriately filled with his merchandise. "Think I could pick up another forty or fifty by then?"

"You know where to find us, and you know the ticket," Ortega said.

The rustling of the plastic became rhythmic, telling Doroz that their informant was now walking toward the exit.

"He's outside," Carter said over the radio. "Carrying two white grocery sacks. He's in his car, backing out."

Fifteen minutes later, the van, the Buick, and the Ford Taurus driven by Peewee James were side by side in a parking lot on the grounds of Gallaudet College. Doroz and Carter took the marijuana and put it in an evidence bag while Crawford retrieved the transmitter from Peewee, who seemed to be enjoying his new role.

"How'd I do?" he asked Carter.

"Fine, just fine."

"Lemme know when you want me to wire up again. Next week, maybe?"

"We'll see, Peewee," Carter said, shooting a glance at Doroz, who immediately read the look and smiled. It always seemed to go this way. Junkies were junkies, even for adrenaline. They never wanted to get involved, but once they were, they got a kick out of being *a spy*. The trick was to make sure they didn't brag about it to their homies or girlfriends. That could blow an investigation, get them shot, or both.

"Did I help myself?"

"Everything you do will go to the judge and be taken into account at your sentencing," Doroz said. "Yeah, you helped yourself. Just remember: anybody else hears about this, and your cooperation all turns to obstruction. No braggin' to the ladies or even your momma. If you do, a big positive turns into a big negative and maybe even more charges. Got it?"

"Yeah, I got it." Peewee's voice reflected just enough disappointment to tell Doroz that the warning had been necessary.

They did another search on Peewee's person and his car, a repeat of the one performed prior to the buy. No unauthorized dope, money, or weapons going into the operation, none coming out. Everything was kosher.

"Nice work, everyone," Doroz said. "Let's go home."

He followed the Buick out of the parking lot, heading back on New York Avenue toward the FBI field office. The Buick made the light a few blocks later, but the van didn't.

"Shit," Doroz muttered to himself. It was already another late night, and he still had a report to write. His eyes followed the taillights of the Buick as it headed southwest toward the center of town. Those taillights suddenly swerved violently to the right and off the road.

August 30, 1:47 a.m.

The low, steady growl woke Trask, and he raised his head from the pillow to look at the clock on the dresser. There was no digital display in the dark. He turned toward what should have been the red indicator light on the alarm control panel on the wall. Nothing there, either. There was just enough light from the gas streetlamp outside filtering through the bedroom curtains to keep it from being pitch black in the room, and as his eyes adjusted to the darkness, he saw that Boo was by the door, teeth bared.

Oh hell, not again!

He shook Lynn awake, putting a finger over her mouth to warn her to stay quiet.

"The power's out," he whispered, "and something has Boo stirred up."

She nodded, and he saw that she had already retrieved the .45 from its place in the headboard. He rolled quietly out of bed and pulled the Glock from the holster on top of the dresser.

A loud knock on the door made Boo start barking, a chorus that Nikki immediately joined.

Lynn had located the flashlight that had become their other headboard accessory. "Assassins don't usually knock," she said.

Trask opened the bedroom door slowly. *No machetes this time.* He climbed the six steps to the landing and the front door. The knocking resumed just as he put his eye to the peephole, and Trask's nerves almost sent him tumbling backward down into the lower level.

"Jeff?" It was the voice of Barry Doroz.

Lynn came up the steps in her robe, holding the flashlight in one hand, the .45 in the other. His own robe was over her left arm. He pulled it on and opened the door. Doroz stepped inside, then lurched backward as Boo made a lunge up the stairs, growling.

Trask dropped, grabbing the big dog by the collar just before she got to Doroz. "It's OK, girl," he said.

Boo sniffed at Doroz' feet for a moment, then relaxed and headed back down the stairs, satisfied that there was no threat.

"Whoa! That's one big dog there, Jeff," Doroz said. "Thanks for not letting her eat me. What kind is she?"

"A giant Yorkie," Trask said. "Very rare and very dangerous. What's up, Bear, and what time is it?"

"About two. Power's out all over your neighborhood."

"I'm glad it's not just us," Lynn said.

"Did the buy go south?" Trask asked.

"No, it went down like clockwork. I'll have a report to you on Monday and you can start writing the application for the bug."

"Then why—?"

"It's Dixon Carter, Jeff. He had a heart attack driving back from the buy. Ran off the road and hit a tree. Tim was with him, and he's OK, but Dix is in rough shape. I thought you'd want to know."

"Where is he?"

"Medstar, at George Washington. Tim and Crawford are there with him, and Willie Sivella's on the way. I just thought you'd want to know."

"Of course. Thanks."

"You can ride with me if you want."

"We're both coming," Lynn said.

They rushed through the automatic doors from the entrance to the emergency room at George Washington Hospital. Trask saw a doctor speaking to Sivella and Crawford.

"It could have been worse. He only got some bruises in the crash."

Trask was relieved to hear the words, and was also glad that the ER doctor looked like he was old enough to have attended medical school. The man had some gray around the temples and spoke with the quiet authority of confidence.

"I'd call this a big warning," the doctor said, now directing his words to the group. "Preliminary tests don't show much damage, and there doesn't seem to be any arterial blockage. We see these things sometimes in cases of acute exhaustion. He admitted he hasn't been getting much sleep."

"If he's been where I think he's been, I'm gonna kill him myself," Sivella said.

"You'll have to wait a while," the doctor said. "I'm keeping him for at least a week. Make him rest, run some more tests to make sure we haven't missed anything."

"Keep him as long as you like," Sivella said, calming down. "Maybe this will be the wake-up call he needs."

"What he needs is *no* wake-up calls for a few days," the doc countered. "I'm about to knock him out. He needs sleep more than anything."

"No visitors for now, then?" Doroz asked.

"Not tonight. He's already had a mild sedative. He'll be OK. Just give him a few days."

The doctor headed back toward the row of ER beds separated by drawn curtains. Trask saw Tim Wisniewski emerging from one. He had a butterfly bandage across his forehead.

"My airbag didn't work," Tim said. "Goddamn rundown police car. I gave the windshield a tap with my Polish skull."

"You OK otherwise?" Trask asked.

"I think so. I just seem to keep needing a ride home every time I go out with Dix."

Wisniewski rode home with Sivella. Trask and Lynn were transported back to Waldorf by Doroz, who crashed on the couch in their den, his arm resting on the back of a very large dog.

"Boo seems to have found a new friend," Lynn whispered as she slipped under the covers.

"'Love the One You're With.' Stephen Stills, I believe."

She swatted him. "Turn off your jukebox and go to sleep."

Chapter Eighteen

Saturday, September 2

Trask knocked first, but pushed the door open and entered the room without waiting for an invitation. "Been getting some sleep?"

"Chemically induced." Carter more than filled the hospital bed, and he did not look pleased to be doing so. "They knock me out about two hours after every meal. Give me a while to eat and hit the head, then it's time for the zombie juice. No telling when it wears off. I wake up in the middle of the night and watch some really bizarre TV. Seems like half the stuff on A&E is based on swamp people in Louisiana doing some really crazy stuff. You grew up down there, didn't you?"

"Not in the swamps." Trask laughed. "About ninety miles northwest of New Orleans, not south of there in the bayous. University town in Mississippi. Hattiesburg."

"Mississippi, huh? That's why all us black folks love you so much."

Trask chuckled again. "Northern bias and mythology. Mississippi is two states. It's actually the northern half that's still fighting the War of Northern Aggression. The southern half of the state has long had strange things the northern half only recently acquired. Population, education, Catholics, Republicans. Even when the state was dry, we got real booze from Slidell and New Orleans... didn't have to brew our own and run moonshine."

"What happened to your accent?"

"It was never that thick. Dad didn't really have one. When I first met Lynn, she thought I was from the Midwest. My *mom* could give you a real good Scarlett

O'Hara when she felt like it." He cleared his throat. "Jeeahfrree, would youuu go owwt siiide and mow the graissss?"

Carter laughed hard. "I never understood how you could get three syllables out of a one-syllable word."

"If you ever decide to venture into our primitive little backwoods from this fine mecca of civility with its ever-increasing homicide rate, I'll be happy to translate for you."

"Ouch. Point taken. Speaking of the case—"

"I'm not going to speak of the case, Dix. Big as it is, I just came by to see if you were following orders for once and getting some damn shut-eye. We're making do, and it will still be there when you're back on your feet. Any idea when they'll let you out?"

"Not yet. Lots of tests on the ticker. Nothing serious, so I'm told. Dodged the big one. I *am* resting a lot…hell, too much. I walk the halls once in a while to keep from getting bedsores. Have to drag this pole on wheels with me everywhere. I think Willie Sivella hid a GPS in it."

Trask laughed. Carter finally cracked up at his own joke.

"Tim's been in and out quite a bit," Carter said.

Good! Trask thought. *He actually appreciates that.*

"I have to chase him out some nights, make sure that HE gets some rest," Carter continued. "We watch swamp and duck and gator and catfish shows together until they kick the visitors out. You aren't a Cajun are you?"

"It's Trask, Dix. No 'eaux' in the name."

"Good. That makes me feel better, I think."

"You'd *want* some good Cajun folk with you if you were in the bayous. And a Louisiana cop would want you on his six if he had to look for a perp in Anacostia."

"I might pay to see that. *Detective Boudreaux Goes to Washington.*"

Trask laughed again. "Glad to see you're feeling better."

There was another knock, and Tim Wisniewski walked in carrying what smelled like some very good barbeque in some sort of flat container. "They try hard, but it's still hospital food," he said.

Trask nodded and looked over his shoulder at Carter as he headed for the door. "Shift change, Dix. I'll stop by again."

Wisniewski waited until the door closed behind him to pull the folder from under the tray. "Here are the other report copies you asked for, Massa Dixon."

"When I'm out of here—"

"When you get out, I'm driving. This lump on my head still hurts. Where's my list of assignments?"

"Right here." Carter rolled to one side and pulled another folder out from under the sheets.

"Wonderful. You've been lying on that," Wisniewski said. "You don't have a back on that gown yet, do you?"

"No," Carter smiled. "And I had cabbage for lunch, too."

It was a Saturday, and Trask was startled when his phone rang at the Triple-nickle.

"Jeff Trask."

"I hoped you'd be in your office today, Mister Trask. It's Mitchell Clark. I represent—"

"Santos. I remember, Mitch." *I have no idea if that's what your friends call you, but I think I know why you're on my phone.*

"Yes. As you recall, it's my first case here, and I wanted to see if there was anything my client could do to help himself out of the hole he's dug."

"There could be. Let me first ask you, however, if you've spoken to him about this yet?"

"No. I wanted to check with you first, to see if it's even worth the effort to try and persuade him to cooperate in some manner."

"Good. My answer is yes, he can help himself, and no, you should not talk to him about it."

"I don't understand."

"You couldn't be expected to on your first case. Let Mr. Santos get used to the idea of spending a significant chunk of the rest of his existence in a federal maximum security facility and hear of the joys of such a life from his current roomies, some of whom have already been to those resorts. Let him come to you with *his* idea that he wants to help himself. That way you don't have to try and hard-sell him, and more importantly, if he never has this epiphany, you don't end up on our victim list."

"I'm glad I called. Thank you, Mr. Trask."

"It's Jeff, Mitch. See you around."

Chapter Nineteen

Monday, September 11

The dilemma—even after Trask's application for the installation of a bug in the car wash office had been approved by the Department of Justice—had been how to install the damned thing. Ortega's *Salvatrucha* clique always had someone at the place, since the precious marijuana crop in the attic always required tending and guarding. Several straight nights of continual surveillance had failed to identify any periods of time in which an FBI black-bag team could get into the building. Everyone was losing sleep over the problem, both mentally and physically, except for Carter, who remained on periodic injections of "zombie juice" in the hospital. The doctors and Willie Sivella still couldn't trust him to get any rest at home without the knockout shots.

The break finally came thanks to some creative thinking on the part of Barry Doroz, who had a good contact in the security section of the regional office of AT&T. In discussing some hypotheticals with his phone guy, Doroz learned that the car wash had no phone service. The next morning, wearing an official AT&T sales outfit and equipped with business cards and order forms, Doroz—calling himself "Mike Long"—sold the basic service for a hard-line telephone to Mr. Esteban Ortega, the proprietor of the Qwik Shine Car Wash.

While Ortega was initially a reluctant customer, Mike Long sweetened the deal with a special sign-up offer that included the first sixty days free and a free listing in the yellow pages. Ortega signed the papers, and an installation crew appeared on schedule the next morning to install the desk phone in the car wash office. The Washington field office of the FBI reimbursed AT&T for the sixty days of not-really-free service and—as an extra bonus feature—installed a microphone and transmitter inside the desk set. The mic could pick up any conversation in the room, was powered by the telephone line that serviced the telephone, and sent a signal directly to the digital recording equipment in an electronic surveillance facility: the "wire room" of the Washington field office of the FBI.

The first call received by Esteban Ortega over his new business equipment came from one Timothy Wisnieswski, who told Ortega that he had just moved into the area and was looking for a good place to clean seven hundred miles of road dirt off his prized Dodge Charger. When Ortega hung up the phone, he was pleased that his new listing was driving business to the establishment, providing both some modest income and some cover for the real business being cultivated in the attic. He would not have been pleased to know that by picking up the receiver, he had switched on the concealed mic, which, by order of the United States District Court, was to be allowed to transmit any pertinent conversations in the office for a period not to exceed thirty days. Timothy Wisniewski was pleased to get the dirt, tossed by bucket onto his vehicle by Mike Long, off the Charger, and he opined that the MS-13 clique actually did a respectable job of cleaning cars.

The first week was spent monitoring the normal pattern of conversations in Ortega's office and provided few surprises. In addition to two prearranged visits from Peewee James, there were sixteen other encounters between Ortega and residents of the nation's capital who desired something a little stronger than a natural high. The potent marijuana was walking out the back door at the rate of more than two hundred pounds per week, generating a weekly gross income for the *Maras* of $1,400,000 at $7,000 per pound.

The squad monitored the mic twenty-four hours a day, rotating in eight-hour shifts. Ortega did most of his business in English, since most of his customers (both for marijuana and car washes) were American by birth. The conversations usually shifted to Spanish in the after-hours chats in the office, so Wisniewski and another Spanish-speaking agent were assigned the four-to-midnight shifts to provide real-time translations. Trask monitored the calls and the shift summaries as they came in, returning every day to his office computer to prepare the required status reports for the court, and for one very interested Ross Eastman.

The first "tickle" orchestrated by Doroz was an ATF arson team. As expected, when the two agents pressed Ortega for any information about the fire at the deli, they came away with nothing but denials and assurances by Ortega that the deli had been a profitable business, one he never would have thrown away had it not been for his enemies torching the place. The agents' conversations over the bug were duly recorded as several knowing nods and eye-rolls were seen around the wire room. It was the follow-on session between Ortega and his lieutenants that they wanted to hear.

They weren't disappointed. Within minutes after the ATF agents' departure, Ortega and two others were laughing it up in the car wash office. Wisniewski had the office on speaker for a moment, then switched the speaker off to concentrate on the conversation through his headphones.

"*What a couple of morons*...That's Ortega speaking," Wisniewski translated, doing his best to provide a real-time interpretation. "*I told them we were turning a profit and had no reason to burn the joint down. I told them I had enemies in the Eighteenth Street gang. Real criminals. I'm an honest businessman, I said, and I just couldn't take that neighborhood any longer. They just nodded and apologized for disturbing me.*

"*Yes, it was the Eighteenth-street girlies, Esteban.*" Wisniewski explained there was a second voice, unknown speaker. The three *Mara* troops in the office were laughing their asses off.

"*Yeah*...This is Ortega again...*Me and a gallon of gas from my own pumps. Best torch job the Eighteenth-Street idiots ever did. Those stupid bastards would have probably just tossed the gas on the concrete wall and scorched it a little while they ran off like little girls.*"

Wisniewski looked at Trask and grinned.

"There it is," Trask said, smiling and nodding in acknowledgement toward Doroz. "Nice work and two counts on the indictment even if we get zilch from now on. Arson and insurance fraud. If your other tickles work as well, we'll be adding some dope deals and a few homicide counts. What's next on the agenda, Bear?"

"Run Peewee back in at the end of the week for some more dope conversation, I guess. Build the drug conspiracy evidence pile a little higher. We might be able to ID some more weed customers we can spin later for additional testimony. We'll save any interrogation on the murders for next week. Let 'em get real comfortable about their little sessions in the office."

Trask nodded. He allowed himself to lean back in his chair and took a couple of deep breaths. He finally had some real progress to report to Eastman, who would then report it to the Department bigwigs, who would then stay out of their hair a little longer. He watched Wisniewski making notes on the shift report.

"Ortega's leaving for the day," Wisniewski said, still listening on the headphones. "He's leaving someone named Mario in charge."

"I'm leaving for the day, too," Trask said. "This office at least. I'm looking forward to giving Eastman and Patrick some good news for a change."

"I'm heading out, too." Doroz was piling some papers into his briefcase. "Tim, you get to match wits with Mario for a few hours."

"I'll give it my best shot."

Trask took the elevator up to the squad room. Lynn was looking at the murder file on the M-18 victim. She looked up and smiled when he came in.

"How's it going down there?" she asked.

"Pretty well. Some good conversation about the arson at the deli. I was just heading across the street to brief the bosses. Anything jumping out at you on that homicide?"

"Nothing other than a couple of loose ends to tie up; I'll work on it. What time are we heading home?"

"Fivish, barring some emergency."

"Great. We need to walk the dogs, and there'll still be some daylight."

"See you at five."

He didn't have to pick up Patrick. The Criminal Division chief's office was empty, and when Trask looked at Patrick's secretary, she nodded in the direction of Eastman's office. They waved him in when he appeared in the doorway.

"How's the bug?" Eastman asked.

Trask recounted the translations Wisniewski had made of the conversation between Ortega and his underlings in the car wash office.

"Excellent." Eastman was nodding. "This ought to keep the buzzards from circling for a while. I was starting to look for them out my window. I'm due to go over and give the AG a status report today." He stopped nodding and looked at Trask. "Any talk about the ambassador's son yet?"

"Not yet. We haven't thrown anything at them to prompt that discussion."

"You might move that up on the timetable, Jeff. I anticipate I'll be asked that question when I make my status report. When do you think you can work that in?"

"Next week, probably. We didn't want to spook the bad guys by throwing every tickle at them at once."

"That should be soon enough. Nice work."

"Thanks. I've got some more reports to write for the judge."

"Of course, thank you for the update."

Trask headed back to his office, getting an approving wink from Bill Patrick as he left.

An hour at his computer left him feeling even more like a cop. For every half an hour of the "fun side" of an investigation (the successful field work), he had to spend double the time writing about it. In this instance, it was the ten-day report required by statute for the bug. The pertinent conversations had to be summarized and presented to the judge who had signed the Title III authorization for the hidden microphone, the Honorable Waymon Dean.

Drawing Judge Dean had been a pleasant surprise. Trask liked the man, and felt that the judge had some positive regard for him as well. Judge Dean was one of the old breed. There were certain attorneys he trusted, and his review of pleadings submitted by those favored few could be very cursory. Trask wondered if the judge would even read the report he was typing.

Probably not. He'll just ask me for a quick verbal summary and sign these thirty pages after I talk for two minutes. It's worth doing, anyway. His signature will say he approves the report, and that's what the law requires. It'll make it easier for me down the road in the case, having these summaries in the can. Electronic cut-and-paste, the new practice of law.

The phone jarred his concentration away from the computer on his desk.

"Did you wear your watch today, hotshot?" Lynn asked.

"Yeah...oops!" Trask saw it was already 5:20.

"I was beginning to think you'd left me."

"Sorry, got buried in a ten-day. I'll see you in five minutes."

"I'll meet you in your garage."

One of the few benefits of being an AUSA who'd been attacked in his home was the temporary underground parking spot that Trask had been assigned in the office's guarded garage. Spaces there were usually a perk reserved for upper management.

Lynn was waiting beside him at the Jeep.

"How'd you beat me down here?" Trask asked.

She kissed him as he held the door open for her. "I called you from here after I took the elevator down," she said. "I figured you just had that brain of yours immersed in some concentration pool."

"Sorry."

"Just take me home, handsome."

He started the car and switched on the radio as they pulled into traffic. A classic rock station was the selection *du jour*.

"Nothing funkier today?" she asked. Lynn's preferences were for heavier beats that gave her happy feet.

"I prefer music with a melody," he said. "Not just bad poetry shouted out by somebody who wouldn't recognize a key signature, backed by a scratcher who can't play anything more than a turntable."

"I suppose it'll do then."

The radio began to blare disco, the high falsettos of "Stayin' Alive."

Trask wasn't talking as he drove. He made the turn southeast on the Indian Head Highway.

"What are you thinking about, Jeff?" Lynn asked.

"I was thinking that at least one of the Bee Gees' parents must have been a sheep, and that disco is the direct and proximate cause of gangsta rap. Somebody *had* to bitch about *this* stuff." He pushed the seek button on the tuner. Led Zeppelin's "Ramble On" filled the car.

Much better. Long John Bonham kickin' syncopated accents on the bass drum. Tolkien's Ring *set to some great rock music. These guys put the Beatles to shame. They just didn't have the same marketing department.*

They pulled into the driveway, and Trask walked to the mailbox while Lynn went to get the dogs and their leashes. He was inside the front door and tossing the mail onto a table as she brought them in from the backyard.

"Anything of interest?" she asked.

"Just bills and what looks like an invitation to the next Air Force Academy reunion in Colorado Springs next month."

"Wanna go?"

"We'll have to see what this case looks like a little closer to the date."

"Some folks you want to see again?"

"Several I'd like to see, sure, even if a couple of 'em are raving liberals."

"Liberals at a service academy?"

"An equal-opportunity institution. I even liked 'em."

"I never would have guessed that."

"You go through enough stress with somebody and you respect how they react to it, even if you're on the other side of a political aisle. Let's load the pups."

The White Plains dog park, just south of the Saint Charles subdivision in Waldorf, Maryland, was open seven days a week, 8:00 a.m. until dusk. With the summer season and daylight savings time, that usually meant about 8:30 p.m. Big as their backyard was, Boo could still lope from one side to the other is about six long strides, and the park's six acres gave her room to run. The Trask family had tried to make trips to the park a part of their regular routine, whenever their routine was at all regular.

Boo and Nikki jumped into the backseat of the jeep on a sling-style blanket that connected to the headrests of the front and rear seats. Five minutes later, the Jeep pulled into the parking lot of the dog park. Trask opened the rear door and endured the usual tow to the gate, straining to hold the big dog back. Once inside, he removed the leashes and watched in awe as both dogs raced happily toward the center of the park.

"Why aren't you running with them?" Lynn poked him in the side.

"You mean chasing them. No way that I could keep up with Boo at full throttle."

"You always told me you were pretty quick."

"Not that quick. Not even twenty pounds and ten years ago."

Both dogs came running back to them, the initial sprint having momentarily satisfied their need for speed. Trask and Lynn started walking counter-clockwise on the paved path that ran around the edges of the park. Nikki trotted along just in front of them, her tail curved over her back. Boo performed her usual scouting duties, running ahead fifty yards, then running back toward them, letting them know she had cleared the way of any threats and that the trail was safe ahead.

They were a quarter of the way into their first lap when Trask noticed a figure approaching them on the path about a hundred yards away. A tall man, dressed in dark slacks and a black windbreaker, was walking a leashed dog that was every bit as large as Boo. As the distance between them closed, Trask felt the hair on the back of his neck start to bristle. The man was wearing an eye patch.

He started to call Boo back, but she was already off on her recon mission. Trask turned toward Lynn.

"I see him," she said before he could warn her.

Boo came loping back. She snorted, and then headed off into the grassy infield.

"Boo doesn't like him either. Should we turn around?" Lynn asked.

"No. Let's see what's happening here."

When they were about ten yards apart, the man with the eye patch seemed to notice them for the first time.

"Mister Trask. A pleasant surprise. And this must be Mrs. Trask?"

"Yes, Señor Rios. My wife, Lynn."

You speak English after all, Rios—or whoever you are. American English.

"It is an honor to meet you," Rios-García said, bowing his head slightly.

Lynn nodded back.

"That's quite a dog you have there," Trask said, looking the animal over. It was three feet tall at the shoulders, with a thick chest and massive head.

"Yes, Franco is a Spanish mastiff. I brought him back to El Salvador after my last visit to Castille. My grandparents still live in Spain."

"Franco?" Trask asked. "After the late Generalissimo?"

"Yes. Very astute of you. I was born in Spain. My parents emigrated to El Salvador after the Generalissimo died."

"Your English is excellent," Trask said, "but not European in accent."

"Thank you. You are correct again. I attended college here in the States."

The conversation was interrupted by a deep growl as the mastiff suddenly lunged toward Nikki. Trask saw the leash slip from Rios' hand, and he instinctively bent down to protect the smaller dog and Lynn, who was also reaching for Nikki. His concern was unnecessary. A large, dark blur flashed between them and Rios, slamming into the mastiff and knocking Franco off his feet. Boo stood over the other dog growling, her teeth bared in warning.

Trask took Boo by the collar and pulled her back. Rios grabbed the mastiff's leash and angrily barked a command in Spanish. Franco returned to his master's side. The dog heeled and sat, looking vulnerable and confused.

"My sincere apologies," Rios said. "That's quite a dog *you* have. What kind is she?"

For a second, Trask considered making up an exotic breed name. He decided against it. "A hundred percent, pure-bred American mutt," Trask said, patting Boo on her side. We're a melting pot, in case you hadn't heard."

"Of course I've heard," Rios responded. "Much like our *mestizos* in El Salvador."

Trask detected a hint of contempt in Rios's voice. "I'll hold her until you put some distance between us," he said, his hand still wrapped around Boo's collar.

"Of course," Rios said, nodding toward Lynn. "It was very nice to meet you."

He turned and gave an angry tug on the mastiff's leash, walking back toward the parking lot. Trask and Lynn waited until Rios was a good distance away before following. They circled past the exit gate, watching as the mastiff was loaded into a limousine by a very large man who seemed to be taking directions from Rios. Trask made a mental note of the diplomatic license plate.

STL-467. S for staff. TL—the country code for El Salvador.

He watched the limousine pull away while Lynn took the leashes off the fence and hooked them on the dog's collars. When they were back in the car, she turned to him.

"That was no accident, was it?"

"Only if you think that members of the Salvadoran diplomatic corps like driving thirty miles out of Washington to walk their dogs."

"Was it another warning? Was he trying to chase us off the case?"

"I don't know. I just know it was no chance meeting. I also know that there's something that doesn't fit about our man Rios being part of the current government of El Salvador or its embassy here."

"That Spanish connection?" she asked.

"Yeah, the Franco stuff. If eye patch's family was connected to Franco and his Nazi-backed goons during the thirties, and if he can't mention the word *mestizo* without sneering, it makes me wonder how he ended up as deputy to an ambassador appointed by the supposedly egalitarian Farabundo Marti National Liberation Front. Mr. Rios, as he currently calls himself, fancies his pedigree to be as pure as the one for that big weenie of a dog he's hauling around."

Trask reached behind the seat while he drove, finding Boo's furry head in its usual place, looking out the front of the car in the gap between the two front bucket seats. He gave her a long series of head-rubs and ear-scratches. "Hell of a body slam, Boo-boo. Nikki owes you one."

"He said he went to college here," Lynn said.

"Yep, but didn't want to tell us where," Trask said. "Normally that would have been volunteered. He didn't want us to have that information. What people hold back is often more important than what they say. There's a lead in there somewhere."

"Sure," Lynn scoffed. "All we have to do is guess what his real name is first, then research historical student roles of every university in the country. Some lead."

Trask felt his cell phone vibrating in its belt holster. He flicked it open. "Hello?"

"You'd better get back here ASAP, Jeff." It was Barry Doroz' voice.

Trask pushed the speakerphone key and handed the phone to Lynn, who held it close to his face while he drove. "Why Bear? What's up?"

"Tim just called. He was listening to the car wash bug when all hell broke loose. Auto-fire gunshots, screaming, the works. Somebody just hit the MS-13 troops again. Patrol units just got to the car wash. Four dead on the scene."

"Shit!" Trask pounded the steering wheel. "Any witnesses left alive, Bear?"

"Nope. They're all dead."

"We're on our way. We'll drop our dogs at the house and meet you there in about thirty, traffic permitting."

The car wash was a bloodbath, with four corpses perforated by multiple, high-velocity rounds. Trask, with Lynn following in his footsteps, was careful not to tromp on anything that might be considered of evidentiary value as he picked his way toward the hallway that ran parallel to the wash track. His right hand began tapping out a bass line on the seam of his jeans.

"Song?" she asked.

"'Dead Man's Party.' Oingo Boingo, 1985. Danny Elfman. Very tight horn line."

The first body lay inside the door to the hall from the waiting area. One hand stretched toward the other end of the hall, and the smeared trail of blood that ran from the waiting room to the corpse's feet showed that he'd been able to crawl a few feet after the bullets found their mark. Someone had finished him off with a shot to the base of the skull, the entry wound indicating that a small-caliber handgun hand been used for the kill shot. Trask looked back at the dead man as he made his way down the hall. The empty eyes stared past him, toward the room at the end of the hallway. The mouth was stretched open, as if calling out.

He was trying to get to the office. Trying to warn the others.

Two other victims were sprawled across the floor in the office doorway. The crime scene techs were looking over a fourth corpse slumped over the blood-soaked desk inside the office. The body was half-sitting in a swivel chair, the back of which was turned sideways.

Hello, Mario. Wish we could have met under better circumstances. Maybe you can tell us a couple of things, anyway.

Barry Doroz was busy retrieving the bug from the desk telephone. He looked up from a notepad when he saw them. "Welcome to Hell 4.0," he said.

"I'm getting tired of these multiple homicide scenes. I called in some of our guys from the drug squad. Puddin's with 'em upstairs. They're processing the marijuana operation in the attic."

"Did the shooters grab anything upstairs?" Trask asked.

"Not that we could tell. There's packaged product and a lot of maturing plants. Doesn't look like anyone was interested in it. Of course, the stair steps weren't dropped down for access. We had to do that."

Trask looked at Lynn. She shook her head.

She's thinking the same thing I am. Other gangbangers would've looked for the dope, run off with it.

Frank Wilkes was in a corner of the office, holding a shell casing up to the light. He answered Trask's question before it could be asked. "Common 7.62 rounds. The cheap stuff again."

Trask nodded. He leaned over the desk and looked at the wall behind the body. There were two holes in the sheetrock about four inches apart, each about thirty inches above the baseboard. The hole on the left had some small blood splatter marks encircling it. The one on the right did not. "Frank..." Trask called Wilkes over. "Take a look at this."

Wilkes peered at the wall over Trask's shoulder for a moment, then looked at the photographer standing behind them. "You get your shots of the body?" Wilkes asked.

The crime scene tech with the camera nodded. "Yeah, you can move him now."

Wilkes stepped around the desk, and using hands covered in latex gloves, gently pulled the corpse back into the swivel chair. Trask saw two entry wounds in the man's torso, one in the center of the chest, one below the left ribs about an inch inside the edge of the body.

Wilkes looked up. "Want to take a stab at this?"

"Three-shot burst, fully automatic AK clone," Trask said. "The first round hits the victim dead center, and is either still in the vic or in the chair back. The second shot is a through-and-through, causing the wound in the side and then following on into the wall, with the splatter around it. It might have caught the chair back, too, except the victim wasn't sitting straight when hit...probably starting to stand up, or trying to run. The third round of the burst missed the vic and is in or somewhere behind the wall."

"One hundred percent, so far," Wilkes said, nodding with approval. "Here's the hard part, gangbanger shooters or pros?"

"Pros. I'm sure of it," Trask said.

"I agree," Wilkes nodded again, "but tell me why."

"I've fired a Norinco before," Trask said. "ATF invites us to their little shooting demos once in a while. If you're not well trained on an automatic weapon like the AK—or one of the Chinese knock-offs—and you're right-handed, you'll always pull it up and to the right when you're firing fully automatic. You'll also probably crank off six or seven rounds in the burst. This was a three-shot, controlled burst by someone who knew how to keep the barrel down while firing the weapon."

"And why wouldn't a gang member be that proficient with the weapon?" Wilkes asked.

"He could be, professor," Trask smiled at him, "but it's not as likely, since they don't usually have the time or place to practice. These fully automatic weapons are illegal, and you can't just take them to your friendly local firing range to mow down cinder blocks or cut targets in half, emptying banana-clip magazines in three seconds. I've seen gang drive-by scenes before, and it's always the same. Seven or eight round bursts pulling up and to the right."

"Excellent," Wilkes said. "May I assume that this eliminates the need for a trial prep interview on the subject?"

"Yeah, for now," Trask said. "That is, if we ever have a trial. You have to identify defendants and arrest them to have a trial."

"Speaking of defendants, Bear," Lynn asked, "is one of these dead guys Ortega?"

"No. Tim said he'd left for the day before the fireworks started."

"Then," she said, "I'd suggest we find him. Whoever did this may be still looking for him."

"Good point," Doroz replied, sarcastically. "Got any ideas where we might find him tonight?"

She shook her head. "No. Sorry."

"Wherever he is, if he's heard about this, he's got his head down. He won't be easy to find," Trask observed. "No point in chasing ghosts if we don't know where to look."

"Agreed," Doroz said. "We've got this, Jeff. You two go home. We'll see you in the office tomorrow."

Ortega was sitting in the basement by a tool bench, waiting for the ringtones to stop. The party on the other end of his call would wait for him to speak first.

"El Gato Grande, por favor."

"Momento."

A different, but familiar voice replaced the one who had answered the call. They spoke in the Salvadoran dialect of *voseo* Spanish.

"Esteban?"

"Yes, Jaguar."

"I heard about the raid on your car wash. Very sad."

"We lost four good men, and all of the product as well."

"So I heard. Any idea who is responsible?"

"Mario was on his cell phone with me when he was killed. He said, '*La sombra*.'"

"It is true, then. You are being hunted. I will send help. I would come myself, but I have seven more months to spend behind these stinking walls. La Esperanza never changes." There was a short pause. "Did you say Mario called you on his cell?"

"Yes."

"Did he call *your* cell?"

"Yes. The phone I'm using now."

"Throw it away as soon as you hang up. In a river, preferably. You must assume that *La Sombra* has Mario's phone and that they are looking for the person he was talking with when they killed him. They have your number now and can track you through the GPS in your phone, Esteban. Pull the battery out and get rid of it immediately."

The line went dead. Ortega reached for a hammer hanging on a pegboard and smashed the phone. He had only been on the line for a few seconds.

Surely that would not have been enough time...

A noise from outside startled him. He was out the rear door of the basement and into the alley in seconds.

Chapter Twenty

Tuesday, September 12, 9:05 a.m.

The mood in the squad conference room had returned to a somber confusion.

"Now I'm beginning to hate this room as much as my office," Doroz quipped. "Just when we think we're getting a handle on this, somebody blows away the only location we've got a read on and scraps a bug it took everything we knew to get authorized." He looked down the table at his squad. "Any ideas?"

"Are we prepared for another retaliation raid by our MS-13 targets?" Carter asked.

"Sorry, Dix. I meant to welcome you back," Doroz said sheepishly. "I called the cops on the Maryland side and gave 'em a heads-up. They tried to do the humane thing and warn the few 18ers they knew in the area. Couldn't find any of them. Seems the word got out in the Salvadoran community, and none of the Barrio 18 boys wanted to be held accountable for this last mess."

"Can't say as I blame them," Carter responded. "That guy the MS-13 dumped on your doorstep looked a bit worse for wear."

"Not much flesh left on the bones," Doroz agreed. He paused, looking around the table.

"So…anybody have any suggestions?"

"Just one," Trask said from the other end of the table. "We need to redecorate." He nodded at Crawford. "Puddin' old pal, would you run down to the supply room and bring me about six boxes of pushpins, please? They're easier on drywall than tape." He pulled out a briefcase from under the table, and from that he retrieved a stack of typed pages.

"I'll bite. What do you have there, Jeff?" Carter asked, speaking for the group.

"Jigsaw puzzle pieces. If two heads are better than one, then the collective wit and wisdom of this group ought to be a miracle-working marvel, and that may be what we need right now," Trask replied. "Besides, everyone in here, with one exception of which I am very certain, is a male." He nodded at Lynn, while the others laughed. "I am also very confident, being a male, that most of the minds in this room are sparked by visual aids."

Crawford entered the conference room with the requested pushpins and slid the boxes across the table to Trask.

Trask opened a box of the pins and stabbed four into the corners of the first sheet of paper. "Puzzle piece number one," he said.

Incident One

Monday, August 8

Headless corpse of Armando Lopez-Mendez, son of Ambassador of El Salvador, found in front of Embassy of El Salvador
Suspect: Diego Morales of MS-13 (now deceased)
(Freshly "beat-in" shortly after victim's murder)
Victim had "18" tattoo
Cause of Death—Decapitation
Ligature marks on wrists and arms noted at autopsy
Place of death—Undetermined

QUESTIONS:

1. **No proof victim killed by MS-13**
2. **Who else had motive?**
3. **Inconsistencies with other known local MS-13 homicides?**
4. **Who ordered murder?**

Trask stepped back to give the others a view of the paper now pinned to the wall.

"That's where Dix and I came in, but if that's a puzzle piece, we're screwed," Wisniewski volunteered. "It's got all kinds of holes of its own."

"No doubt about that," Trask responded. "But maybe there are answers to this piece in the other ones. That's what this drill is all about. I won't pretend for a minute that I've found many of the answers, but I want everyone's best ideas. The next puzzle is really two."

"Can't hurt." Doroz shrugged his shoulders. "Next piece of wallpaper."

Incident Two

Early Morning Hours of Wednesday, August 10
Convenience Store (Managed by MS-13)
Langley Park, Maryland
Two MS-13 victims killed by high-quality rifle firing NATO rounds
No specific suspects to date

QUESTIONS:

1. **Barrio 18 involved?**
2. **Ballistics indicate rounds probably fired by US-made sniper rifle. Who has those?**
3. **Motives?**
4. **Related to #1? How?**

"And the next one," Trask said.

Incident Three

Early Morning Hours of Thursday, August 11
Convenience Store (Managed by MS-13)
Langley Park, Maryland
Store burns down. Fire investigators say arson.
MS-13 (Esteban Ortega) uses insurance $ to buy car wash

QUESTIONS:

1. **Barrio 18 again? Why?**
2. **Who else swould have a motive?**
3. **Related to #1 or #2?**

"I'll take both questions on that last one," Lynn said. "Ortega loses troops in front of a business that's indefensible if he's in a street war. He's got cover for an inside arson because somebody's already killed two of his guys. He points the finger at his 18th Street bogeymen, cashes the insurance fraud check—which he already admitted on our short-lived bug—and buys the car wash—"

"Which is more defensible—if you're not asleep or high—and is suitable for use *and* an ideal cover for that marijuana grow," Carter chimed in. "I agree with our analyst on all of that."

"Me too," said Crawford. "And if I'm one of the outnumbered 18ers, I'm not going to see much point in revisiting the scene of my successful raid the night before just to chase my arch-rivals out of a bad location. Too much risk versus too little reward. The 18ers are not the ones who torched the store."

"Bear?" Trask asked.

"Sounds like we've got Incident Three pegged," Doroz said. "I haven't heard a word about Incident Two yet." He looked around the table and got only shrugs and shaking heads.

Trask grabbed some more pushpins. "Incident Four may definitely be related to Incident One, *if*..." he paused, "*if* we are correct in our deduction that Diego Morales bears some responsibility for the murder of the ambassador's kid."

"Do you think we're wrong on that?" Lynn asked. There was a slight edge in her voice. "I don't know," Trask said. "Everything you've suggested on it makes sense that Morales *was* involved. The timing certainly fits, and that's why I have him listed as a suspect in #1, but that's all we have right now. Can't afford to assume we've got it right, though." He put the next paper on the wall.

Incident Four

Thursday, August 11, about 0300

3100 Block of Georgia Avenue, NW
Three MS-13 killed; one is Diego Morales (suspect in #1)
No suspects
Sniper rifle and NATO rounds; MO consistent with #2, but not same weapon
QUESTIONS:

1. **Barrio 18?**
2. **Who else has motive? Ambassador and staff?**
3. **Does Salvadoran Embassy staff have sniper rifles?**
4. **Probably related to #1 and #2**

"Discussion?" Trask asked.

"I don't think the 18th Street boys are riding around with sniper weapons and ammo," Carter volunteered. "But I also don't think the ambassador is the shooter, even with his son being the first victim in this little war, if that's what it is. He doesn't strike me as the type. And for what it's worth, I did some checking of my own with a contact I have at ATF. The Salvadoran bodyguards for the ambassador are allowed their sidearms. They're required to register them when they enter the country, and they've registered handguns only. They don't have a true stand-alone building, so it's not like they're guarding an enclosed compound."

"That hospital must have had a nice big laptop beside the bed," Doroz quipped.

"I had a nice big Polish gopher who knew how to smuggle one in," Carter shot back.

"One of the time-honored traditions of the Polish people," Wisniewski said as he stood and bowed. "A natural hobby of a nation without natural borders."

"What about our pirate friend?" Lynn asked. "Old Eye Patch?"

"He *does* feel wrong to me," Trask replied. "That, unfortunately, is not my standard of proof in court. He stays on our list of suspects until we can either *prove* he's wrong, or we can eliminate him as a doer with other proof. If he or any other embassy staff member is involved, we have another problem because we'll have to deal with the diplomatic immunity issues. At any rate, there may be more than one crew shooting up our MS-13 bangers."

"If it's someone from the embassy, what exactly are the diplomatic immunity issues?" Carter asked.

"Depends on the individual," Trask replied. "As the number two at the embassy, our friend Rios-Garcia would enjoy absolute diplomatic immunity for anything, even including murder. Our only recourse would be to ask El Salvador to revoke and waive his status so that we could prosecute him; otherwise we'd be reduced to asking State to declare him *persona non grata* and send him home."

"And State means Murphy," Doroz added. "He's sitting on the Central American desk."

"Exactly," Trask nodded. "I'm not sure we actually have a friend in court with Mr. Murphy." He grabbed another sheet of paper and more pushpins.

Incident Five

Wednesday, August 17, 0216

Two MS-13 dead in drive-by shooting at Car Wash, 2110 Bladensburg Rd, NE

SKS Norinco AK knock-offs, 7.62x39 steel core ammo

No suspects

QUESTIONS:

1. **Barrio 18?**
2. **How did shooters know of MS-13's new location so fast?**
3. **Related to #1 thru #4? How?**
4. **Different MOs to #2 and #4—no sniper rifles used.**
5. **Evening of same date—MS-13 bangers arrested in attempted retaliation raid.**

"Thanks for not putting me asleep at the scene on that one," Carter said. There were a few chuckles.

"No problem, Dix. Thoughts?" Trask asked.

"Round 'em all up and deport 'em," Crawford quipped.

"Really Puddin'? All of them?" asked Doroz. "I was certain you might want to make at least *one* exception to that rule, assuming you could get those clowns at ICE or DHS or whatever immigration calls themselves today to actually deport *somebody*. Maybe a certain pretty secretary?"

"I wasn't talking about embassy personnel," Crawford said, blushing.

"Wow, there's something I just thought of," Lynn said. "Woodin' Puddin.' How much wood could a wood-pud wood, if a wood-pud could pud wood?"

"God, Lynn, that's not fair," Crawford whined while the others snickered.

Trask waited for the laughter to die down. "Anything constructive, to get back on track?"

"Only because I always start with the obvious, since there are *reasons* for things being obvious, we have to consider that there really is some involvement in this by the 18th Street gang," Carter offered, "with the caveat that it just doesn't feel right. Lynn was correct in saying earlier that there's no reason for the mice to tug on the cat's tail. They're so outnumbered here, they'd have to be suicidal to keep doing it."

"If it is the18ers, they could have known about the new place a number of ways," Wisniewski said. "Loose lips in a restaurant, somebody's old Salvadoran girlfriend switches sides, a floater between the groups who isn't tied to either but speaks the lingo. Hell, it could even be a weed customer like Peewee who brags to one group about the smoke he got from the other one."

"Good points," Trask said. "But if it's not the 18ers, Dix, then who?'

"I don't know," Carter said. "I've been sick."

He ducked as a few loose wads of paper and empty cups flew across the table.

"At least our MS-13 friends thought it was the 18ers," Wisniewski noted. "That's why some of Ortega's boys are in jail."

"Yeah," Trask said, "with dead lawyers. Which makes me glad the next one didn't go as somebody had planned it." He put another sheet of paper on the wall.

Incident Six

Friday, August 19, about 0230

Machete-Wielding Thugs Assault AUSA and FBI Analyst, then Die
QUESTIONS:

1. **What the hell were they thinking?**
2. **Hadn't they read our press clippings?**
3. **Who were those guys?**
4. **Seriously, connections???**

After the chuckling subsided, Trask looked around the room. "Like it says there for question four, seriously, anyone have any idea just *how* this is related to all this other stuff? For now I don't know, but until someone proves otherwise, I know in my gut that it is. It might ultimately get me kicked off the case."

Doroz thought for a moment, and then spoke up. "Jeff, all that we know as far as a connection goes is that somehow, some way, they all have to do with El Salvador and with MS-13. That's where we have to start for now."

"Agreed," Trask nodded. "We have to start with what we know, put those puzzle pieces together, and work outward from there. Now here's the rest of it." He started putting the rest of the puzzle on the wall.

Incident Seven

August 21

Defense Attorney Darren Regan Murdered;
Represented MS-13 Van Driver Santos
MO Consistent with Salvadoran Death Squads

Questions:

1. **Who is/are killers?**
2. **Who had motive?**
3. **Embassy personnel involved? Why?**
4. **Connections?**

"Here we go with the embassy thing again," Doroz mused. "Couldn't it just be the gangs?"

"You were there for our meeting with CIA and DEA, Bear," Trask replied. "There's no history of the gangs using these methods—the thumb tying and the back-of-the-head shots—and they've never whacked their own attorneys before."

"But those were ARENA government, or ARENA-allied death squad tactics, not FMLN government methods," Lynn said. "That's what doesn't make any sense here."

"Unless the MS-13 was worried that some of these attorneys were urging cooperation, and they just adopted tactics from old adversaries," Carter added. He shook his head. "Forget I said that. Too much of a stretch."

"All food for thought," Trask said. "Let's look at the next two."

Incident Eight

August 23

Murder of 18er by MS-13, Body Dumped at FBI WFO
MO consistent with known MS-13 homicides

Questions:

1. **Retaliation for Incident 5?**
2. **Why the body dump at the FBI field office?**

"No doubt in my mind that it *was* retaliation for the car wash raid." Carter led off on the discussion. "It's another case of accepting the obvious when there's no reason to reject it. The method of the murder is textbook MS-13 gang torture. I think it would have happened earlier if we hadn't intercepted the *Maras'* raid team on their way to Bladensburg. We just delayed the inevitable for a few days."

"Why dump the body out front on the sidewalk, Dix?" Trask asked. "Why not in front of Main Justice or FBI headquarters? Why not your police department's HQ, for that matter? Why not the Triple-nickle? We were all involved in stopping the Bladensburg raid."

"Maybe somebody was tailing us back here after a court hearing," Carter answered. "Beats me. At any rate, they're telling us they're not afraid to respond, not afraid of any of our esteemed and storied agencies."

"And they may be watching us, collectively or individually, so let's be careful out there." Doroz looked pointedly at Carter.

"Got it," the detective responded. "I've already been tagged as a maverick, had a GPS slapped on my wheels, and have a Polish ninja watching my back. Like I said, got it."

"See what you—or anyone else—has on this one, then," Trask said, reaching for another sheet of paper. The entire eastern side of the squad conference room was beginning to look like a badly papered tenement wall.

Incident Nine

August 23

18er Shot to Death in Apartment near RI Ave

Single Bullet Wound to Center of Head

Questions:

1. **NOT MS-13 MO, so who killed him and why?**
2. **Status of crime scene investigation**
3. **Connected?**

"Ballistics aren't back yet on the round Kathy pulled out of his head at the autopsy," Wisniewski volunteered. "There's some DNA that Frank Wilkes is waiting on as well."

"DNA?" Trask asked. "Do we have evidence of more than one victim?"

"Dunno yet," Wisniewski said. "Frank told me there was some dried blood around the joints of a chair in the room. He swabbed it, because Frank is Frank. He wasn't real happy with the area canvass the uniforms did on the scene either. Said they were lazy. Apparently there were some other Hispanics living in the building, and the guys who rolled on the call couldn't speak the language."

"I know someone who can—" Trask began.

"And that someone has already been assigned that lead by his venerable senior partner," Wisniewski said. "I'm on it."

"Ride with him, Dix. You're out of the hospital now. Nobody rolls alone." Doroz was looking at Carter again.

"Like I said before, got it." Carter nodded deferentially. He looked at Trask. "You see any connections on this, Jeff? Might just be a dope rip, or maybe the vic had been sleeping with somebody else's baby-momma. We haven't seen this MO anywhere else in this case." He paused. "Or in these cases, whichever it is."

"No evident connections other than the victim's status as an 18er, Dix," Trask said. "One dead 18er in return for the MS-13's losses at the car wash probably doesn't balance the scales the way Ortega's boys see it. Maybe it just wasn't the right time or place to carve him like a turkey. Too much noise and too many people around in the other apartments. Could be that they couldn't manage a snatch on the guy so they just put him down with a quick one to the head. One shot. May have used a silencer, may not have needed to depending on the noise level in the building. We just can't afford not to check." He smiled. "Wilkes might think we're getting lazy, too."

"Can't have that." Carter nodded in agreement. "We'll finish questioning the neighbors and check on the ballistics and DNA." He flipped through a copy of the incident reports. "I just noticed one thing. The round from the Regan shooting was a .22. This one was, too. So is the one for the Boydston shootings. Like I said, we'll check the ballistics. The 18er's autopsy was done later, so the lab just got that slug."

"Speaking of Boydston," Trask said, "he's next."

Another summary went up on the wall.

Incident Ten

August 23

William Boydston and Lynette Morris murdered
MO matches Regan murder, ARENA death squad methods
Bank's ATM camera across street blocked to conceal crime scene

Questions:

1. **Motives?**
2. **Ballistics match with Regan shooting, so same MO and weapon means same shooter, but who?**
3. **Any ARENA government operatives in country?**

"We may need to talk to our CIA friend again to answer question three," Doroz noted. "Other than that, I've got zilch. Why would our *Mara* defendants start whacking their own attorneys? Makes no sense. From what we've heard, this is an ARENA-era stunt, and one *they'd* probably deny, too."

"Somebody is just doing anything and everything they can to hit the MS-13 goons and anyone associated with them," Lynn volunteered. "We identify that somebody, and the picture gets clearer."

"Any ideas on that, babe?" Trask asked.

"Babe? *Babe*?" Wisniewski parroted.

"Jealous, Tim?" Lynn shot back. "Maybe you need to go home and spend some time with your Tootsie Pops and Trojans."

"With his what?" Doroz almost screamed.

Wisniewski shook his head at Carter. "There's been a major breach of partner confidentiality here," he said.

"An admission if I ever heard one," Trask added. "You can explain yourself later, Tim." He tacked one more sheet to the wall.

Incident Eleven

September 11

MS-13 car wash attacked, four killed
AK/SKS ammo and weapons
??????

"I've got nothing but questions on this one," Trask said. "The arms and ammo used don't match the prior attacks on the Ortega crew. If I thought our friend with the eye patch was involved, I'd have to disqualify myself from this case because Lynn and I saw him while we were walking our dogs southeast of Waldorf. In other words, Rios-Garcia was thirty miles away when the car wash got hit, and we'd be his alibi witnesses. We've all seemed to agree that this was too big an operation for the Barrio 18 boys to take on at this point. Any ideas?"

"You've just given me one, BABE," Lynn said, shooting Wisniewski a warning look that caused him to hold both hands up in mock surrender. "What if that's exactly what Rios wanted? To DQ you and establish an alibi? It's all that *does* make sense."

"Your question is its own answer. I agree." Carter was nodding.

Before Trask could comment, he felt a double vibration on the cell phone holstered on his belt. He pulled the device out and switched on the screen to see a Google alert for MS-13. After reading the news bulletin, he glanced around the table. "MS-13 and Barrio 18 have declared a worldwide truce," he said. "The gang leaders are being transferred from Zacatraz to medium security facilities like the one at Quezaltepeque, wherever that is. They get conjugal and family visits in return for dropping the murder rate in El Salvador. It looks like the FMLN government is finally following through on its election promises."

"If it's worldwide, we may get some time to connect the dots on your wallpaper before the DOJ and Bureau know-it-alls descend upon us," Carter offered.

"Let's hope so," Trask said. "Let's get to work."

In the kitchen of his hotel suite, the man with the eye patch slammed the lid of his laptop closed in disgust. "FOOLS!" he screamed. "*A truce? A fucking truce!?*" He picked up his cell phone and growled after the ring tone stopped. "Hugo, get ready. We pay a visit to some old friends tonight."

Chapter Twenty-One

Tuesday, September 12, 5:40 p.m.

Lynn Trask drove south on Maryland Highway 5 toward Waldorf. She hadn't really said anything to Jeff before leaving. She *had* left a short message on his office voicemail, knowing that he'd probably never check it. He'd stay in the task force bullpen or in the conference room until it dawned on him that it was past time to leave. The voicemail would cover her if he bothered to ask. He'd check her cubicle and see that her purse was gone, and then he'd figure it out.

He IS *a freakin' genius, after all. That's why he's right 99 percent of the time, and why he was asking questions about Armando's killer again in front of the squad, even after I'd figured it out. GOD, he pisses me off sometimes, always analyzing, re-analyzing. Sometimes I think I married one of those Vulcans from* Star Trek. *Logic, logic, and more logic, with a memory like a damned computer. When he's focused on something like this, I can't break into his hard drive, even when I'm helping input data. I'm right about Armando's murder, damn it. It all makes too much sense to be wrong. "Can't afford to assume." DAMMIT. He might as well have been cross-examining me on the witness stand. It's not an assumption; it's a solid inference based on proof.*

She stopped at a shopping center when she reached the Saint Charles subdivision. Boo and Nikki were almost out of dog food. She picked up a forty-pound bag of the expensive stuff, and continued the debate with herself as she pushed the cart back to her car.

Calm down. You know he didn't mean anything personal by asking everyone else about it. He probably agrees with you and doesn't want it to look like he's playing favorites. No, he's really weighing other possibilities and letting the chips fall where they may, even with his own wife. It's still not personal, though; he's just doing his job, the one he's so good at. That concentration will stay focused until he solves this, then he'll be human again. GOD, he pisses me off sometimes. He'll miss dinner for sure. He can find his own tonight.

She turned into the cul-de-sac marked Amwich Court and pulled into the driveway of the house at the end. Throwing the sack of dog food over her shoulder, she opened the door to the split-foyer entrance and headed downstairs. She filled the bowls and walked to the sliding glass doors, which opened onto the patio in back. She pulled one side open and paused at the screen door, seeing the two happy faces and wagging tails on the other side. She couldn't help but smile and felt her mood improving.

"Hi, girls. Mama's home. Ready for dinner?"

The low growl from Boo caught her by surprise.

"What's the matter, Boo?"

She knew as she asked that she should turn to look behind her, but that realization came too late. A large gloved hand covered her face, and she had time for only one thought before she blacked out.

Chloroform!

"Embassy of El Salvador, Ms. Moreno speaking. How may I help you?"

Crawford opened the door to his car in the parking lot as she answered. He sat down in the driver's seat but didn't hit the ignition, not wanting to miss a word of the call. "Marissa, it's Michael. Sorry I didn't call earlier. We've been swamped and I was stuck in meetings until five minutes ago. Can I see you tonight?"

"Of course, my love. This night and every night. Your place or mine?"

"It should probably be mine tonight, if you don't mind. I probably have a stack of bills waiting on me, and I'll get evicted if I don't pay some of them."

"Not a problem," she laughed. "I'll see you soon."

Trask slumped into the chair of his office at the Triple-nickle. His hope that the gang truce would buy them some time had not materialized. Patrick had called him in to tell him someone from Main Justice would be in the next Monday to conduct an "assistance visit" to see how things were progressing with the investigation. He leaned back and closed his eyes.

Six days to solve all this mess. Guess I'll be spending a lot more time in here in the near future. If they let me stay on, it'll be as a second fiddle at best. Even more likely, they'll use the attack on Lynn and me to disqualify us from the case. Lynn! I didn't see her when I left. Nuts. He glanced at his watch. *6:00.* Then he saw the red message light flashing on the desk phone. He picked up the receiver and hit the button.

"Hey, it's me. I'm heading home to feed the dogs. OK, bye."

Uh-oh. Something's wrong. I only get the curt 'OK, bye,' when she's pissed about something. Better head out quick. He was halfway out the door when he saw the vest hanging on a peg on the wall. He'd ignored it lately, too hot and bulky. CCR's "Bad Moon Rising" started playing in his head. He grabbed the vest and headed for the parking garage.

She woke up slowly, still tasting the chloroform, but when she tried to lick her lips, they were taped shut. She leaned forward, but felt constrained. As she came to, she realized that her feet were bound. Her shoulders were pinned to the back of the chair, and she felt her wrists pinned together by the rope. She tried to feel the cords, hoping to recognize the knot, but she couldn't move her hands normally.

My thumbs are tied together!

He stepped in front of her then. A huge, Hispanic man, grinning at her.

Not a grin, a fucking leer. What's up, big boy? Planning to untie me and have your way with me before you finish me off? Give it a shot. I'll take all the time I can get, and I'll fight dirty as hell. You're not wearing a mask, so I know you don't want to leave me here alive.

She looked past him, trying to put a plan together. She saw the window on the far wall and recognized the curtains she'd hung around it.

I never really liked those. Need to replace them. She shook her head. *Get with it, back to your senses.* She blinked her eyes and concentrated. *I'm still in the den. He's got me facing away from the door. Where's Jeff? Oh, God, don't let that voicemail be the last words he ever hears from me.*

The man looked at her, still smiling. His eyes dropped to her breasts. His hands moved to the buttons on her blouse, opening the first two. Then he stopped and stepped back.

Don't stop there. I hate everything you just did more than you'll ever know, but I need time now. What are you thinking about, you bastard? Jeff, where are you?

The man shook his head from side to side as he pulled a small caliber pistol from his belt and began screwing a silencer onto its barrel.

No, no! It can't end like this. He's more afraid of whoever it was who sent him to do this than he is horny. He has his orders, and they were to kill me. I've just lost all my time. Jeff, I'm so sorry.

The man stepped behind her, and she felt the silencer touch the back of her head. There was a gunshot; she felt an impact on the back of her head and felt herself falling.

Trask turned onto Maryland 5. He called her cell but got no answer.

I'm probably getting the silent treatment for whatever sin I committed.

The traffic was a little lighter than usual because he'd left the office late. He weaved in and out of traffic, earning more than one dirty look from his fellow commuters. *Most federal employees don't donate much time to the government; I wonder how many actually fudged five or ten minutes today. I'm lucky not to be in gridlock tonight.*

He glanced down at the speedometer. *I'll risk ten over. If one of the county boys pulls me over, I'll have him escort me home.* He thought about calling the sheriff's office to have one of their units check on her, but decided not to waste a call on what was probably just a domestic tiff. *Don't want to cry wolf in case I really need 'em later.*

He couldn't get the Credence tune out of his head. *Oh, well, at least it's not "Proud Mary." Wish I had a nickel for every time that thing hit my radio. Way overplayed.*

When he turned onto Saint Charles Parkway, the music suddenly stopped. *Something's wrong!* Trask floored the accelerator, passing two cars with his horn blaring. He pulled in behind Lynn's car, grabbed the Glock from the glove compartment, and bolted to the door. To his horror, it was unlocked and ajar. For a microsecond, he thought about the vest he'd left on the passenger floorboard.

Screw it! He pulled the Glock and flung the door back. He looked up the stairs toward the living room on the left. *Nothing.* Then he heard a whimper coming from the den down the stairs. He took the six steps in two strides and saw her. She was on the floor, tied to a chair, her back to him. There was a small pool of blood staining the carpet behind her head and spots of blood on the back of her blouse. The dogs were sitting beside her, Boo licking her face. Trask froze and heard himself calling her name. His legs failed him, and he dropped to his knees.

Crawford had expected her for dinner, but she was late. He was about to put her portion of the lasagna in the fridge when the doorbell finally rang.

"I'm so sorry," she said. "I got stuck at work on a last-minute report that Rios wanted out tonight. He insisted that I stay late, even though I'd been invited to dinner at Tio Juan's house. I had to call and cancel it." Her nose caught the scent. "You made your lasagna for me? I love you, and I'm starved!" She kissed him and pulled him back toward the dining table.

Trask sat on the floor, numb and unable to move. Then he saw her legs twitch. In a flash he was dialing 911 and asking for an ambulance and police while he was untying her. When her hands were free, she ripped the tape from her mouth. She hugged him and started crying softly. She pointed to the pistol with the silencer lying on the floor almost hidden by the shadow of the couch.

"Is he gone? Is he gone?" she cried.

Trask instinctively pulled the Glock from his waistband and whirled around, expecting to see the attacker. The machetes sliced across his memory again. There was no one there this time. He turned back to her, checking her head, her back. "There's blood here on the floor. Are you hurt? Were you shot? Cut?"

"No, just dizzy, and my head hurts. Chloroform, I think. I feel like I'm going to throw up." She grabbed a wastebasket from beside the corner of the couch, and did.

"If this isn't your blood, then…?"

"Check Boo," she said. "I heard a shot, I felt something hit my head, and then the chair got knocked over. I hope he didn't hit her. The dogs were outside when he grabbed me."

Trask called the big dog over, and she walked to him without difficulty. He checked her all over and found no injuries. "She's fine," he said. He pointed toward what had been the sliding screen door to the patio. "That's not."

The frame of the door was bent inward, almost in half. The screen hung from the twisted aluminum in tatters.

Trask hugged the big dog's neck. "It's OK, Boo. I can fix that. Thanks to you, we don't have to fix your Mom." He heard sirens outside. "Here we go again. The neighbors are going to hate us." He pointed to the bloodstain on the carpet. "We want them to cut that out and find out who it belonged to. I want ballistics on that pistol, too." He looked around the room, and found the bullet hole in a corner, near the ceiling.

"USAA," she said, laughing a little. "Our insurance company's going to hate us, too."

The medics came barreling down the stairs with a stretcher, freezing when they saw the Glock.

"Sorry, guys," Trask said, returning it to his belt. He motioned toward Lynn. "She needs to be checked out."

"I'm fine, Jeff," she protested.

"You don't know that. They need to do some blood work, find out how much of that gas you inhaled, and check out that bump on the back of your head," he said.

They had her on the stretcher in a matter of seconds. He kissed her and told her he'd be at the hospital shortly, then she was gone, and he was alone for a moment. He started shaking and sobbing.

A Saint Charles County Deputy Sheriff was standing at the top of the stairs.

"Mister Trask? You all right?"

He nodded, still choking back the tears and rage. "Yeah," he heard himself saying. "But I'm going to find out who did this, and he won't be."

Trask sat beside her bed at the hospital, watching her sleep. It was past midnight. The doctors had checked her out and said everything would be fine. A little more nausea, perhaps, until she got the rest of the crude anesthetic out of her system. The attacker hadn't wanted to kill her with the drug, so it wasn't a heavy dose. That's what the pistol had been for. He shook his head. *It's not worth this. Nothing is worth this.* He felt a large hand on his shoulder.

"How you holding up?" Bill Patrick asked.

Trask saw that Barry Doroz was standing behind Patrick.

"I'm OK, Bill. She was very lucky. Just a concussion, and the doc says it'll just require some rest. As best I can put it together, our big dog came plowing through a sliding screen door just as the creep was about to put one in the back of her head, just like the defense counsel murders. The shooter turned toward Boo—our dog—but she got to his arm before he could get the gun trained on her. The shot went up into a corner of the room, and the gun went down to the floor after bouncing off the back of Lynn's head. She went down, and the shooter ran away." He shook his head. "I never should have let her leave the office by herself."

"Apparently you didn't, Jeff," Doroz said. "You left her in the capable paws of that wolf you brought home. She *is* lucky, though. Much luckier than some others tonight."

Trask looked up at him. "Who is it this time, Bear?"

"The Salvadoran ambassador and his wife. Both carved up like turkeys. MS-13 style. I just came from their house. Our friend Murphy showed up and started cussing me—and you—up and down. Blamed us for it, said we were incompetent, promised he would have us both off the case by morning. I guess your friend Rios is the new ambassador, for the moment at least."

"Wonderful." Trask looked back to Patrick. "How much time can you give me, Bill?"

"No longer than Monday." Patrick thought for a minute. "I can leave you in place that long. We'll have Eastman tell the guys at Main Justice that we realize that as victims, you and Lynn will be disqualified, and that they'll need to bring our office in Northern Virginia or Maryland on board to take over the case. We'll DQ our whole office on the conflict of interest, but tell Justice that we'll just leave you there in the interim to run the transition. Sorry, but we've got no choice now."

Trask nodded. "Understood. Thanks."

"I've got two guys here to watch her room tonight, Jeff," Doroz said. "What about you?"

"I'm going home, Bear. Like you said, I have a wolf and another dog, and I need to feed them. That process got interrupted by our friend with the silencer. Feel free to have the sheriff park a unit outside if he wants to, but I'm staying at the house tonight. Lynn's sedated, and your boys are watching her door."

"Get some sleep," Patrick said, patting him on the shoulder again as he turned to leave.

Doroz waited until Patrick was gone. "Plan?" he asked.

"The first time, I think they came for me," Trask said. "Whether they came for Lynn tonight or were trying to get to me through her, it doesn't matter. My *plan* is to solve this mess in the next three or four days and take it down, then hand my successors a gift-wrapped, bulletproof package that even a moron couldn't screw up at trial. This is personal now."

"Normally, that doesn't work very well."

"I realize that, but I'm not normal."

"Yeah," Doroz chuckled. "I know. You OK to drive?"

Trask nodded soberly. "Absolutely." He looked back at Lynn and kissed her on the forehead. *Sleep well, Babe. You're safer here than at home for now.* He squeezed her hand gently before he left the room, tears in his eyes.

The house was still being guarded when he got home. The Maryland State Police had processed the scene and left. Trask talked the deputies outside into limiting the sentries to two marked units, got them some coffee, then went into the house. He put the Glock back into a holster and pulled out the .45 from the headboard before loading two of its magazines with hollow-point rounds. *More stopping power. The hell with the regs.* He went to the bar and knocked back a stiff double of Crown Royal, then returned to the bedroom and lay down. Nikki jumped onto the bed and curled up at his feet. Boo sprawled across the doorway. The dogs were snoring in five minutes. Trask joined them in ten.

Chapter Twenty-Two

Tuesday, September 12, 8:30 a.m.

"Any signs of forced entry?" Trask asked, looking over the crime scene photos spread across the conference table.

"Nope," Doroz said. "Looked like whoever pulled this one walked in through the front door."

"Doesn't make sense," Trask said. "Their government signs a truce with the *Maras* and takes the heat off them—exactly what the gangs have been looking for—and the local chapter of this crew whacks the ambassador and his wife, leaving their calling cards carved into the corpses? Good way to bust the truce your bosses just agreed to, don't you think?" He looked across the table at Crawford. "How's your girlfriend, Mike?"

"Pretty messed up. She was supposed to eat dinner with the ambassador and his wife last night, but had to work late on something for Rios. She's taking it hard. She was real close to the ambassador, called him her Tio, her uncle."

"She have any ideas about this?" Doroz asked.

"Just that it's the MS-13. Her cousin killed herself years ago after being gang raped by them. Marissa hates their guts."

"We either have a rogue clique operating under their own set of rules, or someone who wants us to think they are," Trask mused.

"I may have something!" Lynn shouted from her cubicle out in the bullpen.

Doroz shook his head. "I can't believe you brought her in here today, Jeff."

Trask looked back at him and smirked. "If your two stalwarts couldn't stop her, what makes you think *I* was going to? The docs cleared her, and she called me before six. I couldn't trust her to stay home, and I wasn't going to let her drive herself in after last night. Let's see what she's got."

They walked into the bullpen and looked over her shoulder.

"Look at this first," she said, cueing up a photograph of several young men posing on risers. "It's a photograph of the UCLA Salvadoran Student Association about twenty years back. I pulled it off an online yearbook collection. The club charter said that membership was open to students from El Salvador and any others who wanted to promote good relations between the US and Central America."

She highlighted a tall young man standing in the center of the group.

"The future and now late ambassador from El Salvador and president of this association at the time, Juan Carlos Lopez-Portillo," Lynn said.

"Prominent even while a student," Trask said. "Meaning what?"

She shot him a familiar glance.

"Sorry," he said. "What else do you have?"

She moved the curser to another tall young man standing to the right of Lopez-Portillo, blowing up the photo to the point where the goateed face of the student filled the screen.

"Anybody want to take a stab at this one?" she asked.

"Looks familiar, but I can't place him," Doroz said, shaking his head.

Trask took a moment longer. "Sorry, same here." He stepped aside for a moment to let Crawford, who had joined them, venture a guess.

"You got me. No idea," Crawford said.

"Watch this." Lynn pulled the photo of the face onto a second computer monitor on her desk. "First I gave him a shave, using some of this high-tech Bureau Photoshop stuff. Then I aged him twenty years with the facial recognition software. Finally I added a fashion accessory. An eye patch."

"Holy shit!" Doroz exclaimed. "It's Rios-Garcia."

"Not exactly," Lynn said. "His real name is—or was—Luis Moreno-Montillo, according to the caption under the photo."

"Amazing work, Lynn." Trask was massaging both her shoulders. He saw that Crawford was heading for the door. "You OK, Mike?"

Crawford nodded and waved, but continued toward the exit.

"Now check this out," Lynn said. She pulled the face of the man standing on the other side of Lopez-Portillo from the photo to the second monitor. "I'm aging this one too, and since the yearbook shot was a black-and-white, I gave it some color."

Trask looked at the red-haired face in the new portrait. "Murphy." He shook his head. "We have a college reunion here. The ambassador pulls one college bud up as second-in-charge and has a ready-made plant at State with Murphy, another member of the club. Phenomenal." He turned to Doroz. "Bear, can you get our CIA and DEA boys back in for another sit-down? Give 'em the real name of the new acting ambassador and see if it means anything to them, please."

"Tomorrow afternoon all right?" Doroz asked.

"Sure. That'll give 'em time to do a file search on Moreno. Maybe they'll actually have something this time, now that we have his real name." Trask looked around the room. "What happened to Puddin'? He left looking like he'd seen a banshee or something."

9:30 a.m.

Carter and Wisniewski climbed the stairs to the second floor of the apartment building on Rhode Island Avenue.

"That was the vic's apartment," Carter said as they passed a door with the number 206 on it. "The canvass notes indicate that the patrol guys tried to talk to the lady in 208, but she didn't speak English."

Wisniewski nodded and knocked on the door to 208. A small, Hispanic woman of about sixty opened the door cautiously, but smiled broadly when she saw their badges. She began to explain that she did not understand English, but when Wisniewski answered her in Spanish, she invited them inside.

"Did you know your neighbor in 206, *abuela*?" Wisniewski asked her.

"Yes, a nice young man. His name was Adan Sarmiento. Very troubled."

"Troubled? How do you mean?"

"Something bothered him very much. I never saw him at ease. When I asked him what was wrong, he would only say that he worried for his family back in El Salvador."

"Are you from El Salvador?" Wisniewski asked.

"No. Guatemala," she said. "But close enough to know the troubles in El Salvador. Our countries seem to share them."

"Do you mean the gangs?"

"Yes." She nodded, paused, and then nodded some more. "Always the gangs."

"Did Adan say why he was worried for his family?"

"Not specifically. He just said they were not safe, and he had to do something to help them. Then he got worse."

"Worse? What do you mean?"

"He came to me one morning and asked if I could take him to the church. I am one of the few in the building here who has a car. He said he needed to see a priest, and that he had done something very bad to help his family. He was very upset."

"Did you take him to the church?"

"Yes, of course. But the confession did not seem to help him. He was always very serious, but he seemed to be very scared and sad after that."

"Do you remember what day it was when you drove him to the church?" Wisniewski asked, pulling a small notepad and pen from his sport coat.

"It was the ninth of August," she said. "A Tuesday. I go grocery shopping every Tuesday. Just a habit. I remember telling Adan it was no inconvenience because I was going out anyway. I dropped him at the church, did my shopping, and picked him up on my way back. He was waiting outside, but he was standing in the shadows until I pulled up in front of the church. I did not even see him until he stepped out into the sunlight."

"It was August, a hot day," Wisniewski offered.

She smiled and patted his hand. "A *warm* day. We are from what you *Norte Americanos* call Central America. It is always hot at home. We came back, he helped me carry in my groceries, and he sat in that same chair where you are now. He wanted to talk to me."

He smiled. "I understand. You are an easy person to talk to, grandmother. Did he ever tell you any more about these things that bothered him so much?"

"I asked him what he was so very afraid of. He told me that if anything ever happened to him, it would be because of the *sombra tuerto*."

"Are you sure that's what he said?" Wisniewski asked her. "*Sombra tuerto*?"

"Yes," she said. "It was a strange thing to say. It made no sense to me. I asked Adan to explain it, but he would not. He only said that he had said too much already, then he got up and left."

"Thank you, grandmother. You have been a very big help."

"I hope so," she said.

"What was that?" Carter asked as they headed down the stairs. "*Sombra tuerto?*"

"Yeah," Wisniewski said. "The one-eyed shadow."

"Really," Carter said. He started nodding. Trask would have something else to scribble on his jigsaw puzzle pieces. "Really."

They got into the car and pulled away from the curb. There was a traffic light at the first intersection, and it was changing to yellow.

"Don't run it," Carter warned him. "Look. It's got one of those citation-generating eye-in-the-sky cams on it. Cap'n Willie will make you pay it. Department regulations, you know. No special privileges."

Wisniewski applied the brakes. He looked at Carter. They were thinking the same thing. "What day was it when our man Adan got shot?"

"Wednesday the twenty-third. It's a long shot that we'll recognize any vehicles, but we'll pull the images anyway. The Traffic Enforcement Office will still have them on file."

5:30 p.m.

Crawford sat in his car, looking at the rear of the embassy, the exit he knew she'd take leaving for home. He felt like the fabric of his soul had been ripped. *Has she been playing me all along? That SOB with the eye patch is her uncle, for Christ's sake. The guy in the photo in her apartment is the same one in that yearbook Lynn found, and I can't even tell her I know that because it'll blow our lead. Have I told her anything that would get back to him? I don't think so. How do I play this? How the hell do I get her to talk to me about it?*

She saw his car and waved, rushing over with a smile on her tired face. She got in and kissed him hard. "I've missed you all day."

"I've missed you, too," he said quietly.

She pulled back a little. "What's wrong, Michael?"

"It's nothing, really. A little headache. Some minor things at work."

"Want to talk about it?"

"I can't, Marissa. Classified stuff."

"It's OK." She leaned forward and kissed him again. "It is the nature of our jobs. I understand. There are things I can't talk about sometimes."

He nodded. "Where would you like to eat?"

"Wherever you are going. I am going there with you."

They opted for a small café in Old Town Alexandria, close to the river. After ordering, he noticed that her smile was gone and that her eyes were starting to fill with tears.

"Your Tio Juan?" he asked.

She nodded, unable to speak for a moment. She sipped some water and composed herself.

"If I hadn't had to work late, I might have been killed with them," she sobbed. "The deputy ambassador saved my life."

He saw what he thought might be an opening and took it, even though he felt ashamed for doing so. "You told me that Rios-Garcia arrived just after the ambassador's son was killed. Did he bring anyone with him when he came?" he asked her.

"Some personal staff," she said. "Why?"

"I just wondered if he brought any family with him. He might want to protect them in light of what happened to the ambassador. Did his personal staff include any security personnel?"

"I think so." She stood up. "I need to go to the ladies' room. My makeup is running." She pushed her chair under the table and patted his shoulder. "You don't have to worry about me. I'm just a secretary. Rios is the ambassador now. He has good bodyguards. He will be safe, and I will, too."

He watched her as she walked toward the back of the restaurant. *She's gorgeous. She's also either very good, or she's not to blame for any of this. Maybe both. Maybe there's a legitimate reason for her uncle's use of an alias. To protect her, for example. If their enemies didn't know she was the new ambassador's niece, she'd be less likely to be kidnap bait or worse.*

She was back in five minutes.

"I'm sorry," she said. "It's been a sad day for us."

"I understand. It's tough to lose people you care about."

She nodded and tried to smile. "You seem to be feeling better. Is your headache gone?"

"Almost."

"Good," she said. "I need to be with you tonight."

———

7:20 p.m.

Dixon Carter opened the front door and headed for his refrigerator. He hadn't gotten six feet when the doorbell rang behind him. A process server handed the thick envelope to him when he opened the door. The return address was for a local law firm, one that specialized in domestic relations litigation. Carter merely nodded. *She's finally done it.*

He threw the papers on a table in the foyer, not bothering to open them. He reached for the cell phone on his belt.

"Yes, Massa," Wisniewski answered the call.

"Knock that crap off, and get your wise Polish ass over here."

"What's up?"

"I just received some legal documents from the future former Mrs. Carter. I believe I will require a designated driver this evening."

"You OK, Dix?"

"I am at the moment. I might not be later. I do not know if I'll be celebrating or lamenting. I haven't decided that yet. I *have* decided that I will be drinking."

"I'll be there in fifteen. What's the saying? 'That which doesn't kill us only makes us stronger'?"

"They got it wrong, my friend. I've been shot, both physically and otherwise. That which doesn't kill us only leaves us wounded."

———

10:45 p.m.

"There's still a marked unit out front, and the wolf is at the door, which—in our case—is a good thing," Trask said. "The alarm's on, too." He rolled over in the bed and kissed her. "How's the head?"

"Better. Just a little sore now."

"Good. That was a helluva break you gave us today, babe," he said. "What made you think to do that?"

"A couple of leads you gave me without realizing it," she said.

"Really?" He propped himself up on one arm. "How'd I accomplish that?"

"Work from what we know. College friends who are still friends, even though miles apart politically. I just took your advice and concentrated on the late ambassador. Once I saw the pictures, I thought I saw something familiar about the guys standing next to him."

"It's still fantastic work. I won't take credit for it. Your idea, not mine. Now we only need to make it lead to something conclusive in five days or less."

She rolled over to face him. "What happens if we can't?"

He lay back, staring at the ceiling. "If we make a lot of headway, some lord high executioner from Main Justice steps forward to take the credit for solving what we could not. If there's any real doubt left, they probably just send in the next squad of line prosecutors to save us from our conflict of interest. The politibrats don't want hard cases; it can wreck their careers when they lose them."

"What will you do if someone else takes over?"

He was back on his elbow, smiling. "I shall continue to sally forth as a loyal musketeer, true in my sworn duty to the crown. I have Porthos Doroz, Athos Wisniewski, and Aramis Carter to watch the back of their young and reckless friend. You may call me D'Artagnan."

"So which part do I play in your musketeers movie?"

Trask tucked both arms under a pillow behind his head. "You don't. Don't worry about it. Although Dumas did write some dangerous women into the book, they didn't have female musketeers."

"Why not?"

"Because—even if sexual equality had been in vogue, and it wasn't—seventeenth century muskets weighed a ton, and when you got off your single shot, you had to engage in swordplay. Brute strength stuff. Swashbuckling."

She put her head on his chest. "What does that mean, swashbuckling?"

"I have no idea, but I can't imagine it would have been a good thing to go around with your swash unbuckled. You'd probably trip over the damned thing and hurt yourself in the middle of a duel."

She rolled onto her back, laughing.

"I love you," she said. "You're nuts. And funny."

"And I love you," Trask said. He paused. "There's not really a character in the book that fits you."

"How about the girl in the movie?"

"Which version? There've been several."

"The one with Michael York."

"Oh, you mean the Raquel Welch character?"

"Yeah, her."

"That would be Constance Bonacieux." Trask flipped up the blanket and stared for a moment at her bare breasts. "Yes, there's a certain resemblance there."

He ducked just in time to avoid being swatted with a pillow.

"You can't be Constance," he said.

"Why not?"

"She was already married to somebody else, and she got killed. We can't have that." He shuddered for a moment. "I can't believe I came so close to losing you. No more close calls."

"No disagreement there. But I'm disappointed."

"Why?"

"I'm just feeling kind of French tonight after all that silly talk."

"We could think of *something* French to do," he said, rolling toward her.

Chapter Twenty-Three

Wednesday, September 13, 8:15 a.m.

Trask ducked under the yellow tape that now encircled the ambassador's residence. There was no music playing in his head for the moment. It was Lassiter instead, talking to him as if he had his hand on his protege's shoulder. *Don't ever pass up an opportunity to visit a crime scene. There's no substitute for seeing it yourself. Photographs help, but they don't really give you scope or distance. Let the sights and the smells, the walls and the shadows speak to you. They will if you let them, and if you listen long enough.*

He re-examined the frame to the front door. The crime scene techs had done their thing, and they were good, but they wouldn't be carrying the case in court. *Hell, I won't either,* he thought. *Conflicted out. More likely to end up on the witness stand than at counsel table.*

His cell phone rang.

"Jeff? It's Doroz. Frank Wilkes is here, says he has some things for us to see. When can you be back?"

"I'm up in Bethesda at the ambassador's house. Give me thirty minutes."

"OK. Willie Sivella's here, too."

"Really? Anything wrong?"

"Our two favorite cops—my TFOs—almost got arrested at the Fraternal Order of Police last night. Seems they had a little too much to drink and got out of control. Dix would probably be looking at charges in district court for assaulting a federal agent if Willie hadn't called in some favors."

"*What!?*"

"Yep. Willie said some guy from ATF made the mistake of asking how many Metro detectives it took to solve a gang murder or screw in a lightbulb or something like that. Dix had just gotten served his divorce papers and wasn't in the mood for taking any gas. He grabbed the guy, flipped him over, and was holding him upside down by the heels over the balcony from the second floor staircase. Tim was pouring beer down the dude's pants leg and commenting on his apparent loss of bladder control. They were also inviting other officers to deposit the condiment of their choice in the guy's shirt while he was upside down. Ketchup, mustard, maple syrup, even some tomato soup, from what I understand. Willie had to spring 'em. He's here babysitting them for now."

"That should be a sight," Trask said, laughing. "See you in thirty." He smiled. *Congratulations, Dix. Looks like you have a new partner.*

He returned the phone to its holster. He paused and took a last look at the entryway before heading back to his car. *No signs of force at all. They either knew the killers or just weren't careful enough in opening the door. But this doesn't tell me who they were. Scenes are like witnesses, Bob. Some talk, some don't.*

He started the drive back when the phone went off again. He hit the Bluetooth control on the steering wheel.

"Trask."

"Mr. Trask, it's Mitchell Clark, on the Vincente Santos matter."

"What's up, Mitchell?"

"I think Mr. Santos is close to cooperating on your case, but he wanted me to ask what assurances you could give him that he would not be incarcerated with other MS-13 members. He's concerned for his safety while serving his time."

"As he should be. Tell him that in every case I get an email from BOP—the Bureau of Prisons—asking about any separations from other inmates that are required. BOP doesn't like having to break up gang fights in their facilities, or having to clean up murder sites in their showers or cafeterias. If they have a non-*Mara* facility in general population, we'll request that for him. If not, we could sponsor him into one of the witness security program pens. Everyone in those facilities has cooperated. They're more restrictive, however, and most inmates don't want to be there unless they have to. Less visitation, even from family members. General pop is actually a little easier time."

"Thanks. I'll talk with him again and get back to you."

"One more thing, Mitch. Get your guy to give you some piece of information that will let me know he's actually willing to do something for us. At this point it's not for attribution; he tells you and you pass it on to me. His name never gets attached to that information unless we agree to pursue this. I need something to know he's with us for real and not just wasting my time. I don't have any to waste right now.

"OK. I'll see what I can do."

"No problem. Later."

Trask checked his watch. *It's the thirteenth. Five whole days left. Not much time at all.* Stevie Ray's "Tightrope" started playing in his head.

When he reached the squad room, Trask was surprised to find Willie Sivella in a very upbeat mood, even though he was sitting between detectives Carter and Wisniewski, both of whom were still wearing sunglasses and looked to be in substantial need of headache medication. Doroz, Lynn, and Crawford were also seated at the table, as was Frank Wilkes.

"Commander," Trask nodded to Sivella. "You're looking very chipper today."

"Why shouldn't I be?" Sivella grinned and leaned back in his chair, slapping Carter and Wisniewski on the back. The detectives each winced in pain. "My boys here withstood an onslaught from a federal bully last night, taught him a lesson, and between them and another Metropolitan Police Department employee," he nodded in the direction of Frank Wilkes, "I believe we have some major contributions to make to your federal investigation. Real police officers at work. I might have even brought you some decent evidence myself."

"Excellent," Trask said. "We could use some good news, even though we had a major breakthrough yesterday." He smiled at Lynn. "Who wants to start?"

"That would be me," Wilkes said, standing as he passed copies of a report around the table. "Two major developments from the shooting of the Barrio 18 gang member in that apartment off Rhode Island Avenue. The first one actually came from Commander Sivella, or more accurately, from Kathy at the medical examiner's office."

"I *did* drive it over here," Sivella noted.

"Anyway," Wilkes continued, "as you all know, the ME routinely runs a toxicology screen on the blood from any homicide victim. It takes a while for those to come back from the lab. It's not *CSI* around here."

Trask and Doroz exchanged glances and grins.

If you want a tirade, just mention CSI to Frank Wilkes, Trask thought. *The real world here. No instant lab results with five-minute turnarounds.*

"The lab found a pretty high concentration of zolpidem in the blood taken from Armando Lopez-Mendez," Wilkes continued. "The usual brand name for zolpidem is Ambien. It's a sleep-aid, but we've seen it used as a date-rape drug in the past. Slip it into someone's drink, and bedtime. Especially if the victim has had a couple of shots of alcohol."

"Wait a sec, Frank," Doroz said. "You said that was for the blood from the ambassador's kid. I thought we were talking about the 18er from Rhode Island Avenue."

"We are," Wilkes said. "In my opinion, he's your killer on Incident One here." Wilkes pointed to the sheets of paper on the wall summarizing the murder of the ambassador's son.

"How do you figure that?" Lynn asked.

"Quite a leap, Frank," Trask nodded, agreeing with the skeptical tone in his wife's voice.

"I arrive at that conclusion from the fact that blood found in the dead 18er's room, more specifically, in the grooves of a chair in that room, is a conclusive DNA match for the blood taken from the body of Armando Lopez-Mendez at autopsy."

"Are you sure about that?" Lynn was still defending her theory.

"Virtually certain," Wilkes responded. "In addition to the DNA evidence, the autopsy report for Armando indicated that he'd been tied up in a chair, with his hands bound behind him. The vertical bruising on the inside of his arms is almost a perfect match to the chair from your Rhode Island Avenue 18er's apartment."

Trask looked at Lynn and shrugged. She tossed her hands up in the air.

"How'd you find the blood on the chair, Frank?" Carter asked quietly. "You'll pardon me if I don't speak too loudly."

"Blacklighted the room after I sprayed the luminol," Wilkes answered. "It was obvious that someone had wiped the chair down to an extent. It was clean except for the joints where the chair back met the seat. Those joints lit up pretty brightly."

"If that's your first bombshell, what's your second?" Doroz asked.

"I gave you two already," Wilkes stated flatly. "First, it was Armando's blood on the chair, and second, the lab found that he had been sedated before he was killed."

"Sorry. I miscounted," Doroz said, rolling his eyes.

"There is more, however," Wilkes said. "The ballistics are back on the projectiles and weapon used to kill the Rhode Island Avenue 18er."

"I didn't know we had the weapon," Trask said, puzzled.

"You've had it since Tuesday night, Jeff," Wilkes said. "I mean you, literally. It was left in your house by whoever it was who tried to kill Lynn. It was also the same gun that was used to kill the defense attorneys. We test-fired it and the slugs from the victims were a match. No question at all."

Doroz shook his head and started a low, slow whistle. "What the hell?"

"I'm still on Armando," Lynn protested. "Why would one 18er whack another one? Didn't Armando have an 18 tattooed on his shoulder?"

"He did," Wilkes confirmed. "I can't speak to the motive. I can only say that a chair in the one victim's room had the blood of the other victim on it."

"So someone else could have killed Armando in that room, or for that matter, in that chair, and the chair could have been moved into the apartment after Armando's murder," she said.

"That is certainly possible," Wilkes said.

"But not likely, Lynn," Carter said. "We're stretching now. Besides, Tim and I have something else to throw on this little fire."

Wisniewski flipped open the top of a laptop computer, and the forty-inch LED screen on the conference room wall came to life.

"This is from the red-light camera at the intersection on Rhode Island Avenue just east of the apartment building where the 18er took the bullet to his forehead," Carter said. "You can see the date and time in the lower right-hand corner. August twenty-third, 3:07 p.m. It's consistent with what the ME found to be an approximate time of death for the victim. Watch."

The digital video began to run and showed a large, dark sedan running the stoplight and turning left through the intersection.

"Go back and freeze it." Trask was out of his chair and next to the screen. The screen froze, revealing the red and white and blue license plates on the front of the car. "STL-467. Those plates were on the car that Rios—I mean Moreno—had at the dog park."

"Watch the rest of this," Carter said.

They fixed their stares on the screen. The sedan ran the light again, turned left again, and then—after a moment or two—reappeared at the same light, traveling in the same direction as when it first appeared on the screen.

"He made the block," Wisniewski said. "He's at the building at about the same time our vic gets shot, and he makes the block around the building."

"Picking up the shooter?" Trask asked.

Carter nodded. "That's my guess. And just in case there's any doubt about whose car it was, we blew up the best still-shot of the driver."

Wisniewski hit some buttons on the laptop, and the screen showed the photograph. The driver was wearing an eye patch. "The 18er's neighbor said he was afraid of someone he called the 'one-eyed shadow.'"

"He's got a motive, working for the ambassador. Avenging the murder of the ambassador's kid," Lynn said.

That's my girl, Trask said. *Open mind, no tunnel vision. She knows not to try and cram every round fact into a square hole, even if her initial theory made all the sense in the world.*

"But how did he know that? How'd he find this guy?" Carter asked. "Why suspect that an 18er did it instead of one of the MS-13 punks? Your question there was very valid, Lynn."

"Great," she said. "At least my questions are valid even if my answers aren't."

"Lynn, if we had all the answers, we'd have all these mopes locked down already," Doroz said. "Your first shot was a good one."

"It was." Trask agreed. "But now we've confirmed our other problem. Our friend Moreno is now the acting ambassador. If he didn't have complete diplomatic immunity before—and he probably did—he's certainly got it now. We've just solved some of our murders and run into a brick wall at the same time." His cell phone rang again. "Excuse me." He hit the answer icon on the touch screen. "Trask."

"It's Mitchell Clark again, Mr. Trask. Mr. Santos asked me to pass along what I believe may qualify as your requested indicator of his good faith. He told me that he heard from other members of his gang that the rival gang member whose body was dumped at the FBI office was killed by Esteban Ortega at the car wash. He also said that if we can agree on a plea, he can provide you with the whereabouts of Mr. Ortega. He said you'd know what that meant."

"I do. Thanks, Mitch. We'll get back to you shortly." Trask looked at Wilkes. "Feel like doing some more work on our case today, Frank?"

"Of course."

"Great," Trask said. "Who has the keys to the car wash?"

"Our forfeiture guys have 'em," Doroz said. "The property was subject to becoming the property of the government since it was used to facilitate the marijuana grow. I'll get the keys and meet you in the parking garage."

"Call our DEA and CIA friends and tell 'em we'll see them tomorrow morning, Bear," Trask said. "We need to get to that crime scene now, before what evidence may be left disappears, and I need a little quiet time to think about what we can do with Moreno."

"Sure. Any ideas for now?"

Trask shook his head. "Not a damned one."

He followed Doroz to the squad supervisor's office. "Santos' attorney said that his guy can tell us where Ortega is holed up," Trask said. "I'll try and get some plea terms approved and then we'll roll on that. If Frank Wilkes can do his magic at the car wash, we may have a homicide we can actually prosecute."

"Just give me some lead time to write the arrest plan. You know how detailed the Bureau wants its operations plans these days. You'd think we were planning D-Day the way they want everything triple-checked in advance. I'll have to get the SAC and ASAC on board."

"Sure. Maybe we can give Ortega a nice heads-up so he won't move in the meantime. You know, an invitation to remain in place, awaiting arrest."

Doroz shot him a warning glance. "It's not my FBI anymore, Jeff. We've forgotten how to do crim work. Everybody just sits at computers and chases terrorism ghosts now. We have a War on Terror, in case you haven't heard."

"Sorry. I know it's not your call. We'll give you as much lead time as possible. See you downstairs."

———

Trask and Doroz watched as Wilkes walked the length of the car wash floor, spraying luminol, then waving his UV light over the areas he'd sprayed.

"Who was that old Greek guy, the one with the lamp?" whispered Doroz.

"I heard that." Wilkes didn't even look up from his work.

"Diogenes of Sinope," Trask said. "The original Stoic. He carried a lantern in the daytime, looking for an honest man."

"Yeah, him." Doroz looked at Trask and shook his head in disbelief.

"I'm looking for an honest clue in the dark," Wilkes shot back. "I didn't actually expect to find much here in the middle of the track, even though it's a great place to cut somebody up. You run the wash after you're done, and there are torrents of soap and water to wash everything down the drain. The more washes, the fewer clues." He stood up, looking around the building.

"Quiet, genius at work," Doroz said, smiling.

"Only if I find something, Mister Special Agent." He pointed toward the door where cars would enter the wash. "There, I believe."

"Because?" Doroz asked.

"Because they needed to load the body in a vehicle to dump it. The corpse thrown in front of your building had been used as a cutting board. It would have been leaking like a colander. If you are a functioning, thinking criminal, and you're using a pickup, you can wash the blood off the side of the truck by running it through the wash after you've dragged the bleeding corpse down there and thrown it into the truck bed. You don't want to do that in the middle of the wash while it's running. You'd get yourself soaked. There may be some dried blood in the concrete seams at that end. If they didn't hose it down well enough, we might get lucky."

Trask watched Wilkes get down on all fours, crawling the length and width of the entrance to the wash. Spraying, lighting, spraying, lighting. *I wonder if obsessive compulsive disorder is a prerequisite to being good at that job,* he thought. Then he smiled. *Or to my job.*

"Bingo!" Wilkes pointed to a corner of the wash where the walls met the floor. "Looks like they hosed it down some, but just shot the blood into this corner. They didn't think to hose the corner out." He pulled a swab from a small plastic bag, ran it along the joint, and returned it to the bag, marking it with a number and his initials. He then stood up and took a series of photographs of the area.

"Enough for some DNA, Frank?" Trask asked.

"I think so. Hope so," Wilkes said. "It'll take a while. It's not a TV show. I'll let you know."

Trask nodded. "Thanks, Frank."

7:15 p.m.

Crawford handed her the wine bottle as she answered her door. She was cooking for them this evening.

He sniffed the aroma as he walked in. *Another gourmet meal from the most beautiful girl on the planet. I should pinch myself, but I can't.* "That smells wonderful, as usual," he said.

She smiled, turned and kissed him long and hard. "I have many more dishes from my country to share with you," she said. "And many more days and nights, if you will let me."

"I'd love all of that, and all of you."

She smiled, kissed him again, then pulled back a little. "Have you ever thought of living in another country?"

"Not really, why?"

"I love you and your country, but I love mine, too. I don't know that I can keep this job forever. I may have to go home soon, depending on the situation at the embassy. I'm sure the government will name a new permanent ambassador, and he may want to bring a new staff with him."

He nodded, frowning.

"You could come with me, Michael," she said. "We—my family—have connections. You could be a permanent resident, and someone with your background would have no trouble finding work. The cost of living is very cheap compared to America. We could be together."

"There's nothing that means more to me than being with you, Marissa. But that would mean the end of my career here, and leaving *my* country is a lot to think about."

"You could have a similar career in El Salvador. We know many people there. I will help you with the language." She smiled at him and kissed him again, pulling herself tightly against him, her head on his shoulder. "I love you, Michael," she whispered. "We are so much alike. We love each other, like the same things." She looked into his eyes. "We even hate the same things, like criminals and murderous gangs who have no respect for order or society."

A timer on the stove went off.

"Dinner is ready. Will you at least think about it?"

"I already am," he said.

"Good!" She kissed him again. "Don't wait too long to give me your answer." She smiled at him over her shoulder as she walked toward the kitchen.

Luis Moreno-Montillo, also known as Jorge Rios-Garcia, also known as His Excellency, the acting ambassador of El Salvador to the United States of America, sat cleaning his sniper rifle at the desk formerly occupied by the late Juan Carlos Lopez-Portillo. He looked up as the big man entered the office.

"How is your wrist, Hugo?"

"A little sore, Jefe. It is healing, but bruised. The dog bit through some blood vessels."

"A pity you were not able to take care of both the woman *and* the dog." Moreno slapped the bolt assembly. "It is an impressive animal, however, even if not a purebred. At any rate, you may get another chance."

"Tonight, Jefe?"

"Perhaps. I don't know yet. I do know the FBI expects to learn of Ortega's whereabouts very shortly. As soon as we learn where he is hiding, I want the full team moving within minutes. Understood?"

"Of course, Jefe." The big man hesitated before leaving the room. "Jefe, you said the full team. We are short two men."

"I know. Have our alternates briefed and ready to participate. If they are willing to share in our venture's bounty, they must also be willing to share in the burdens."

"Jefe." Hugo bowed slightly as he left the ambassador's office.

Chapter Twenty-Four

Thursday, September 14, 9:30 a.m.

Despite the pressure of the impending deadline, Trask was in a relatively good mood when he got to the squad conference room. *No reason to get down today. Either we'll make some real progress, or we won't. Not much else that could go wrong or make things worse at this point.* Lynn walked in with a cup of coffee, and he smiled at her. *We're both alive, after all, and there's a lot to be said for that, given all we've been through lately.*

She saw his fingers drumming on the table. "Song?"

"'Second Chance' by .38 Special. Best slow song of the rock era, in my opinion. Poetic lyrics, soaring lead vocal, a dialogue between the vocal and lead guitar, and a gorgeous melody line and hook."

"I know the song. You have something to apologize for?"

Trask laughed. "No! You're focusing on the lyrics too much. I think they're good and heartfelt, but with the music in that song, they could be singing in Hungarian and I'd love it."

She nodded. "It *is* a great song." She sipped her coffee.

Carter and Wisniewski came into the room and sat down.

"No sunglasses today?" Trask asked. He got only sharp looks in return.

Willie Sivella was the next to enter. "Morning, Jeff, Lynn. Barry wanted me to tell you that the DEA guy is bringing someone with him. Somebody who's been in-country in El Salvador. He went down to the entry desk to let them in. Should be here any second."

"Good," Trask said. "Like Lassiter used to say, 'Info is ammo.' I've been feeling a bit unarmed lately. At least I was before Lynn uncovered the true identity of our Mr. Moreno."

"He's likely to be the main subject of our conversation today," Doroz said. He was standing in the door, motioning three other men into the conference room.

Trask recognized two of them: Steve McDonald from CIA, still wearing the bad sport coat, and Kevin Hall from DEA, still looking like a chemistry professor. The third man was carrying a laptop. He was shorter than McDonald or Hall, but he looked like he could have been a bouncer from a bar in a bad neighborhood. He was solidly built and dressed in a form-fitting polo shirt that accented every muscle in his arms and torso. Trask shook hands with McDonald first.

Hall was the next to extend his hand, and as he did so, he made the introduction. "Jeff Trask, this is Jason Mays, DEA's current station chief in El Salvador. When the name of Moreno-Montillo came up in our inquiry, Jason decided to fly up for the meeting."

"Nice to meet you," Trask said, barely avoiding a wince as Mays almost crushed his hand.

"You, too." Mays said. He put the laptop on the table. "How do I hook this into your display screen?"

"Puddin'!" Doroz barked. Crawford came into the room within seconds.

The three visitors glanced at each other.

"Just a nickname," Doroz said. "He has a real one. Gentlemen, Michael Crawford."

There were more handshakes.

"Mr. Crawford, please be so good as to work your Wi-Fi magic and connect Jason's computer to our wall monitor." Doroz shrugged. "Sorry guys, but too many new tricks for an old dog. I often require help in the digital age."

McDonald nodded in agreement. "I get left behind myself." He quickly shot a glance at Hall. "No comments required."

Trask saw that Crawford had apparently entered the required passwords. "Let's get on with this. What do you have for us, Jason?"

"Luis Moreno-Montillo," Mays began, pushing a key. A photo of Moreno flashed onto the monitor, the first in a series of PowerPoint slides. "He first came to our attention as one of the opposition activists, one of the FMLN opponents of the ARENA government. We also had street intelligence tying him to one of the smuggling operations in San Salvador, some real bad asses involved in the coke trade. I think you've already figured out that he went to UCLA with Lopez, the late ambassador."

"Yes, thanks to an incredible analyst whom I personally selected for this squad," Doroz said, nodding in Lynn's direction.

Lynn smiled at Trask, who saw that Mays noticed.

"She's my wife," Trask explained.

"Interesting," Mays said flatly. "Anyway, both Lopez and Moreno were part of the opposition for years and actually had contacts within the gangs in El Salvador, first with Barrio 18 and then later with MS-13. They certainly weren't members themselves, but they viewed the *Maras* as victims and byproducts of the ARENA government policies. Again, we had files on them because Moreno kept coming up as a money man for the coke smugglers and because Lopez was very close to Moreno."

Trask looked across the table at McDonald. "Did CIA have anything corroborating this?"

"Some," McDonald replied. "The activism, yes. The dope stuff, no."

"Looking the other way again?" Hall jabbed.

"Up yours, Kevin," McDonald shot back. "We weren't concerned with every two-bit snort merchant. We were trying to keep a friendly government in control."

"No two-bit ops here," Mays replied, fixing a stare on McDonald. "Tons of coke. Enough to help fund a lot of the FMLN politics, once the cash got washed a little. Our info is that Moreno was hooked into the Texis Cartel, the guys who control the smuggling routes from Colombia through Central America into Mexico. So if you'd followed the money—even though it was dope money—you'd have been interested in this, too. Moreno just kept his dope contacts after he switched sides politically."

And checkmate, Trask thought. *I think I'll be listening primarily to my new friend Mays for a while.*

"Anyway," Mays continued, "the fiction that the *Mara* punks weren't as bad as the ARENA government made them out to be hit the Moreno family before it came back on the Lopez family."

Mays hit a key on the laptop. The photo showed the body of a teenage girl. The top half of her head was missing.

"This is a Salvadoran police photo of Carolina Moreno—Luis' daughter—after she ate the wrong end of one of her daddy's shotguns. She'd been getting closer and closer with some of the *Mara* toughs from her school, and they invited her to a party one night. Her initiation party. She was gang raped and couldn't live with it. Her father found her body, heard what had happened to her at the hands of the MS-13, and went looking for the gangbangers who'd raped his daughter. He hunted them alone and did pretty well, all things considered. The Salvadoran cops I've talked to said he managed to kill five of the six who'd been involved in the rapes before the sixth one decided not to wait on his own fate and ambushed Moreno with some other *Maras*. They shot up his car pretty good, and the leader of the group hauled him out of his car and took out one of his eyes with a machete. They left him for dead, since he'd been shot seven or eight times. To everyone's surprise, he lived."

"Any idea who the banger was that slashed his eye?" Carter asked.

"Yeah. A real tough kid named Ortega. Esteban Ortega."

"Son of a bitch," Wisniewski exclaimed. "We've got Central America's Ahab up here hunting his whale!"

Dead on, Tim, thought Trask. *Melville, not Dumas. I should have figured it out before now. Blind rage is all that explains this. That's why it made no sense before. No political motives, not even gang warfare. Blind hatred and revenge is the only thing that explains all the indiscriminate killing.*

"Did Moreno stay affiliated with the FMLN after his daughter's death?" Trask asked. "I'm just wondering how he ended up here in their embassy."

"No," Mays said. "The cops in El Salvador, who'd been closely allied with the ARENA party, had been turning their heads while Moreno hunted the *Maras* who'd raped his daughter. Hell, they were probably feeding him leads. They were the ones who scraped him off the road and got him to a hospital after he got ambushed. When he was back on his feet, the ARENA guys recruited him to their side. He even started running some of their black shadow death squads. Mr. Hall here told me you'd done your homework on them."

"Yeah," Doroz said. "Moreno has left some of their calling cards in the area."

"So how does he wangle an appointment as the number two in an FMLN embassy?" Wisniewski asked.

"Through his buddy Lopez, after Lopez' son gets murdered—ostensibly by the MS-13—and only then by using an alias," Trask offered. "Lopez is facing the same grief and rage that Moreno did after losing a child, and knows that—despite the broad gulf in their current political views—Moreno has considerable expertise in *Mara* hunting. So Lopez imports 'Jorge Rios' into the embassy, and the next thing you know, we've got a wall full of murders. What do you think, Mr. Mays?"

Mays nodded. "Makes sense. There's no way the new government would have approved Moreno as an embassy official if they'd known who he really was. They really weren't prepared for the success they had in the election, no appointment systems in place since they hadn't been through it all before. They probably took Lopez' vouching for this 'Rios' guy and didn't ask many questions."

"Any way of finding out who he brought up with him?" Carter asked.

"As a matter of fact, yes," Mays said. "We were up on some coke deals involving Moreno and his people and even thought we'd be able to arrest Moreno himself, all with the blessings of the new government. In fact, I was at the airport in San Salvador with an ops team about to take him off when his goons start slapping diplomatic pouch tags on all their luggage, including the cases with the coke in it. I wasn't willing to risk alienating the new government when I saw the stickers. I figured somebody in the new regime was either on the take or knew something I didn't. Maybe Moreno was still on their side, a double agent or something. Anyway, I aborted our op at the airport, came away with nothing but some pics. Here they are."

The monitor image changed to show a photo of a large, dark blue sedan parked at the airport curb. Moreno was pointing to some bags at the rear of the car and an entourage of six men appeared to be carrying out his instructions.

"Do you have files on any of Moreno's goons?" Sivella asked Mays.

"Just a couple. The big guy there at the back is Hugo Vaca. I'll see if I can get a close-up out of this." Mays zoomed in to get a better view of the big man's face.

Lynn was suddenly standing, pointing at the monitor. "That's the asshole who tried to kill me!"

"*What?*" Mays asked. "Are you sure? If Hugo Vaca tries to kill you, you usually die. He's been with *La Sombra Negra* for years and—"

"You bet your ass I'm sure," Lynn said. "I was just lucky because—"

"Because they have a wolf," Doroz tried to explain.

"She's not a wolf, she's. . .never mind," Trask said, noting that Mays seemed to be very confused. "Can you zoom in on the other faces in that crew?"

Mays moved the cursor.

"Hold it there," Trask said as the zoom highlighted the face of another member of Moreno's team. Trask went to a file cabinet and pulled out a folder. He took an eight-by-ten photograph from the folder and slid it across to Mays. "A match?"

Mays looked at the photo, then the screen. "I'd say so. How'd he get the bullet in the face?"

"From me," Lynn said, "as he was trying to decapitate Jeff with a machete. That's actually an exit wound. I hit that one in the back of the head."

"That one?" Mays asked.

"There should be another one in that crew who we have in the morgue with an entry wound to the *front* of his head," Doroz said.

Mays moved the cursor again.

"Yep, him," Trask said, pulling another photograph from the folder.

Carter saw that Mays looked totally off balance, unaccustomed to a world in which attorneys and analysts chopped down thugs and escaped certain death. "Lynn is a former OSI agent," he tried to explain, "and a very good shot. She and Tim here took out a Jamaican hit man last year."

"We are overwhelming Agent Mays, guys," Trask said.

"Yeah, I'd say so," Mays acknowledged. "I don't know what I walked into here, but I'm glad that I could help. I think. Is there anything else—"

"Possibly," Trask said. "How are your contacts in the Salvadoran diplomatic corps?"

"I know some people," Mays replied.

"Good," Trask said. "Let's talk."

Trask excused himself from joining the others for lunch, saying he had a loose end or two to tie up at his other office. That was only partially true, as the single loose end he could think of was there in the squad room.

Puddin's been too smitten, and Lynn too busy with other things, to do a real review of that pole camera at the lawyer's office. I need to have a chance to look through it myself without offending anyone.

He found the disc and loaded it into one of the computers in the bullpen. Setting the video on fast-forward, he watched the hours roll by to see if any vehicles at all stopped at the law offices of the late Victor Scarborough. He saw one sedan pull into the parking lot, turn around, and re-enter the street.

Probably lost or looking for another address. He marked the time anyway. *I'll come back and check it if nothing else turns up.*

No other vehicles even entered the parking lot. After putting the video on double fast-forward for several minutes, Trask moved the cursor back to the point of the single turn-around.

He slowed the speed until he got the best angle of the driver's window, then zoomed in. A splash of red hair showed through the window.

Murphy! The son-of-a-bitch keeps turning up in the wrong place at the right time. He was either listening to us while we were at the embassy, or someone else was and sent him to check out the office. He's wired in to the old college clique a lot tighter than he should be, and he's been dirty from the moment I met him in Bear's office.

The thought hit his mind like a brick.

Bear's office!

The door to the room was not locked. Trask began with Doroz' desk, looking under and behind each edge. *Nothing there.* He stood up and looked around the room. *Why would there be anything there? It wouldn't be like Bear to leave him in here unattended, even if he was supposed to be a friendly. Where was Murphy when I first saw him in here?* His eyes darted to the chair closest to the door. *He sat in that same chair when he came back in to bring me that bogus file.*

Trask dropped to a pushup position, not wanting to move the chair or give any indication at all that someone might be looking for it, if in fact it was there. He rolled quietly on the floor and moved so his head could see the bottom. *There! On the inside edge toward the front!* He started to reach for the bug, but then quickly pulled his hand back and away. He got to his feet and left the office, shutting the door.

What did we say in there? What would they have heard? Bear's been in the conference room a lot more than he's been in here, thank God. Lynn did come in here to mention the MS-13 moving to the car wash from the convenience store. That's how they knew to hit the place the first time, and how they knew that the Maras were still using the car wash after the first drive-by. That's when they hit it again. They had to hear me earlier today when I told Bear that Santos was going to give us Ortega's location.

Trask heard the others returning from lunch. He motioned them into the conference room. McDonald wasn't with them.

"We seem to have lost our CIA representative," Trask said.

"He didn't feel loved in present company," Hall quipped.

"Probably doesn't matter," Trask said. "I think we have everyone we need for the moment. Bear, remember our little play in the ambassador's office?"

"Sure," Doroz said. He saw the questions on the faces around the table. "We were in the embassy after all the *Maras'* defense attorneys started turning up dead. Jeff planted the seed that one of the replacements might be a guy named Scarborough. Anyone listening probably didn't know that Scarborough was already dead. We put a pole cam on his office."

"And then this happened." Trask cued the video from the pole camera, again freezing it as the car turned in the parking lot and zooming in on Murphy's face.

"Shit!" Doroz stood up and pounded his fists on the table. "You had him pegged, Jeff. I just thought he was a typical State weenie."

"It gets better…or worse," Trask said. "He bugged your office. I found the mic while you were at lunch. It's under the chair he was sitting in the first day he came in. Their bug was listening to us discussing our bug. Theirs is probably a slap-on glue job."

"That sounds familiar," Carter remarked, shooting a glance at Sivella.

"Did you pull the damned thing?" Doroz asked.

"No," Trask said, "and I don't think we should. It explains how they knew to hit the car wash after the MS-13 crew moved in there—"

"You want me to leave their freakin' bug in my freakin' office?" Doroz asked. He caught himself. "Ohhhhh."

"Yep," Trask said. "They don't know we found it, and they had to overhear me telling you earlier that we had a source for Ortega's location."

"I get it. You can set 'em up," Mays chimed in. "Bravo. That ought to be quite a show. Moreno and his whole crew." He looked at Lynn and shrugged. "Or what's left of 'em."

"We need a good location and a whole lot of heavily armed good guys," Trask said. He looked at Doroz. "You have time to set up an operation with your SWAT guys? I lose control of this on Monday, and I'm not sure my successor—whoever that may be—will agree with this."

"It's already Thursday," Doroz noted. "No way. This has trouble written all over it, and I'd have to write the short version of *War and Peace* just to try and get it approved, then some clown up the command chain would disapprove it."

Trask looked at Hall.

"Same here," the DEA agent said. "Maybe if we were in-country in El Salvador, but not here."

"Your friendly local police can provide the requested services," Sivella said.

"Your SWAT guys can handle this?" Mays asked.

"We in the nation's capital do not have a SWAT team," Carter answered for his boss. "Being more politically sensitive, we have an ERT, an Emergency Response Team. They work out of our Special Operations Division and do seem to resemble what other city authorities would call a SWAT team or tactical unit. At any rate, our Kevlar Cowboys are quite good, and our operations plans do not require Department of Justice approval, unless, of course, the Assistant United States Attorney assigned to the case thinks that DOJ should weigh in on it."

"My neck's out as far as it can be already," Trask said. "Might as well try to bring our little murder spree to a close, even if we're just going to be deporting someone." He looked at Doroz, who had an eyebrow cocked. *He's thinking the same thing I am.* "I don't know if Moreno and his crew will go down without a fight. All we can do is corner them as well as we can and try to make it happen with a minimum of casualties."

"I know a spot," Sivella said. "My girlfriend has a brother in commercial real estate. How does an empty warehouse sound?"

"As good a spot as any, as far as I'm concerned, Willie," Doroz said. "But it isn't up to me anymore. This looks like your show from here on out."

"Accepted, then." Sivella nodded. "We'll need to brief the ERT guys and get them set up in place before Jeff and Barry issue the invitations. How does late Friday night sound? Can you two tailor something credible for our listening audience?"

"That shouldn't be a problem." Trask looked around the table for any signs of disagreement. There weren't any. "Sounds like a plan."

Everyone stood to leave the room.

Trask motioned to Crawford. "Mike, have a minute?"

Crawford came around the table. Doroz came around the other side.

"I don't think you should see her tonight," Trask said.

"And I agree," Doroz said. "If you have to, tell her you're sick or something. We can't risk a single wrong word on this, for any of our sakes, but especially yours."

Crawford nodded. He headed for the bullpen and his desk.

Trask turned back to Doroz. "You and I have a script to iron out."

Chapter Twenty-Five

Friday, September 15, 10:00 a.m.

The ERT briefing was held in Sivella's building, enabling both FBI and DEA assets to claim they were merely observing and assisting a Metro Police operation. Since neither federal agency had the time to clear everything with their command chain, those involved could not take the chance that something could go wrong. Without the required T-crossing and I-dotting, heads would roll. Better to let the cops play it out and pick up the pieces, if necessary.

Trask recognized the police captain in charge of the ERT from some prior cases. Chester Halsey Williams was a Naval Academy grad whose father, a Navy captain and Annapolis grad before him, had named his son after two World War II admirals. Somewhat to his father's chagrin, Midshipman Williams had chosen to accept a commission in the Marine Corps upon his graduation instead of aiming for a command in the surface fleet. After performing admirably in Iraq, where he had earned a purple heart for a leg wound, Captain Williams the marine had decided to become an officer of a different kind and had entered his second academy—the one that graduated metro cops. After a rapid rise through the ranks, he was a captain again, and his knowledge of urban warfare tactics had made him a natural fit to command the Emergency Response Team.

Trask received a pleasant nod from Williams as he entered the room with his command. "Colonel," he said, addressing Trask by his rank in the Air Force Reserve.

"Captain," Trask said, smiling back at him. "Good to have a marine on board for this one."

I mean that, too. No outfit I'd rather be with if I had to be in a ground fight.

Mays from DEA was the first to address the group.

"I'm happy to contribute what I know of your targets for this evening, gentlemen. These guys are not gangbangers or street thugs. You will probably be facing a squad—exact number unknown—of paramilitary operatives who know something about combat themselves. These guys have been through a civil war in their country, have probably been trained by US military or CIA instructors, and they'll fight hard and dirty. The plan I've seen gives you your best shot at forcing them to surrender, but do not assume they will. I wish you luck."

Sivella was next. He grinned, looking around the room at the faces of the officers. He knew many of them from their prior assignments in the department. They smiled back at him.

Everybody loves working for Cap'n Willie, Trask noted.

"You'll be setting up in a vacant warehouse in the 1300 block of 5th Street, NE. It's part of the farmers market area near the intersection of Florida and New York Avenues. I know a lady who knows a guy who knows the owner."

Trask smiled as the cops laughed. *And everybody knows about Willie and Kathy.*

"There's a back door, but it's blocked," Sivella said. "One way in for the bad guys, and—hopefully—no way out except unarmed and cuffed. They'll have to come in the front door. They'll be expecting a few undisciplined gang thugs. We've even arranged for a radio to be softly playing the greatest hits of El Salvador in a little office off to the side."

More snickers from the cops. *Willie has 'em at ease.* Trask glanced across the room at Captain Williams. *He isn't laughing. Going over the ops plan one last time before it's his turn. He's focused. Good.*

"There's plenty of cover inside, and you'll have plenty of time to set up before the subjects hit the front door. There may be a little wait involved, in fact. Don't get too relaxed or careless. As our friend from DEA said, these are serious people and they will mean you serious harm. Let's be safe and careful." Sivella looked at Williams. "Your show, Captain."

"Thank you, Commander." Williams swept the room with his eyes. The eyes that looked back at him were all business now. "Like the man said, our subjects may be well trained in combat tactics. If they choose not to lay down their weapons, even faced with an ambush and overwhelming force, we can expect them to charge and attack a point in our perimeter inside the warehouse. Expect automatic weapon fire. AK clones. Some of you have been in combat before. You know the sound."

Trask saw several heads nodding in agreement.

"We have a couple of bright spotlights centered in the warehouse that should serve to surprise and blind them. I don't want anybody using laser sights tonight. These guys will know to return fire at the sights. Expect them to shoot out the spotlights right off the bat if they want to fight it out, so don't set up by the spots. Pick your targets while they're lit up and before they realize they've been had. We'll demand their surrender in both English and Spanish when the lights go on. After that it's up to them. We don't know if they'll be wearing body armor, so expect it. If we take fire, don't assume that one shot will knock these guys down. Everybody clear?"

All the heads nodded again.

"Good. We'll roll in well after dark, give the area a chance to clear out. It's usually pretty deserted on a Friday night after about twenty-two hundred. We'll use the vans instead of the armored cars so we don't get noticed. The vans'll move out after we unload. We go in the warehouse, then everybody sits tight and quiet. I'll have a radio link to the commander and a mobile command post, and he'll have eyes outside. Like the commander said, safe and careful, guys."

They didn't know exactly when the listening end of the bug would be manned. Trask suspected it would be twenty-four hours a day, with some poor schmuck wearing the headphones even when nobody was in the whole FBI field office building, much less Doroz's office. Such was the nature of work in a dictatorial environment, and he strongly suspected that Moreno ran his group in such a fashion. Still, they couldn't take any chances, so they had to bait the hook before they set it. It was 3:00 before Trask and Doroz closed the door to the office.

"Looks like we got lucky," Trask said. He was sitting in the chair under which the bug was planted. "The attorney for Santos called me again. He has an appointment to meet with his client late this afternoon. His guy is supposed to give him the current location where we can find Ortega. That's the good news."

"That *is* good news," Doroz said. "What's the bad?"

"That we'll be working late again tonight. I don't expect to hear from this guy until after he has a chance to grab some dinner. He doesn't look like he misses any meals, if you know what I mean. I've got some errands to run myself, and you'll need a couple of hours to get an arrest team together and your precious ops plan written."

Doroz flipped him the finger.

"That being the case," Trask continued, returning the gesture, "what time do you want to meet back here tonight?"

"Why don't we say nine or so? That will give me time to get everything lined up. Once we get an address, it will still take some time to set up the ops plan. We can probably roll on Ortega about midnight."

"See you at nine, then," Trask said. He rose from the chair. "Open or shut?"

"I'll follow you out and get something to eat myself."

They shut the door after they were out of the office. Sivella was in the bullpen, grinning.

"Oscars for my friends," he said softly. "Jeff, you are a righteously evil guy. I knew Bear was an actor from all his undercover stints. I guess your courtroom theatrics gave you the background, too."

"Willie," Trask said, "I *never* act in court."

It was Lynn's idea. Dinner for everyone not wearing Kevlar at her favorite eatery, a giant, all-you-can-eat seafood place that had peanut shells for a floor and picnic tables and benches for furniture. Trask finished his huge plate of fried cod and waited patiently as his spouse, Sivella, Carter, Wisniewski, Doroz, and a very subdued Crawford did their collective best to rid the world of crabs. They were in a side room off the main dining floor, since Sivella "happened to know the owner."

"Jeff doesn't eat seafood," she explained.

"Not true," Trask said. "I eat fish, not bait. Those ugly things you are all devouring are nothing more than sea spiders. Arachnids. Eight legs, count 'em. Anyway, I'm working on the mental script for my next act in Barry's office."

"What's the plan after that, Cap?" Wisniewski asked.

"Mr. Trask and I will be climbing up the back side of an electrical supply company at the north end of the block," Sivella explained. "Jeff will have a view of the alley behind our target building if our target bad guys want to get fancy on us. I'll be looking straight down 5th Street watching the front of the building. ERT will all be inside. They're probably setting up already." He stopped for a moment to suck the meat out of a crab leg. "We'll have ERT helmets and radios on to stay in communication."

"Dix, I want you and Tim to take the surveillance van. Park it in the lot of that motel on the northwest corner of the block behind the alley. Bear, you're welcome to ride with them. Puddin' too, just in case we need extra eyes or guys on the street. There'll be extra helmets and radio packs in the van, too."

Lynn was fidgeting in her chair. "Jeff can't go," she said. "He might start throwing rocks at somebody with a gun."

"I *am* going," Trask corrected her. "I have the .45, if I need it—and I won't—and a vest, if I need it—and I won't. I'm staying on the roof, above the fray, just monitoring, but if any of these creeps have something to say, I'm going to make sure our evidence is properly taken and preserved. We've only got six hours for the interrogations after any arrests. So sayeth the Supremes in their collective wisdom. Anything longer is presumed to be a violation of the perp's rights. I trust Williams and his guys to do everything *tactically* correct, but I want to make sure we have it all *legally* correct. We're going to hand this over to some unknown stiff on Monday, and I don't want him or her having to even consider *not* charging something or somebody because of some proof problem."

Trask looked at Lynn. "*You* on the other hand, will be remaining at the field office squad room because you are still recovering from a concussion. End of discussion."

"The hell I will—"

"Supervisor's orders, Lynn," Doroz said, his mouth only half full of a hush puppy. "Doctor's orders, too, if I recall correctly. I'd trust you like my best agents on the street if you were healthy and had a badge, but Jeff's right on this one. Besides, I need someone to man the phones in case we have to call in more cavalry."

"Shit," she said. She turned to Sivella. "Willie, if my favorite prosecutor tries to get off that goddamn roof too soon, you have my permission to shoot him in the butt."

"I'll be going out in front of him if we go," Sivella said. "But if he outruns me, I could probably manage that."

Trask looked at his watch, then at Doroz. "Had enough sea spiders?"

"Not really, but it's about that time." Doroz wiped his face with a napkin and downed what remained of a glass of iced tea. "Come on, Lynn. You're heading back with us."

"I'll get the check," Sivella said. "Dix, you and Tim take Puddin' and get the van. You can pick Bear and Jeff up after they play scene two, then head for the motel. Everybody gears and arms up, understood?

"I just heard from the mouthpiece," Trask said. "Ortega's holed up in an empty warehouse on the west side of the 1300 block of 5th Street, NE. I brought it up on Google maps. The warehouse front has metal bars, with a door cut in 'em. Center of the block, the only front with no sign above the door. There's a chain and a padlock on the door. Santos told his attorney that Ortega locks himself in at night to help slow down any rival gangbangers, so we'll need some bolt cutters on the entry team. Santos said they've pulled a dumpster against the back door in the alley so nobody can sneak up on 'em from behind. Ortega has about three other *Maras* with him. I printed a photo of the warehouse front and the block. You can use these to brief your arrest team."

"Sounds good," Doroz said. "They're in the conference room. I'll get started. We should be able to roll on this about midnight."

They got up and left the office. Trask made sure to give the chair a nice noisy scrape across the floor on his way out. *Hope you have the goddamn headphones on yourself, Moreno.*

They took the elevator down to the waiting van.

Chapter Twenty-Six

Friday, September 15, 10:14 p.m.

An ocarina was playing in Trask's head. The theme from *The Good, The Bad and The Ugly.* He was on a roof staring southward through the binoculars down the alley that ran between the 1300 blocks of 4th and 5th Streets, NW. *I know who the ugly is. I'll figure out the rest later. This must be the scene in the flick where the Blue and the Gray fight over the river bridge. Wonder how old Hugo Montenegro came up with that ocarina idea?.*

The supply building they were on faced southward on Penn where 5th Street T'd into it. At the far end of the block to the south was Neal Place, running parallel to Penn and crossing 4th and 5th Streets. The motel was on his right, across Penn, and he could see the surveillance van in the parking lot in front of the place. Sivella was about forty feet to his left, also looking over the edge of the roof with binoculars. Trask heard him start the communications check.

"ERT set?"

"We're in place, Commander." Trask heard Williams' voice loud and clear through his headset. *Once a marine, always a marine. That sounded like he was about to brief an admiral.*

"Bear, you read us?"

"Gotcha, Willie."

"Good. Dixon?"

"Yes, sir, Cap."

"Good. Everybody relax. We'll let you know when we see anything. Jeff, keep a lookout for vehicles approaching from the north and the west. I'll watch east and south."

"Will do," Trask said. *Twenty-eight years in blue. I almost said, "Roger." Some things get burned into your brain if you do them enough.* He trained the binoculars southwestward down New York Avenue and rolled onto his right side to follow the route to the north. *What am I looking for exactly? Anything big enough to hold an assault team. Six to ten people, probably. A large van or stretch SUV, maybe even a panel truck. If they're coming from my side, they'll have to come up on Florida Avenue from the south or get off New York onto 4th Street.*

Trask turned his attention back to the south and west. He saw a pair of headlights turn off New York onto Florida, heading south and east, toward where 4th and 5th crossed Florida, the larger street. The lights turned northward onto 5th Street. The vehicle was close enough now to make out: a long bed van. "Willie, I got a—"

"I see him," Sivella said. "Van heading north on 5th off Florida. Everyone saddle up." Sivella watched the van as it drove straight toward him, approaching the target block. When it reached Neal Place, however, the truck turned left. "Turning your way, Jeff. Watch him."

Trask trained the binoculars southward down the alley. The van slowed, and Trask saw a single figure wearing a ski mask and dressed in black from head to toe jump from the front passenger door. He was carrying a very long-barreled rifle. The second the man was out of the truck, it was rolling again.

"One shooter just bailed at the south end of the alley," Trask said. He turned the binoculars toward 4th Street. His view was obscured for a moment by the roof of the motel, but the van appeared again, headed north on 4th, then made a quick right onto Penn, right below them.

Sivella saw it, too. "Here we go, guys," he said.

The van slowed again at the north end of the alley, and a second figure with a long gun ran southward down the alley along the back wall of the motel. The van continued eastward, then turned south down 5th Street toward the warehouse. Trask was about to announce the second shooter's location, but Sivella beat him to it.

"Second shooter setting up in the north end of the alley," Sivella said. "They didn't believe Jeff when he told them the back door was blocked. Dix, you and Tim circle around behind the shooter at the south end of the alley. Bear, you and Crawford take the one on the north end. Be careful, guys. Captain Williams, your party guests are about to ring your doorbell."

Trask froze and listened. The ocarina wasn't playing anymore. He saw Carter and Wisniewski disappear across the front of the motel, heading south. Doroz and Crawford came out of the van behind them and started making their way to the north end of the alley, moving slowly along the north wall of the motel. Trask saw the closest sniper set up behind a crate along the west side of the alley, his back to Trask and the north, training his rifle southward toward the back of the warehouse. Doroz looked up at him, and Trask held his hand up. Doroz froze, Crawford behind him. Trask held up one finger and motioned it forward and to the right. Doroz nodded.

"Main raid team's out of the van. I count five. Point man has bolt cutters," Sivella said. "Dix, Bear, hold until they go in. If there's action inside, it'll divert your shooters' attention."

Trask strained to hear, his gaze fixed down the alley. Four or five seconds passed, and he heard Williams' voice again, shouting this time.

"Police! Drop your weapons! Policia——"

The warnings were interrupted by the low, guttural chatter of the AK clones, followed by a steady scream of higher-pitched automatic fire, the Colt submachine guns used by the ERT. Trask looked down into the alley and saw that Doroz and Crawford were already close behind the north end sniper, screaming at him to drop his weapon. The would-be shooter dropped the rifle and raised his hands in surrender. Doroz bent down to cuff him while Crawford stood to the side, his gun trained on the subject. *You're too exposed, Puddin'!* Trask raised the binoculars toward the south end and to his horror saw the other sniper, half standing now with the sniper rifle drawing a bead on Crawford.

"*MIKE, GET DOWN!*" Trask yelled.

Crawford spun toward him instead, looked up for a moment, and then dropped into a crouch at the instant two gunshots flashed and echoed from the south end of the alley.

"Our shooter's down." Trask heard Wisniewski's voice report.

"Clear inside, Commander," Williams reported from the warehouse. "I've got one of my guys nicked. Nothing serious. Four targets down. One wounded in custody. We're calling for two ambulances and some body transports."

"Got it. I'll start Crime Scene." Sivella stood up and walked toward him. "Nice work, Jeff. Let's go see if anyone wants to talk to us."

They climbed down the fire escape at the back of the building and walked around to the front. Doroz and Crawford were escorting their prisoner to the curb. Trask heard the sirens of the ambulances as they approached the area.

"Jeff, Commander, I think you better see this before you go in." It was Carter's voice in the earphones.

Trask followed Sivella down to the south end of the alley where Carter and Wisniewski were standing by the body of the other sniper. A blood-soaked ski mask lay on the concrete beside the shooter's head. Sivella took a flashlight from his belt and pointed it down into the lifeless eyes of Marissa Moreno.

"She recognized Puddin'," Wisniewski said. "That's why she didn't shoot. Goddamit. I didn't know."

"He *didn't* know, Cap," Carter said. "She had the mask on. Tim did the right thing. I was two steps behind him and saw it, too. I thought she was about to fire. I'd have taken her down myself."

Sivella nodded. "You guys back out a bit. Somebody's got to tell him. I'll do it."

Trask watched as Sivella walked back up the alley, speaking first to Doroz. The lights from the streetlight by the motel silhouetted them. Trask saw Doroz pat Crawford on the shoulder. They started walking toward him.

"Sorry, Mike," Trask said as they approached. "I saw it from the roof. That's why I yelled at you to drop. She had a bead drawn on you and was masked up. Tim and Dix couldn't have known who she was. They were protecting you."

Crawford didn't say a word. He sat down beside the body and started stroking her hair and face. When his tears started flowing, he pulled the gun from his holster and handed it to Doroz.

There's nothing I can say that will mean anything here. I was almost looking at Lynn this way. Trask left them and walked around to the front of the warehouse. Williams was barking instructions to his team and waving one of the ambulances over.

The good guy goes to Medstar, Trask thought. *The bad guy...who is the bad guy? He said he had a survivor.*

Trask stepped through the framed hole in the bars that passed for a door into the warehouse. He looked down to see a chain—cut open by the bolt cutters lying beside it—and a padlock lying on the sidewalk. He noticed as he entered the warehouse that Williams' team had already pulled the masks off the bodies, but left the corpses in place for the crime scene guys to photograph. Even though the cops were the shooters this time, everything had to be documented as if it were any other homicide. Trask stepped carefully around any shell casings he saw on the concrete floor. He asked one of the ERT guys for a flashlight.

The first face he saw meant nothing to him. *Looks to be Central American. One of Moreno's squad from the airport, I think.* He stepped a few feet to his right, and the light's beam fell onto a more familiar face. *Murphy. Can't say that I'm surprised at this point.* The third face also looked familiar. *So you're the one who was going to kill my wife.* He saw what appeared to be the edges of a bandage sticking out from under the black sleeve on the corpse's right arm. *I hope that Boo bit the ever-loving shit out of you and that you cried like a schoolgirl all the way home.* He scanned the other body's face, not recognizing it. *Dammit. Where is he?*

Trask looked up to see two of the ERT troops escorting a man out into the lights in the street. He followed and waited for them to turn the man toward him. It was Moreno.

"Read him his rights, guys," Trask said. He saw blood oozing from Moreno's right shoulder. "Get him to the hospital as soon as you can. Go ahead and take him to the ER at Howard. It's the closest. At least three of you with him in the ambulance." He looked at his watch. *10:48 p.m. My six hours are running.* He phoned Lynn, told her he was OK, and told her to meet him at the hospital.

"Jeff?" Sivella stopped him as Trask was getting in a squad car. "Think it might be time to give your boss a call? We just shot up a bunch of foreign nationals, killed a State Department employee, and wounded an acting ambassador."

"Thanks for thinking about me, Commander. Not yet. That call will go much better if what we have planned at the hospital actually works. I've got one other call to make."

The staff at the Howard University Hospital Emergency Room, a Level I Trauma Center, was not unaccustomed to the treatment of gunshot wounds. The hospital staff was not, however, accustomed to treating such wounds without the use of anesthetics or with providing treatment in the presence of large, black-clad ERT officers who refused to leave the patient being treated.

"We have him in a private room now, as you requested," the doctor told Trask. "The bullet went through the shoulder; some tissue damage but nothing major. All we had to do was sew him up. He's still in a lot of pain, of course, since he refused any anesthesia. He wouldn't even let us use a local. Are you sure this can't wait until morning?"

"Is there any danger to him if I speak with him now?" Trask asked.

"Probably not. Still, tomorrow would be better, if you can wait."

"Sorry, it can't." Trask was already on his way to the room. He passed the nurse's station where Lynn and Jason Mays were waiting with another man. "Ready?"

Mays nodded and gave him a thumbs-up; Lynn smiled and winked at him.

Trask walked past the ERT guys into the room and shut the door. *Helluva breach of normal procedure, being in here without a witness, but I'm already conflicted out of the trial team. No harm in being a witness myself at this point.* Moreno was lying in the bed, one hand cuffed to the rail. He looked at Trask, expressionless. Trask pointed at the bandage on Moreno's shoulder. "You should have let them give you a local."

"So you could drug me? Question me with sodium pentathol? Are you wearing a wire now?"

"No." Trask pulled up the hem of his shirt. "See? No wire. As for the drugs, our Constitution doesn't allow that for criminal cases. This is a criminal case, and you appear to be the criminal, or at least one of two surviving criminals. The other one—your Mateo—is down at police headquarters singing like a bird."

"Mateo is a good man. You are lying. He would not talk."

"I *could* be lying. We are actually allowed to use ruses and trickery in interrogations as long as we don't violate the rights of a prisoner. We have to carefully guard those rights, regardless of how many people an arrested criminal may have killed, or tried to kill."

"You have proven very difficult to kill, Mister Trask."

"So you admit that? Remember that you have been warned of your rights. Are you waiving them?"

"Why not? My rights go far beyond your Constitution. I am the ambassador from El Salvador. I have complete diplomatic immunity, as you are aware. I demand that I be transported to your Reagan Airport immediately so that I can return to my country."

"That's not going to happen, Moreno."

The man with the eye patch frowned.

"Yeah, we know who you really are," Trask said. "You're going to be charged Monday morning with importation and conspiracy to distribute cocaine. You're not going anywhere."

Moreno snorted in contempt. "You have no authority to deny my request."

"You're right, but I told you that Mateo is singing. You thought I was lying. He was very worried when we told him that he could be locked up with hundreds of *Mara* inmates unless he cooperated with us. He's just a staff weenie, if he's on the diplomatic list at all. No immunity for him. As for your status, those cocaine charges will be the tip of the iceberg, but they'll hold you for now. Assuming that the ballistics on those two sniper rifles we recovered from the alley match the rounds from the *Mara* victims, there will be murder charges added later."

"You have no right to hold me for any charges," Moreno shrugged. "I have full diplomatic immunity, as I said." His face showed a hint of concern. "One of my party was a girl—"

"Yes, your niece Marissa. Thanks to you, she is also dead. Your hunt for those who attacked your daughter has killed far too many."

Moreno's arm jerked against the cuff that restrained him. "You have no right to even mention her," he growled.

"Don't rip your stitches," Trask said calmly. "I have every right to question you about each aspect of this little crime spree you've run, including your motives. When did it start? With the murder of the Barrio 18 kid in Northeast? Is he the one who killed Armando Lopez?"

"Yes, he killed Armando." Moreno's face contracted into a sneer. "At my direction."

Trask kept his poker face despite his surprise. *I'm in control of this little duel, you psycho, not you. Why? Oh, I get it.* "Yes, we thought that might be the case. Frame the MS-13 for that murder, get your college buddy the ambassador to invite you up to solve the problem, and now you're in the country and free to pursue your hunt of Esteban Ortega. You just had to kill the 18er to tie up a loose end. Is that how it went?"

"Yes. Precisely. It was our only way to get into your country, and the diplomatic immunity was a considerable bonus. I demand transportation to the airport immediately."

"Pretty sloppy, Moreno, using the same gun on that kid and on the attorneys, then leaving it in my den. You had to know the ballistics would tie the gun to you and your guys."

"The plan was to leave it in the dead hand of Ortega after I killed him. You would have thought him responsible for all of the murders."

"Maybe. Did you kill Armando's parents, too, Moreno? Was that just another frame job to make us think the *Maras* did it? Must have been at least a little bit difficult carving up your friend and his wife like that."

"I *was going* to kill them. The idiots in the new government had signed a truce with the gangs. A *stinking truce* with the vermin that ruined our nation and killed my daughter and so many more." He looked at Trask defiantly. "I would not have cut them, I would just have shot them like the dogs they had become. The *Maras* must have beaten us to them. They were already dead when we got there."

"I'm sure Ortega blamed them for bringing you and your crew into town and declaring open season on them. And the defense attorneys, Moreno? Why kill them? They were just doing their jobs. They were innocent. They had families, too."

"They were trying to free the *Maras*. They spoke for them."

"And me? *My wife*? We were trying to prosecute the gangs, get them off the streets." *Explain that to me, you sick son of a bitch.*

"You were interfering. If you got to Ortega first, you could have put him out of my reach. You should have just let us manage it in our own way. We would have cleaned up quite a bit of your local gang problem and then returned home."

"Cleaning it up for us? Is that what you call those slaughters at the car wash?"

"Call them what you like. I prefer to call them eradications. Pest control, I think you call it. I wish to return home now. If you will not honor my request to provide transportation to the airport, please connect me with someone in your State Department so I may make an official demand."

"I will not do that, Moreno. Your State Department mole is in the morgue with the rest of your team. Murphy can't help you anymore. What was his stake in this, anyway?"

"Money. He just wanted money, always more money. He didn't want to come with us tonight. I made him, told him he was going to earn his money like a man, for once. You can call someone else at your State Department."

"Like I said, I'm not going to do that. I *will* introduce you to someone in your own Ministry of Foreign Relations. Bring him on in, Jason."

"What? Who are you speaking to? You said you were not wearing a wire!"

"I'm not, Moreno. There's a microphone above your bed that can be monitored from the nurse's station up the hall. Getting out of a hospital bed can be tricky. We wouldn't want you falling and hurting yourself without being able to send help right away."

Trask opened the door. Mays and the other man entered the room.

Trask stepped aside, but he never took his gaze off Moreno. "May I present Miguel Navarrete-Ponce, very recently named the new ambassador to the United States from El Salvador. He has something to say which I believe will be of interest to you."

"Luis Moreno-Montillo," Navarrete announced officially, "as the officially delegated representative of El Salvador in this country, I now inform you that any diplomatic status which was previously conferred upon you in your true name, *or* in the name of Jorge Rios-Garcia, is hereby revoked and waived." He turned to Trask. "He is your prisoner now, Mister Trask, and may be prosecuted according to the laws of your country." He handed Trask an envelope. "The written waiver has been signed and sealed by the president of El Salvador."

"This is a violation of international law!" Moreno screamed.

"I assure you that it is in accordance with the provisions of the Vienna Convention on diplomatic relations," Navarrete said. "If you were a real diplomat, and not just a murderous disgrace to your nation, you would know that."

Trask turned to Mays, who had produced a small metal object from his pocket. "Did your little digital recorder get it all?" he asked.

Mays nodded. "Every word of it. These hospital mics are actually very good. I might have to pick up a few of 'em."

Moreno continued to scream at them in Spanish, the sounds of fury from a defeated madman.

Trask walked into the hallway and spoke to one of the ERT guards. "Nobody in or out except for *verified* medical personnel. *Verified*, OK? Tell the doc he can shoot this guy up with whatever he wants to now, as long as it's medically justified. He probably needs considerable sedation, and the rest of the patients on the ward will need their sleep."

"Got it, Colonel," the man said.

Colonel, Trask smiled to himself. *It's going to take some time to shake that one.*

Navarrete had followed him out into the hallway.

"Thank you, Mister Trask. You have served both our countries well today."

"As have you, Mr. Ambassador. How is the truce going with your gangs back home?"

Navarrete almost spit on the floor. "It is a sham, of course." He noticed the surprise on Trask's face. "I am a realist, Mr. Trask. There *are* some of us in the new government. Thugs are thugs, regardless of their political affiliations. We had several schoolboys murdered a few days ago in Las Colinas. The MS-13 had been trying to recruit them at their school, and when the boys refused, they were taken out and stabbed to death, then dumped into a mass grave. The youngest was fifteen. I am afraid that both our countries will be fighting them for some time to come." He reached into a pocket of his sport coat. "Here is my card, with my cell number. Please call me at any time if I can be of further assistance."

Trask nodded. "Mr. Ambassador." He followed Navarrete up the hallway.

Sivella was standing in the hall by the nurse's station with Lynn. Both were beaming.

"Nice work again," Sivella said. "Think it's time for that phone call yet?"

"Yeah," Trask said, reaching for his cell phone. "This won't be pretty."

Chapter Twenty-Seven

Saturday, September 16, 9:30 a.m.

Ross Eastman, the United States Attorney for the District of Columbia, sat behind his desk staring at Trask. "I don't know whether to fire you or pin a medal on you, Jeff. If you'd called me to let me know this was going to happen—"

"Ross, we didn't *know* what was going to happen," Willie Sivella said. "We had it planned as a controlled arrest scenario. Moreno and his goons were the ones who refused to surrender."

"The press is going to claim it was a staged massacre and an ambush, Willie. You know that." Eastman walked around to the front of his desk and leaned against it.

He's relaxing a little, Trask thought. *I might get out of here alive.*

"And you know we can't control what some of those freaks write," Doroz chimed in. "They're going to spin it the way they want to spin it, regardless of the truth."

"He's right, Ross," Bill Patrick said. "We can defend everything that's been done here, and these guys were trying to protect you in case something went bad."

Eastman stared at Trask again. "You've got a lot of defenders here, Jeff. I want to hear from you." He shot a look back at Patrick before returning his stare to Trask. "Convince me that this didn't 'go bad,' as your *current supervisor* calls it."

Trask measured his words for a moment. "We found the bug in Barry's office. We certainly suspected who was on the other end, but didn't know for sure. The bug explained a lot, but left dozens of questions unanswered. Did we set a trap? Definitely. Did we know things could get hot out there? Of course, given the fact that we've had executions popping up all over town. I saw it as a chance both to answer some of those questions and to apprehend the killers. We controlled the situation with as many tactical boundaries as we could to protect the public. Moreno and company decided they didn't want to be apprehended. In the final analysis, we had one good guy wounded, and we took down or apprehended all the perpetrators."

"That sounds like your response to the press, if you ask me, Ross," Sivella said.

"It's a start, Willie, but I didn't ask you," Eastman said curtly. "The least Mr. Trask could have done is to have followed your suggestion to call me from the warehouse. We have a wounded ambassador and a dead State Department employee, for God's sake. Do we have enough evidence to lock them down as being involved?"

"Ross, if I had called you from the warehouse, you would have been in the same mood you're in now, and rightly so," Trask said. "You'd have probably jerked my remaining chain so short that I would not have been allowed to follow up at the hospital with Moreno. With his taped confession and other evidence in the case, we do have more than enough to answer any questions the press, or the AG, or State, or the White House may have, and we even have the backing of the Salvadoran government. It was also my goal, Ross, to keep you and my 'current supervisor' out of this until we could make it right."

"I assigned you to this case, Jeff, and I don't need protecting from myself. And if this big walrus," Eastmen gestured toward Patrick, "told you otherwise, he was wrong." He took a long breath. "Thanks for your concern, anyway. Both of you. Bill, your job now is to convince some of those press hounds in our conference room that one of them could win a damned Pulitzer if they get this story right. If you figure out how to do that, let me know. It'll help me answer the questions coming from upstream. We have ten minutes before the press conference that I had to call before I knew what the hell I was going to say."

12:20 pm.

"What did Ross tell the press?" Lynn asked.

"He basically quoted your husband's answers to his own questions," Doroz said, chewing a bite of his burger. "I think he calmed down. Everybody's safe with Ross, including Jeff's 'current supervisor.'"

"Ross dressed down *Bill Patrick*?" she asked.

"Just for a minute," Trask said. "They go back a long way. I think he was just pissed at being kept out of the loop and wanted Bill to know that. Point taken. Anyway, we get to stay on the case of Esteban Ortega. No conflict there. I just have to hand off everything on Moreno to the Prince of Alexandria. The Department gave the case to G. Gary Gray from the Eastern District of Virginia. I'm briefing him after lunch."

"You're shitting me," Lynn said. "Isn't that the guy who walked out on that terrorism case in Phoenix?"

"Yep. The G unit charged a dozen defendants with financing terrorist activities, got a mistrial, and then left that appointment to get closer to Washington and the big money firms. He left his former office holding the bag, and they had to scramble to get ready for the re-trial. At least they won it. My spies in Alexandria think he lobbied for this one because it can be the feather in his cap that gets him a high-six-figure job on K Street with one of the big lobbying firms. He figures he can get the first death penalty in the District in the last century."

"You think he's got a shot at that, Jeff?" Doroz asked.

"There are plenty of bodies and statutory aggravating factors for the Department to certify the case as capital," Trask said, "but in the final analysis, I doubt it. Odds are that Magistrate Noble will appoint J. T. Burns to represent Moreno. He won't be able to stop a conviction—there's too much evidence—but he'll eat Gray alive on the sentencing phase. Moreno's dead daughter is a powerful mitigating factor, and Burns will pull a high-dollar shrink in to say that the loss of his little girl snapped something in Moreno's mind. This is a predominantly black town, and our jurors don't think that capital punishment has ever been fairly applied. I'll probably end up having to testify to get Moreno's confession admitted."

"You did pretty well against Burns in the Reid case," Lynn said. "You can handle him from the witness stand, too."

"I don't think it's going to matter," Trask said. "Moreno will get convicted here, then he'll get life. The wild card is what happens in Maryland after the first trial. If Gray doesn't get a death verdict here, the Maryland guys get a shot at Moreno for the murders he committed there. Depending on the jury pool, a capital verdict there isn't out of the question. Anyway, you guys need to give Gray all the help he needs, whether or not you think he deserves it. He'll be a pain in the ass to work with, but the goal is convicting Moreno. Remember that."

"Not a problem," Doroz said. "You've just spoiled us a little. At least we can still work on Ortega. What's the next move there?"

"Finding him," Trask said. "Hopefully our friend Santos can get a lead on that. It's my guess that Ortega's got his head down somewhere in Fairfax County on the Virginia side. That's where that heaviest concentration of MS-13 types live around DC. Santos' attorney is supposed to get back with me on that." He looked at Doroz. "How's Puddin'?"

"He's gone, left his credentials on my desk with a letter of resignation. He had some leave on the books, so I signed him out in case he changes his mind. I just don't expect him to."

Trask nodded, looking at Lynn. "If you were gone—"

"Don't say that, Jeff," she said. "This is who you are. You're needed here."

"Still, that had to be a hell of a blow," Trask said. "If you were gone, I'm not sure *who* I'd be anymore."

3:00 p.m.

"I fully expect to get a capital verdict in this case, given the evidence," Gray said as he looked around the squad conference room. Trask's incident summaries were still pinned to the wall.

"Good luck with that," Trask said. "Burns is no pushover."

"I hear you did well against him in the Reid case." Gray was still looking at the wall.

Trask sized him up. Gray was a tall, blond guy who could have had a career as a male model, and had probably been told that by anyone who could hold his attention long enough to pry him away from a mirror.

"We got lucky and found a smoking gun. Even with that, I'm not sure the jury would have given Reid the juice," Trask said. *If you don't get your verdict, you'll find someone else to blame. It certainly won't be your fault, will it?*

"I'm certain I can have the same success that you did, Jeff. I was first in my class at UVA law, was editor of the Law Review, and I've had over thirty trials now. How many have you had?"

"I stopped counting at three-hundred," Trask said. He saw the jolt in Gray's demeanor. It lasted only a second.

"Impressive. How did you come by all that experience?"

"About 275 courts-martial. I had the whole Southeast. Twenty-five bases. On the road for five years, trial to trial."

"Oh, so those were *military* trials."

Trask didn't react. He had expected the comment. "We used the Federal Rules of Evidence, with some small modifications. They were real trials, with judges, juries, and everything. And since you were wondering, I attended Ole Miss Law. Not Law Review though. I decided to get more trial training so I went to the Moot Court Board. They had a higher GPA than the Law Review while I was there. You have everything you need now?"

"Yes, I think so. Thanks for the update."

Chapter Twenty-Eight

April 4, 1:30 p.m.

It was time. And the time had arrived much sooner than Trask had expected. The Department had certified the case for a capital sentencing hearing if a conviction was returned on the homicides. That had not been a surprise. What *had* surprised him was the speed with which the trial date had approached. Burns was his usual crafty self and had pushed the case forward, asserting Moreno's right to a speedy trial instead of asking for the usual barrage of delays.

The old fox knows that the government's case actually gets better *with additional time to prepare; it's just a myth that a delay always benefits the defense.*

Trask paced back and forth in the witness room. At least Gray was doing one thing correctly, saving the confession—the coffin nail—for the close of the case. That's why Trask was testifying last. Gray had used Lynn to testify about the attacks on them in their home, saving Trask to describe the events at the hospital after Moreno's arrest.

Start strong, finish strong, and bury any weaknesses in the middle. . .trial advocacy 101. The jury'll convict him of the homicides, and the judge will then surprise them by telling them that they now have to consider the death penalty or life without release. A bifurcated, or two-part trial. Guilt phase followed by sentencing phase. That's where the challenge will be for you, Gray old man.

Trask wasn't really nervous. He'd been a witness in a couple of other cases, courts-martial to be precise. He'd also prepared hundreds of witnesses for trial before and had mentally split his own personality in order to coach himself while getting ready for this moment. *But it's J. T. Burns. I know I could handle him if I were trying the case, but Gray's sitting in that chair, not me.*

He'd forced himself to separate as much as possible from the task force, leaving them to the tender mercies of G. Gary Gray for the past couple of months. He'd had to do it. It was Gray's case, and if he was to have any chance of prosecuting it successfully, Gray would have to be comfortable with it, massage it, mold it into something he knew. Trask's continued presence would have been too much of a distraction.

He had, nevertheless, been given a nightly update by Lynn regarding Gray's management ability and techniques, usually laced with language that would make a veteran sailor retreat. Trask was somewhat surprised that Gray had survived to see the beginning of the trial. He was convinced that several of the investigators on the task force had been considering the commission of their own perfect crime.

Since Trask was a fact witness in the case, he had been prohibited from watching any of the trial. He had been getting summaries from Barry Doroz, who had been allowed to remain at counsel table with Gray as the government's case agent. He had been told several times by Bear that he could have done a better job, but that the proof was going in with few problems. Trask remembered the Reid case. *Burns is no "springbutt" as Lassiter had called them. He won't be attacking every little thing just because he can. And if he isn't attacking anything yet, he's saving his ammo for what he thinks he* can *attack successfully. That target might be painted on me.*

The knock on the door startled him, even though he'd expected it. Tim Wisnewski had been acting as the witness manager for the trial team.

"They're ready for you, sluggo. Go get 'em."

"Yeah. Thanks, coach," Trask said as he grabbed his suit coat and buttoned it. "If I'm not out in an hour, call the police or something."

The huge oak doors leading into the courtroom of United States District Judge Waymon Dean closed behind him. Trask walked down the aisle separating the two sides of the peanut gallery, the section of the courtroom reserved for spectators and the press. It was full. A sound feed had actually been provided into a second, empty courtroom so the overflow who had not been admitted to the day's proceedings could hear the trial in progress. It was audio only. Cameras weren't allowed in federal court. Trask pushed through the low, swinging double doors into the well of the courtroom, raised his hand and took the oath, then climbed the four steps to the chair in the witness stand.

Gray smiled at him from the podium in the center of the courtroom.

"Please state your name and your place of employment."

"Jeffrey Trask. I'm an Assistant United States Attorney for the District of Columbia."

Gray, to his credit, let Trask tell the story of Moreno's confession with few interruptions, only breaking up the narrative with questions as required by the Federal Rules of Evidence. Narratives weren't actually supposed to happen; lawyers were supposed to ask questions, and witnesses were supposed to answer them. Another legal fiction.

Trask noticed that Burns appeared to be bored with the whole tale. Moreno, seated beside Burns at the defense table, had been well coached. The malevolent stare from the hospital room was disguised for the court proceedings. Only once or twice did the defendant's single, functioning eye look up at Trask, and then it quickly retreated to the papers on the table.

There was a fifteen-minute break following the direct examination. Trask headed for the men's room for a final pit stop before cross. Burns was there when he entered.

"Hello, Jeff."

"J. T."

"New role for you?"

"I've done it before, actually."

"Good. This should be fun, then. See you shortly."

Yes, you will. I just wish you weren't so confident about it. What do you have cooking in that head of yours?

Trask walked back to the witness room and found the half-full can of Diet Coke he'd left there. Wisniewski was reading a newspaper.

"How'd direct go?"

"Not bad. Got the story told."

"Ready for cross?"

"I have no idea. I'm ready for what the cross *should* be, but it's Burns, so who knows."

"You'll be fine. No sweat."

Yeah. Trask walked back toward the courtroom. *That's what my boxing coach at the Academy told me before I got in the ring with the golden gloves champ of California. He just forgot to tell me who my opponent was.*

The jury filed back in. Judge Dean gave them his grandfatherly smile, then nodded toward Burns.

"Cross-examination. Mr. Trask, you are reminded you are still under oath."

"Yes, Your Honor."

Burns took the long way to the podium, walking behind his client to the far end of the defense table and around that. This gave him the chance to give Moreno a reassuring pat on the back en route.

A little theatre, J. T.?

"Good afternoon, Mr. Trask."

"Mr. Burns."

"We've met, haven't we?"

Trask couldn't resist smiling in response to the question. "Yes, sir, I'd say that was an understatement."

There were chuckles from the jury box.

Good. Trask smiled back at them. *A point for me. At least I didn't get shut out.*

Burns was smiling back at Trask. "Some very high-profile cases, wouldn't you say?"

"I think that's a fair assessment." *Where are you going with this, J. T.?*

"Why do you think we keep meeting like this?"

What? Why aren't you objecting to that one, Gray? Trask saw that the prosecutor was writing notes on a tablet. *Wonderful. Clueless and emphasizing all this for the jury. If you're writing, they think it must be important.*

"I'm sorry, Mr. Burns, what was your question?" *Maybe if I get him to repeat it, Gray, you'll hear it the second time.*

"I was asking, Mr. Trask, why you and I keep meeting in these important cases?"

Still no objection, although completely irrelevant, so I have to answer it. "I can only assume, that it is because the court feels confident in appointing you to represent defendants in challenging matters." *How's that, J. T.? "Challenging" means when your client is guilty is hell.*

Burns shot him a wry look and smiled. "Thank you for the compliment, Mr. Trask. I hope that you are correct, and may I suggest that your own abilities are why your office appoints you to cases of considerable magnitude as well?"

It suddenly hit Trask like a punch from that golden gloves champion—the punch that had knocked him into the next county. *He's picked his battle on the ground that he knows he can defend. We're already in the sentencing hearing, before the jury's returned a guilty verdict!*

"I can't speak for my superiors, Mr. Burns." *Earth to Gray, object on the grounds that the question calls for speculation, you moron. Nope, he doesn't get it. Thinks this is all chummy preliminary stuff.*

"Oh, I think it's safe to say that you are a rising star in your office. Otherwise, you would not be trusted to handle major investigations like this one, don't you agree?"

Gray, you're a potted plant. No objection again? How do I answer this without looking like an asshole? "No, Mr. Burns, I'm just mean and they want to see me fail, or get attacked, or killed." Let's try this. "Your assessment is very kind, Mr. Burns."

"Oh, I think it is entirely merited, Mr. Trask. After all, you *are* the one who took my expert apart in the now famous case of the United States v. Demetrius Reid, are you not?"

"We had evidence that did that, Mr. Burns."

"I think you are being very modest, but so be it. At any rate, you would have to agree that your office—the people in your office—may feel like they have a very personal stake in the outcome of this matter, would you not? Especially after you and your wife were personally attacked?"

Gray? Oh for heaven's sake. "Mr. Burns, you are aware that it is because I was an intended victim that our entire office was disqualified from prosecuting the case, and that's why Mr. Gray is handling this trial."

"That is essentially a Department of Justice rule, isn't it?"

"Yes."

"It is also a Department of Justice policy that an attorney should never interrogate a defendant without a witness being present, isn't it?"

"Yes."

"But you did that in this case?"

"Only after I knew I would be disqualified from trying the matter because of attempts on my life and on the life of my wife. The reason we have witnesses at interrogations is so we are not disqualified from trying a case. I already knew I would be disqualified. In addition, as I explained on direct examination, I had multiple witnesses monitoring my contact with Mr. Moreno over a sound feed from his room to the nurse's station."

"And why couldn't someone else—one of your agents or detectives—why couldn't one of them have conducted this interrogation?"

"They could have." *And the way this is going, maybe they should have.*

"But they didn't."

"No."

"And is that because your Department also believes that you have superior investigative skills?"

"Objection, Your Honor!" Gray exclaimed.

He lives, Trask thought.

"And the basis for your objection, Mr. Gray?" Judge Dean asked.

"I. . .withdraw my objection."

You're kidding me. No, you're killing me.

The judge shrugged. "Answer the question, Mr. Trask."

"I do my best, Mr. Burns. What others think of my efforts I can't say."

"It was you, after all, Mr. Trask, and not one of your agents or detectives, who found that critical piece of evidence, that proverbial smoking gun in the Reid case, wasn't it?"

Trask waited a moment before answering, staring at Gray, who was writing notes to himself again. *Relevance, you idiot, relevance.* He looked up at the judge. Their eyes met, and Trask knew he understood, but Waymon Dean was old school. He let the lawyers try their cases. No objection meant no objection, regardless of the rules of evidence. The evidence was coming in; the question had to be answered.

"Yes, I found the evidence that proved Mr. Reid was not insane."

"Thank you, Mr. Trask. I'd like to take you back for a moment to the instant in which you saw your wife bound—and as you described it on direct examination—you thought lifeless, on the floor of your home. If you had seen her attacker standing over her, and you had been armed, what would you have done?"

Again, no objection. Oh well, cat's out of the bag now. To object would be to emphasize it even more, and now I'm back in the election of 1988. Trask looked at the judge again. Dean just nodded. Trask turned back to Burns.

"At that time, and under those circumstances, Mister Burns, I would have shot that man dead."

Burns walked slowly back to his table before turning to face the judge. "No more questions."

Gray finally stood. "The prosecution rests."

Burns was on his feet immediately. "As does the defense, Your Honor."

April 5, 10:00 a.m.

Trask had been allowed to watch the closing arguments, since he was not subject to recall following the completion of his testimony. The guilty verdicts came in fairly quickly, as expected. Burns had barely contested the evidence of his client's crimes and had just asked the jurors to consider all the evidence and viewpoints of the witnesses before arriving at their verdicts. The evidence was overwhelming.

Always tactically sound, Trask thought as he listened to the defense counsel's guilt phase summation. *He won't sacrifice his credibility with the jury trying to lead them somewhere they won't go. They have to be willing to consider what he says about the penalty; if he tries to sell them a crock now they won't even listen to him later.*

The verdicts came back so quickly that Judge Dean moved them straight into the sentencing hearing, breaking only for lunch.

When the case resumed, there was victim impact testimony from the surviving family members of the murder victims who *had* families. The lawyer's widows and children, as well as a sister of the slain legal secretary, all testified that their lives had been shattered by the bullets that took their loved ones. It was the usual gut-wrenching stuff, sudden mortality thrust upon those who were not expecting it. Even lawyers did piss-poor jobs of preparing for their own deaths. One of the attorneys hadn't had a will, and his estate was a mess—a further complication for his wife and kids.

Gray went first in closing argument. Trask listened to what seemed to be a philosophy dissertation. Sure, there were references to the lives lost, but Gray had never studied the true art of prosecution—how to safely say what the appellate courts would not otherwise allow you to say. The courts had decreed that it would be error for Gray to invite the jurors to "place yourselves in the shoes of those poor souls as they were bound and waited for their own executions," so he didn't say it. He did not know how to achieve the same effect without crossing the forbidden line.

Trask mentally rewrote the argument for him. *Mister Boydston, bound and too terrified to scream, watches as complete strangers force Lynette Morris, his trusted secretary of twenty years, to kneel at his feet. He sees them fire a bullet into her brain. He then waits for that sound to be repeated. The sound of a gun masked by a silencer. The last sound he ever heard. These are the crimes committed by, ordered by, repeated by Luis Moreno. See, Gray? You don't have to use the forbidden words, but you can still get there from here. This is why I'll never be a judge. It's why Lassiter said he could never be one. Too tough to watch the incompetents at work with so much at stake.*

Burns' remarks did not suffer from such sterility. He reviewed the evidence, stressed the death of Carolina Moreno in the way that Gray should have described the deaths of the other victims.

"This beautiful little girl, the light of her father's life, was repeatedly brutalized to the point that she could no longer face even the prospect of another dawn. Raped six times, she took her own life. It would not be an exaggeration to say that those six rapists—those barbaric gang thugs who had destroyed so much of Luis Moreno's country and his family—also destroyed his life that night. The decision that he made afterward, to seek revenge, may not have been a lawful one. It was nevertheless an understandable one. Perhaps even one that would have been undertaken by others, under similar circumstances."

As I admitted on cross, Trask thought.

"Ladies and gentlemen, search your memories to try and recall the last execution in this city. Odds are that you can't remember one. We don't undertake such things lightly. There have been terrible crimes, *horrific* crimes, *senseless* crimes committed without the smallest fragment of justification, and we have not inflicted death just because someone else did so. Is *this* really the case in which we should change course? A case in which even a trusted officer of the Department of Justice admitted on the stand that he would have felt just like Luis Moreno upon seeing the lifeless body of a loved one at his feet? Or is this a case in which the Department of Justice has sought the ultimate punishment because one of their own—one of their best—was himself attacked?

"OBJECTION!" screamed Gray.

"SUSTAINED!" shouted Judge Dean, bringing down his gavel with a thunderclap that echoed through the room. "Mr. Burns, there is no evidence to support such a claim, and you know better than that. The jury will disregard the last statement."

Sure they will, Trask thought. *They'll disregard your last instruction, judge. If the prosecution pulls something like that, it's reversible error. The defense gets a meaningless curative instruction, but wins by crossing the line.*

Three hours later, the people of the District of Columbia informed the court that Luis Moreno should go to a federal pen for the remainder of his existence on the planet earth. He would not face the death penalty.

Trask left the courtroom and headed back toward the witness room. He felt a tug on his coat, and turned to face G. Gary Gray.

"This is all your fault, Trask. He pinned you on the stand and your stupid answer sunk us!"

"I was under oath, Gray, and had to tell the truth. That was my job up there. It wasn't to put a notch on your gun. That question—hell, that whole line of questioning—was objectionable, but you let Burns lead me down that little path by sitting on your hands because you've never read the rules of evidence. Besides that, I'd have looked like a liar if I'd said anything else. Go Google Kitty Dukakis and learn something. Don't worry, though, you get your name in the paper again tomorrow, and Moreno's gone for good. One of those big firms whose butts you've been licking will call, and you'll be gone, too. Have a nice life on the civil suit side. You'll be a lot better at settling cases than you are at trying them."

Trask turned and walked away. Gray turned back toward the courtroom and found Barry Doroz standing in front of him.

"Best summation of the day," Doroz said, pointing toward Trask.

Chapter Twenty-Nine

May 5, 11:20 a.m.

G. Gary Gray was packing. He had been invited to be a junior partner in a large firm in Georgetown and was happy to be leaving the office of the United States Attorney for the Northern District of Virginia. He was wrapping a very nice granite desk set with bubble-wrap when the audible chirp on his computer alerted him to the receipt of an e-mail.

Shit! He thought. *Thought I'd cleared them all.*

He grabbed the mouse and opened the e-mail, which was a request from a case manager in the Bureau of Prisons, inquiring as to whether there was any necessity for the separation within the federal prison system of an inmate named Luis Moreno from any other inmates or groups of inmates.

Gray looked at the monitor. *He ought to be on death row anyway.*

He clicked on the reply button and sent a response reading, "No need for separation."

May 7, 2:30 p.m.

Trask looked around the task force conference room. All the incident reports had been pulled from the walls, leaving only the pin holes where the summaries had been before. Weeks of searching for Esteban Ortega had led them nowhere.

There had been an indictment returned, but it would mean nothing without a defendant to be tried. Santos had been debriefed at least four times, but it seemed like the DC clique of the MS-13 had been disbanded. Ortega had most likely melted into the thousands of *Maras* living in Fairfax County, Virginia. If some cop got lucky one day and stopped him for littering or something, maybe they'd roust him and haul him in on suspicion of having an attitude in public, print him, and then there would be a trial. Probably not.

Trask's cell phone rang.

"Trask."

"It's Mitchell."

"Hey, Mitch."

"Just got a call from my favorite client."

"And how is Mister Santos today?"

"He says Ortega just left on a plane for El Salvador. Said he used the alias of Saul Moreno."

"A taste for irony. How'd Santos come up with that?"

"He said his sister knows a gal that's been sleeping with Ortega. The info came from the girlfriend."

"Thanks. We'll check it out."

Twenty minutes later, Trask pulled a card from his briefcase and dialed the personal cell phone of Miguel Navarrete-Ponce, ambassador to the United States from El Salvador.

"How are you Jeff?"

"Been better, Mr. Ambassador. I need a favor."

"Name it."

"We got a tip that Ortega boarded a flight for San Salvador a couple of hours ago. He's using an alias. We checked with the airline and verified that a passenger by that name is on the flight. I'd like some help extraditing Mr. Ortega back to the States for trial."

"I think I can help. I'll make some calls."

"Thank you, sir."

"Certainly. Anytime."

The ambassador dialed the international call from memory. When the voice answered, he did not say hello.

Esteban Ortega walked out the front door of the terminal of the Comalapa International Airport in San Salvador. He held a small duffle bag in his right hand and scanned the line of vehicles picking up passengers for the one he expected. He did not see it. He did see a dark panel truck parked on the curb.

Fuckin' Huey. I told him to be here.

He dropped the duffle bag to the sidewalk. As he took the phone from his pocket to make the call, someone pulled a dark bag over his head. Ortega brought his arms up to fight the bag, but a fist slammed into his diaphragm, and he felt the air leaving him. Strong arms on both sides threw him onto the floor of the waiting van. There was a knee in his back. Ortega tried to fight, but was outnumbered and still struggling for breath. His kidnappers bound his hands and feet and gagged him. He heard them move toward the front of the van, leaving him alone on the floor. The bag was still over his head.

He tried to feel the cords, hoping to recognize the knot, but he couldn't move his hands normally.

My thumbs are tied together!

The van left pavement and rattled over crude roads for what seemed to be an eternity. Ortega felt himself being pulled out of the truck. Someone forced him down into the grass on the side of the road. The bag was pulled from his head. He felt a drop of rain on his cheek.

Acknowledgments

Thanks to my review team for their suggestions and sharp eyes: my sister Jamie, daughter Jennifer, Tania Santander, Carolyn Dean Yeatman, and the editors at CreateSpace.

As always, thanks to my wife, Lea, for believing in this whole crazy ride before it started.

Other Books By Marc Rainer

Capital Kill

A few short blocks from the safety of the museums and monuments on the National Mall, a ruthless killer prowls the streets of Washington, DC. Federal prosecutor Jeff Trask joins a team of FBI agents and police detectives as they try and solve the series of brutal murders. As the body count rises, the investigation leads to a chilling confrontation with the leader of an international drug smuggling ring, and no one is safe, not even the police. *Capital Kill* is a swirling thrill ride through the labyrinth of a major federal investigation and trial, with a gripping conclusion that no one will see coming.

"Lawyer Jeff Trask is just settling into his new job as an Assistant US Attorney when he becomes embroiled in a high-stakes international case that could break an already-strapped legal system. Characters are well developed, and the elements are assembled so seamlessly that the story feels fresh. Rainer's attention to setting also shines through. The streets of Washington, DC, come alive; those who have lived or worked in the nation's capital will recognize Rainer's cunning use of seedy locales to give the action in the book a realistic tone. The book's intense action, realistic tone and memorable characters will keep readers engrossed in this thriller with a superb payoff."

—*Kirkus Reviews*

Readers' Reviews of Capital Kill:

"As a lawyer and prosecutor, I love legal thrillers, with this one caveat: They must be realistic portrayals of the law enforcement community. Sadly, many legal thriller and crime novels do not achieve the level of realism that I demand. THIS book, unlike so many others in this genre, portrays law enforcement and the duties of prosecutors in a very realistic manner, without sacrificing drama or excitement. I recommend this book for anybody who loves crime novels and lawyer novels, and who demands realistic portrayals of the people involved in those professions. Five Stars!"

"I thoroughly enjoyed *Capital Kill.* The plot involves a Jamaican drug gang operating out of DC, and the joint efforts of the Federal Prosecutors, FBI, DEA, Metro Police, and even the RCMP in putting the gang out of business while attempting to nab a serial killer. As a trial attorney, I enjoyed the discussion of tactics of cross-exam of an expert witness. I even picked up a pointer or two after 25+ years of trying cases. The characters are well-drawn and you feel a great deal of empathy for most of the law enforcement characters, and a real chill when the 'evildoer' is in action. Can't recommend Mr. Rainer's book enough."

"Like a spider weaving his web, Marc Rainer spins a great story, drawing the reader in, page by page, character by character. A fast-paced first novel that leaves the reader wanting more! Don't start reading this novel if you don't have time to finish; it is hard to put down! Marc's storytelling skills are excellent and his explanations of the Judicial System and agencies are easy for the layman to follow. I highly recommend this book to ANYONE that enjoys a good read."

"There are many lawyers, I'm sure, who want to be 'the next John Grisham,' but few, if any, come close to Grisham's greatest attribute: the ability to tell a fascinating story incredibly well. It's frankly hard to believe this is Marc Rainer's first novel, the writing and storytelling are so good. The characters in *Capital Kill* are well-drawn and three-dimensional, but it is the story itself—a young federal prosecutor seeking to bring Jamaican drug gang leaders living in the United States to justice—that is so compelling. The story has all the marks of someone who has seen all this 'up close and personal.' As a lawyer, I generally stay away from books about lawyers—mainly because the stories aren't really that interesting. Marc Rainer—like John Grisham—is an exception. Highly recommended."

"This is an enthralling and fascinating read. My favorite aspect of this book is the internal dialog of the assistant federal prosecutor. After all, how many TV crime/legal dramas have we all watched during which we have only been allowed to wonder what the thoughts and reactions of the prosecution (to the defense, to the defendant, to the witnesses, to the jury) are? The ending is 'blockbuster,' and the entire novel would make a terrific full-length film. I highly recommend *Capital Kill* to any reader who enjoys this type of genre."

"The reason other reviewers keep using the word 'gripping' when describing *Capital Kill* is the same reason I use it here: Marc Rainer's prose grabs the reader's attention from the start and doesn't let it go. Whether it's in his characterization of good guys Trask, Lassiter, Carter, Ramirez and Co. as they wind their way through Washington's labyrinthine criminal justice system; his description of calculating, ice-cold serial killer Demetrius Reid; or as he recounts the dying eyes of Reid's terrified victims, Rainer weaves a web of intrigue that will have you turning 'just one more page.'"

"Rainer is so good that you will find yourself questioning the line between fiction and reality. The author's experience and writing skill will wrench your emotion, challenge your imagination, and leave you wondering how much of this he has really lived."

"Wow, what a novel! Fascinating read that kept my interest from start to finish. Too bad I can only give it five stars. Trask is my newest hero!"

23730328R00143

Made in the USA
Lexington, KY
25 June 2013